CW01111482

A SPARK OF SEAS

A LITTLE MERMAID RETELLING

HEART OF THE QUEENDOM
BOOK 3

SUSANNAH WELCH

This collection is a work of fiction. The names, characters, and events in this book are the products of the author's imagination or are used fictitiously. Any similarity to real persons living or dead is coincidental and not intended by the author.

Copyright © 2024 Susannah Welch

All rights reserved. Neither this book, nor any parts within may be sold or reproduced in any form without permission.

Cover Concept and Design by MoorBooks Design
Editing by Nia Quinn

eISBN: 978-1-958568-14-9
Paperback ISBN: 978-1-958568-15-6
Hardback ISBN: 978-1-958568-16-3

www.susannahwelch.com

ALSO BY SUSANNAH WELCH

Heart of the Queendom

A Spark of Storms

A Spark of Nature

A Spark of Seas

A Spark of Harvest (Coming Soon)

City of Virtue and Vice

Dance with the Wind

Dance with the Night

Dance with the Dawn

Fight with the Wind

Fight with the Dark

Fight with the Heart

*For my Dad
Thanks for introducing me to the best captain,
James T. Kirk*

NAERMORE
TSANYIN
Lake Amyrante
LA VERIDDA
Merewyn Bay
VERKESHE
N
W
E
S
Dharijian Sea
ISANDARIYAH
YLIRA
Mt Qira
ISANDINE
YLARA
Mt Qara
ZARIDIA
Uhlirah Desert
THE QUEENDOM OF
ISANDARIYAH
(AND THE SURROUNDING KINGDOMS)

PART I

1

Rhielle stood atop the cliff and stared at the open sea. Her copper hair blew across her face as she peeked over the edge of the cliff, trying to glimpse her dinghy floating far below. Once she spotted it, her clenched hand on her dagger relaxed. Being stranded on land was unthinkable. Time away from the sea was only tolerable if the reward was great enough. The sound of an approaching carriage pulled her attention back to the task at hand.

She peeked through the scruffy pine trees as a single carriage rattled down the path. Most traffic between Naermore and Verkeshe traveled the roads between major cities—only wealthy lords from Verkeshe used this path to conduct business with property owners in the Naermore countryside. And considering the political power Verkeshe wielded over Naermore, the loser in any agreement between the two was clear.

Rhielle held her position inside the cluster of pine trees, her muscles tensed, ready for a fight. The driver slowed the carriage, a natural instinct when approaching a thick forest after miles in the open countryside. Before the carriage could pass into the shadow of the trees, the driver reined the horses to an abrupt halt.

A natural instinct when discovering a woman in the middle of the road with a bow raised.

Rhielle's bow-wielding companion, Chysu, was originally from Tsanyin, though she hadn't claimed that as her home for several decades. Chysu's dark eyes were lined with more kohl than Rhielle's, and the older woman had smeared it in wild streaks, giving her the appearance of a barbarian with a hint of madness. Ironic, considering Chysu was a doctor and the most well read of Rhielle's crew.

As Rhielle exited the trees, the driver's eyes flicked her way, but after noting her still-sheathed sword, his focus returned to the woman in the road. Rhielle huffed out a breath. The man's easy surrender would speed up this expedition, but she was itching for a fight and now she might not get one.

Rhielle sauntered up to the carriage, confident Chysu had the driver well in hand. The carriage bore the sigil of a Verkeshian lord, and aside from some road dust, it looked in pristine condition. Rhielle unsheathed her sword and smashed the hilt through the window.

Glass crunched beneath her boots as she threw open the door. She flung her flared coat as dramatically as a minstrel, with the added effect of revealing the daggers strapped to her corseted waist. "Greetings!" she said cheerfully.

As expected, a pudgy man and young girl sat inside the carriage. They presented no danger to Rhielle, so she sheathed her sword.

The man was in his forties, his thin hair combed precisely to cover his retreating hairline. His too-tight jacket was cut in a military style, though he had clearly never done anything more strenuous in his life than order servants around.

His pasty face reddened, and he brushed broken glass off

his lap with spotless white gloves. "How dare you!" he spat. "Who do you think you are?"

Rhielle leaned closer as if letting him in on a secret. "We're pirates," she said with a grin. "And we've come for your treasure."

"My ... treasure?" Confusion clouded his face, then he threw his head back and laughed. "If you wanted treasure, you should have robbed me on the way to Naermore. It's too late now. I left everything valuable there."

Rhielle clicked her tongue. "So shortsighted, like most Verkeshian males." She finally turned her attention to the young girl cowering against the opposite carriage door. The girl was no more than fifteen, not much younger than Rhielle at twenty-one. But Rhielle had lived several lifetimes since she was her age. "And what about you, girl? Do you understand more than a Verkeshian fool?"

The girl's pale skin had grown even paler with fright. Her strawberry blond hair was woven in an elaborate braid, though her anxious fingers had frayed the end. The girl's lavender eyes dropped to her fidgeting fingers as she whispered, "He's the only person from Verkeshe I've met."

The man glared at Rhielle and hissed, "This woman is my bride. I won't have you upsetting her."

Anger burned in Rhielle's chest, but she held herself perfectly still so as not to startle the girl. "Is it true? Is this man your husband?"

The girl didn't turn her head, but her eyes shot to the man, then back down to the braid she clutched white-knuckled. "Not yet," she whispered.

The man opened his mouth, but Rhielle just leaned further inside the carriage. "What is your name, child?"

The girl bit her lip. "Poppy."

The man swung his fist, a terrible move in the close quarters. And even more unfortunate for him, considering his lack of skill and Rhielle's longing for a fight.

Rhielle slammed him against the seat with one hand, the other holding a dagger carefully against his neck. Once he realized the truth of his situation, Rhielle returned her attention to the girl.

"Listen closely, Poppy. As a girl from the Naermore countryside, you may not have been given many choices in life, but you have one today. You can continue to Verkeshe with this man, become his wife, and lead a quiet life, raising his children and managing his household. That's the option your parents chose for you, selling you off for whatever riches he offered them in exchange for an obedient wife."

The man took a breath to argue, but stopped abruptly as Rhielle's blade pressed closer. She kept her focus on the young girl's eyes. Their lavender shade stirred painful memories, but Rhielle shoved down the grief, stoking her anger instead.

"If you choose to be his wife, I will let you be on your way, and you'll have an interesting story about pirates to tell your future children. But I offer you another choice—something beyond a safe and comfortable life ..." Rhielle dropped her voice to a fierce whisper. "I offer you freedom."

The girl's eyes widened further, but she didn't speak.

"Come with me," said Rhielle. "Leave everything behind and follow me out to sea. It's dangerous, the work is grueling, and honestly, you probably won't live as long as if you stayed tucked away in a lord's castle. But I promise you, Poppy, while you live, you will truly *live*."

Despite the dagger at his throat, the man huffed a laugh. "What a ridiculous offer! Do you think—"

The girl flung the carriage door wide and stepped out.

The man gaped at her empty seat. Rhielle withdrew her dagger and patted his cheek. "Told you I'd take your treasure."

Poppy rounded the carriage as Rhielle slammed the door,

sending the last few shards of glass tinkling to the ground. The girl edged closer to Rhielle, away from the captivity of her carriage, yet unsure how close she should get to a pirate. Rhielle approached her slowly with open hands, to lessen the girl's fear.

A bow twanged at Rhielle's back, and she spun. An arrow quivered in the ground at the lord's feet. He had found a sword somewhere in the carriage, but his sword arm drooped at his side as he stared at Chysu. She had already nocked her next arrow, her bow trained on the lord, while keeping one eye on the driver.

Rhielle had instinctively stepped in front of the girl, who now trembled at her back. She could just dump the man's lifeless corpse into the carriage, but she didn't want to traumatize the girl any further.

"Get back inside," Rhielle growled. When he didn't move, she roared, "Now!"

The man skittered backward and flung himself into the carriage. Rhielle looked up at the driver, his arms still raised in surrender.

"Take him back to Verkeshe, and tell everyone his bride-to-be willingly ran off with pirates rather than marry him."

The driver nodded, then slowly lowered his hands to the reins. Chysu stepped to the side of the road but kept her bow trained on the carriage until it had passed into the forest.

Rhielle turned to the girl, who blinked sightlessly at the road. "You don't have to become a pirate, you know."

Poppy flinched, her focus shooting back to Rhielle. "What do you mean?"

"I mean, we'll drop you off wherever you want. Even back home in Naermore, if you wish."

The girl's eyes clouded, as if she considered the family who had sold her to a foreigner. "I have no home," she murmured.

The sadness in those lavender eyes sent another wave of

memories rushing through Rhielle, but she spun on her heel and headed to the edge of the cliff, throwing her words casually over her shoulder. "Good. Then you are free to join us."

Poppy hurried to catch up, a skip in her step. "Where are we going?"

Chysu joined them at the cliff's edge. "I'll prep the boat, Captain." Rhielle nodded, and Chysu hooked her bow over her shoulder and started the treacherous climb down to the dinghy.

"First, we take this dinghy to meet up with the rest of the crew in town." Rhielle looked out to the sea. "Then, we head toward the horizon."

"The horizon? What's out ..." Poppy stopped talking, gazing at the massive ship waiting in the distance. The girl whispered, "What is that?"

Rhielle's eyes locked on the ship, her lips curving in a fond smile. "That's the *Lady Tempest*. She's your new home."

2

Rhielle strode through the sleepy streets of Lybeck, trying to look inconspicuous, and failing. The small coastal town on the edge of Naermore and Verkeshe received a lot of travelers, but it was surely clear to the inhabitants that Rhielle and Chysu were pirates. It was probably unclear why a young girl trailed after them.

Poppy hunched her shoulders as if she wanted to melt away, but her wide eyes took in every tavern and blacksmith they passed. When Poppy slowed, cocking her head to study the women standing outside a brothel, Chysu nudged her forward with a fierce glare.

Rhielle was relieved to finally arrive at Olga's tavern. Her crew preferred this tavern because of its marginally less sticky floors and the owner standing behind the bar. The brawny woman had the fierce look of a pirate, but was often covered in flour from the warm bread she served with the ale.

Rhielle's first mate leaned against the bar. Jazhara's dark brown skin and tight curls marked her as Zaridian, though as a pirate, she didn't claim her country of birth anymore. The petite woman straightened as Rhielle approached. "Captain, the crew has asked for shore leave here in Lybeck. We've been sailing nonstop for months now, and a few days on land—"

"We leave immediately," said Rhielle.

Jazhara's brow crinkled in confusion until her eyes landed on the young girl hovering behind Chysu. Though Rhielle's first mate was small, the woman had a glare that could intimidate even the fiercest of pirates. "You picked up another stray."

Rhielle ignored her first mate's accusation. "Poppy is our new cabin girl. Find her something to wear."

Jazhara looked at the girl's delicately embroidered dress covered in dirt from her climb down the cliff to reach the dinghy. "You mean something that won't make her look like a kidnapped duchess?"

"Go now," said Rhielle. "Chysu will come with you." The taller woman nodded in silent confirmation.

Jazhara raised one eyebrow, her typical means of confrontation. "And where are you going?" At Rhielle's own raised brow, her first mate added, "Captain."

"I'm researching possible financial opportunities." Rhielle winked.

Jazhara took the girl's arm and grumbled, "Fine. I'll take this scrawny thing and see what I can make of her."

Poppy's lavender eyes pleaded with Rhielle as Jazhara led her away. Rhielle's first mate seemed gruff, but Jazhara's hand on the girl's arm was gentle and her glare warded off questionable strangers. But even though Poppy was in good hands, the girl's eyes haunted her as she turned toward the bar and subtly signaled the owner.

The stout woman brushed her flour-covered hands on her apron and poured a glass of ale, then smoothly deposited it in front of Rhielle with a welcoming smile. "How's the sea today, Captain?"

"Full of treasure for those who know where to look, Olga." Rhielle sipped the ale with her eyes on the smiling woman.

A woman who was also a Resistance spy.

A tavern in a border town saw many traders passing through, and when those lonely travelers cozied up to Olga's bar, her warm bread and fine ale set them at ease. With a slight shift in her posture, the woman could transform her brawny strength into a motherly softness that spilled secrets from travelers' lips.

Secrets valuable to the Resistance in their fight against Verkeshe. And though Rhielle was a pirate with no loyalty to any country, her goals often coincided with those of the Resistance, so they'd formed a wary alliance.

"I know one place to look for treasure." Olga paused—very strategically.

Rhielle slid a coin across the bar. A coin worth much more than a single glass of ale.

The coin disappeared into Olga's considerable bosom, and the woman's smile shifted from soft to businesslike in the blink of an eye. "The Resistance has tracked an Isandariyan envoy sailing the Dharijian Sea with a valuable treasure on board."

"An envoy ..." The queendom of Isandariyah usually held itself apart from the various kingdoms' politics. Was this a sign their queen was interested in an alliance? "What's the treasure?"

Olga shrugged. "No one knows. I've only heard they keep it on deck, wrapped with a red bow."

"A red bow?" Rhielle snorted. "How ... dramatic."

"It's heading directly for King Ruzgar."

Rhielle had to stop her usual hiss at the name of the king of Verkeshe. "Are you suggesting Isandariyah is proposing an alliance with Verkeshe?" The king of Verkeshe and his two sons weren't interested in alliances—only conquest. No one knew that better than the Resistance. Verkeshe had invaded La Veridda and occupied their country for fifteen years.

Olga's shoulders rose and fell. "I'm not sure. But I do know many are opposed to the possibility of such an alliance."

Obviously the Resistance would be opposed, but they wouldn't want to take direct action against Isandariyah. If the Resistance could win back La Veridda from the Verkeshe occupation, they would want to keep Isandariyah on their side.

But what if pirates stole this treasure before a deal could be struck?

Well, that was exactly why she worked so well with the Resistance. She slid another coin across the bar.

Olga began casually polishing a glass. "I've heard of a particular buyer so opposed to an alliance that they will pay an exorbitant sum if someone can procure this treasure from the Isandariyan envoy."

Rhielle batted her eyelashes innocently. "I've got some skills in procurement."

Olga's lips twitched. "So I've heard. If you can procure this red-ribboned treasure, in seven days you will find a buyer waiting for you in Ravenna."

Rhielle's eyebrow crawled up her forehead. The Resistance was welcome in the pirate city, but the location sparked her curiosity about the buyer's identity.

"Thanks for the information, Olga. You're the real treasure." She slid a few more coins across the bar.

The burly woman's cheeks grew pink. "You're sweet to say so. And you already paid me for the information."

Rhielle grinned. "The rest of that is for several loaves of fresh bread. I need to appease the crew because there is no shore leave until we reach the pirate city."

3

Rhielle hopped over the Isandariyan ship's railing, her footsteps quiet as she stalked across the moonlit deck. Chysu followed so silently that Rhielle turned to make sure she was there. The tall woman's sleek black hair was twisted into a messy knot, and her kohl-smeared eyes almost feral. She looked like the perfect character for this midnight expedition to steal from the Isandariyan envoy.

Except for her judgmental look at Rhielle for accepting such a foolish mission.

But at least she stayed silent. Rhielle's first mate would have been equally capable on this expedition, except Jazhara wouldn't have kept her mouth shut. The woman had berated Rhielle the entire time she explained the plan to steal the treasure from the envoy and sell it to an unknown buyer in Ravenna.

Rhielle would suffer Chysu's silent admonition as long as the doctor helped Rhielle steal the treasure and make it back to the ship unseen. They worked well together—guarding each other's backs while stealing gold or weapons from Verkeshian ships. This time, all they had to do was steal the package Olga said was on the deck, wrapped with a red bow, then escape into the night. Stealing from an Isandariyan envoy would be so much easier than stealing from a Verkeshian military ship.

"Suspiciously easy" was what Jazhara had said. Rhielle suspected she was right, but she had to take the chance. If Isandariyah allied with King Ruzgar, it would only make Verkeshe more powerful, and Rhielle would do anything to prevent that.

Plus they desperately needed the money. Feeding a crew of pirates was expensive. Especially when that crew avoided the murdering type of pirating.

She signaled Chysu to take the opposite direction around the piles of secured cargo. As the woman padded away, Rhielle peeked around the tall stacks of crates. Why hadn't they seen a guard on deck yet? The ship was moored in an isolated cove, but they should have posted a guard. Was this crew filled with idiots? It simplified her theft, but increased her uneasiness. She rounded a crate and froze.

There was a man lying on deck.

He appeared asleep or unconscious, but she wasn't foolish enough to check. He lay on his side, an arm curved protectively around his stomach. She recognized the posture immediately—the man was seasick. She chuckled silently to herself. He had the thick biceps and muscular forearms of a disciplined fighter, yet the sea had reduced him to a weakling.

She scooted one step closer. His blond hair glowed in the moonlight, and a single lock had come free of his neat braid and brushed against his cheek. Blond hair was more common in Verkeshe than Isandariyah, so what was he doing with an Isandariyan envoy?

She looked closer at what she'd originally thought were pajamas—he wore a religious garment with a loose tunic and trousers with a wide sash gathered across his chest. She blinked as moonlight filtered through shifting clouds. The fabric was actually a deep red.

The treasure wrapped with a red bow was a man?

How had Olga failed to share this critical piece of info?

No matter how much the job was worth, Rhielle was not in the kidnapping business. She turned slowly, heading back to Chysu. Rhielle would just have to take another job that didn't involve—

Strong hands spun her around and slammed her against the tall crates. Before she could catch her breath, the man had one hand wrapped around her upper arm, his other holding a knife at her throat.

"Who do you work for?" he whispered in harsh Isandariyan.

She mentally cursed herself for turning her back on him. Chysu would never let her live it down, and she dreaded the number of times she would hear "I told you so" from Jazhara once she made it back to the ship.

His grip tightened on her arm, and he whispered again, this time in Riddish, the more widely known language of La Veridda. "Who do you work for?"

"I work for myself," she said defiantly. Why hadn't the man raised the alarm? Was he just as idiotic as the crew who'd left the ship unguarded?

The man scanned her face, taking in her kohl-rimmed eyes and the beads woven into her hair, then glanced down at her jacket—deep purple, fitted across her chest and flared at the waist.

His grip slightly lessened. "You're just a common pirate."

She growled, "What do you mean 'common'?"

He blew out a breath, studying her as if he wasn't sure what to do with her. She studied him right back. Who would consider a religious man from Isandariyah a treasure?

"Who are you?" she asked.

He blinked at the question. "You don't know? I assumed that's why you are here."

The last thing she wanted to admit was she had taken on this foolish mission without knowing the full story. Accidentally falling into a kidnapping scheme was too embarrassing to admit to her crew, much less to this stranger.

"I'm a pirate," she said confidently, despite how tightly he pressed against her. "I go where I wish."

He narrowed his eyes, and Rhielle finally noticed how blue they were.

A drop of rain landed on her cheek, and she flinched.

The man looked confused at her reaction until a raindrop landed on his bare shoulder, and he glanced up at the passing cloud.

Rhielle ground her teeth. Just what she needed.

Rain.

The raindrop irritated her skin as it dripped down her cheek. Another drop fell, landing on her collarbone, prickling her skin.

She had to leave.

Now.

"Well, it was nice meeting you," she blurted. "I really must be going."

He snorted a laugh, glancing at his knife still at her throat. "You think I'll just let you leave?"

"I could've left at any time." Another drop landed on her temple, scraping the side of her face as it trickled past her ear. "I'm not what you think I am."

He gave her an arch look. "I think you're a pirate. What else would you be?"

"A diversion." She winked.

Confusion briefly registered on his face before Chysu slammed her hilt against his head, dropping him to the ground.

4

Rhielle scrambled aboard the *Lady Tempest*, shouting orders while wringing water out of her hair. "Jazhara! Get us out of here!"

Her first mate inspected Rhielle for injuries with a glance, up and down. "On what course, Captain?"

"Away! Fast as she can go." Rhielle dove under the steps leading to the upper deck and slapped her hand beside the empty hook on the wall. "Poppy!"

The young girl from Naermore scuttled forward. Her appearance was more pirate now that she was out of her ruffled dress and wearing pants and sturdy boots, but her lilting voice was still that of a proper lady. "Yes, Captain?"

"Find my hat." Rhielle tried to soften her usual commanding tone, but the cabin girl hopped, then sprinted into the captain's quarters.

Rhielle turned back to Jazhara. "We need to go. Now!" Rhielle had hoped the command would offer a distraction, but her first mate didn't miss the "treasure" Chysu dragged onto the deck.

Jazhara shot Rhielle a fierce look before she started yelling orders of her own. "Helmswoman! Take us about!"

Rhielle avoided her first mate's eyes. It wasn't unusual for Jazhara to be the one to order the crew—the Zaridian woman's voice was much louder than her petite size warranted, and the crew jumped into action.

Besides, Rhielle was in no position to order the crew right now. She could hardly think straight. She should have worn her hat on their ill-fated mission, but she hadn't expected the rain. Water prickled down the back of her neck, triggering the uncontrollable desire to scrape the rain off her skin with her fingernails.

Poppy still hadn't returned with her hat, so Rhielle lingered beneath the overhang, protected from the slight drizzle. She stared at the horizon, trying to give the illusion of confidence, but was uncomfortably aware her posture was more cowering than brooding.

Jazhara temporarily stopped glaring at Rhielle and directed a tall crew member to assist Chysu with dragging the strange man aboard. His head lolled as the two women draped his arms across their shoulders, brought him to Rhielle, and dumped him at her feet. The other woman ran off to assist with rigging the sails, but Chysu remained, standing quietly with her arms tucked behind her back.

Jazhara slowly faced Rhielle, and said calmly, "With all due respect, *Captain* ..." She spoke the title as an accusation. "What in the Four Gods' names have you done?"

It had been a foolish decision to bring him on board. She had fully intended to walk away from this ridiculous mission, and when Chysu knocked him out, he had crumpled to the ground, landing almost exactly as she had found him. She could have left him there, and he would have awoken with a headache but no lasting damage. His memory of almost being kidnapped by a pirate woman would fade until he eventually forgot about her.

But for some reason, she couldn't leave him behind. Maybe it was the bristling rain that had spurred her on, but she had ordered Chysu to drag the man to their boat. And after a brief frown, the woman had complied.

But that was too much to explain to her first mate, so she merely said, "This was the mission. We will deliver him to a buyer in Ravenna in seven days."

Jazhara's eyes hardened.

"I don't like it either," said Rhielle. "But we need the money. Unless you'd rather do some actual pillaging, instead of just raiding military ships?"

Jazhara crossed her arms. "Sure, why not go ahead and pillage? We've already stooped to kidnapping."

Heat rose in Rhielle's chest, both anger at the accusation and embarrassment at the truth of Jazhara's words. Before she could open her mouth, Poppy slid to a halt at her side.

"Your hat, Captain." Poppy's proud smile faded as she blinked at the man crumpled at Rhielle's feet. Her eyes darted between Jazhara, Chysu, and Rhielle, seeking a reason for the lingering intensity.

The embarrassing accusation of kidnapping hit too close to the mark, so Rhielle merely took her hat and shooed the girl away.

Rhielle used the wide brim of her hat to avoid Jazhara's accusatory glare and Chysu's disappointed frown. As she tucked her damp hair inside the leather hat and smoothed back the plume of feathers, she studied the man. Strands of blond hair stuck to his face, and the rain had soaked through his broad sash and thin tunic. "What is he wearing?"

She hadn't expected an answer, but Chysu said, "He's a monk, Captain. Sworn to celibacy while he serves in the shrines of the Twin Goddesses of Isandariyah."

Jazhara twirled her fingers in a warding pattern, writing an invisible symbol in the air. "Four Gods save us," she whispered. "You'll bring the wrath of their Goddesses down upon us."

Rhielle huffed out a breath. "I'm not afraid of the Twin Goddesses."

The man coughed, then rasped, "The Twins harness the power of flame within the heart of their volcanoes. You'd do well to respect them."

Rhielle hunched, looking the man in the eyes. "They may rule *your* land, monk, but they don't rule the sea." She smirked. "I do."

Jazhara whispered another warding prayer.

The man didn't flinch. "Where are you taking me?"

"I've been offered a large sum of money to 'procure' you for a private investor."

He jerked upright, and his skin turned slightly green, though Rhielle didn't know if it was lingering seasickness or from the hit on the head. He grabbed Rhielle's arm. "Who is your boss?"

Rhielle shook off his hand. "I have no boss. I'm captain of this ship, and we go where I want."

His eyes hardened as he glared at her. "Fine. Your 'private investor.' What's her name?"

She bit her tongue on the question that sprang to her lips— *Why do you assume my investor is a 'she'?* Instead she said, "You'll discover that soon enough."

He stumbled awkwardly to his feet. Rhielle didn't move, but she was pleased to see both Jazhara and Chysu had drawn their swords, aiming them at his throat.

"Don't even think of escaping, monk," said Rhielle. "Your envoy was woefully unguarded, but on this ship, you will have eyes on you at all times."

He appeared unconcerned about the two blades pointed at

his throat, and his clear blue eyes pierced her with an intense glare. "You're taking me to her ... to Geeni."

"Geeni?" A prickle of unease crawled across Rhielle's already irritated skin. She spit on the deck. "I don't work for that woman."

He gave her a smug look. "Are you sure about that?"

Rhielle blinked several times in quick succession as she considered the possibility.

He settled back on his heels, seeming at ease. "So, I'm your prisoner. Will you be chaining me to the mast, or whatever it is you pirates do?"

His calmness unnerved her. She imagined him watching her with those intense blue eyes while she bound him to the mast ...

She shook off the image. "There's no need for that. Besides, I assume you'd like to stay near the rail of the ship ... You know, with your tummy issues?" She innocently fluttered her lashes at him.

His cheeks colored. She had guessed correctly about the seasickness.

"I'll allow you to remain on deck in the fresh air if you agree to stay out of the crew's way." She leaned closer. "If not, I have no qualms about tying you to the mast. I'd just prefer to avoid the mess you'd make."

He ground his teeth but didn't respond.

"Jazhara, find him a place out of the way."

"Yes, Captain." Her first mate took him by the arm as ordered, but she aimed an irritated scowl over her shoulder at Rhielle as she left.

The monk also watched Rhielle as he was led away. His sharp eyes reminded her of a caged hawk, but Rhielle had an uncomfortable feeling he had willingly stepped into the snare.

5

The rain still lingered on Rhielle's skin the next morning. After ensuring they had escaped from the Isandariyan ship and setting a rotating guard on the monk, she had passed out without washing off the rain. A bad idea, since she was now exhausted and on edge.

"Captain." Her first mate strolled into Rhielle's quarters and jerked her chin sharply. "You are needed on deck."

Rhielle leaned back in her chair, propping her boots on her desk with a dramatic sigh. "Jazhara, unless we are being attacked, you can handle—"

"It's your prisoner. He's causing a disturbance."

Rhielle ignored the subtle accusation. "He's being guarded by no less than five of our best fighters. Are they not keeping an eye on him?"

Jazhara raised an eyebrow. "Oh, they are definitely keeping an eye on him. At this exact moment, he has nearly every eye on this ship on him."

Rhielle plopped her feet on the ground and stared Jazhara down, waiting for an explanation.

Her first mate pointed toward the deck. "*Your* prisoner is out there, barely dressed, offering his morning prayer salutations to the Twin Goddesses. The starboard deck will be exceedingly clean, thanks to all the women who decided to suddenly start scrubbing the boards."

Rhielle snorted a laugh. "Well, the deck could use a good scrubbing. Move him to the port side before his evening prayers."

Jazhara crossed her arms and shot Rhielle a pointed glare. "I can't believe you're considering handing him over to an unknown buyer. What if he's right? What if it's *her*?"

Rhielle didn't want to admit she had the same concern. Since the moment the monk had said Geeni's name, uneasiness had churned in Rhielle's gut. Was it possible this was another of Geeni's schemes?

"We'll scope out the buyer once we get to Ravenna. If it's Geeni, we both know the *Lady Tempest* will have no problem escaping her. If it's not her, then we will have thwarted an alliance between Isandariyah and Verkeshe while making a load of coin in the process."

Jazhara gave her a shrewd look. "Knowing how much you value your freedom, I'm surprised how casually you are willing to trade a human life in exchange for coin."

Her first mate never pulled her punches, and this time, her sharp words cut Rhielle to the core. As she tried to decide between offering a flimsy rationale or challenging the woman to a fight, Chysu walked in.

"Captain." Chysu's normally calm face showed signs of irritation. "I just stitched up a wound Poppy got from tumbling out of the rigging."

"What was Poppy doing up in the rigging? She's barely learned enough not to trip over the ropes on deck!"

"An older girl led her up there." Chysu's expression flattened into accusation. "They were watching the monk at morning prayer."

Rhielle slapped her hands on her desk as she rose to her feet. "That's it. I'm putting a stop to this." She stormed out of the room, avoiding Jazhara's gaze. Rhielle didn't want her first mate to know how relieved she was to escape that line of questioning.

The situation on deck was just as Chysu and Jazhara had described. A dozen women of all ages meticulously scrubbed the starboard deck. These women were all seasoned sailors, and yet they scrubbed the deck like the newest of recruits. Even with so many buckets and scrub brushes, the deck had hardly been cleaned at all, because the women were focused solely on the monk.

The last time Rhielle had seen him, he had been waterlogged, his hair plastered to his face by the rain. But today, his blond hair was pulled back in a neat braid, with two soft tendrils fluttering around his face in the wind. He had removed his tunic, leaving him in his red flowing pants and the loose sash. He raised his arms overhead, then bent forward in a smooth dive, touching his fingers to the ground, before shooting his feet behind him in a firm plank pose. He lowered his body slowly to the deck, his biceps flexing with the controlled movement. He arched his back, raising his head to the sky, his blond hair sliding between his shoulder blades ...

A woman sighed.

Rhielle snapped her mouth shut, momentarily afraid the sigh had come from her own lips. But the sighing culprit shook her head, as if shaking off a dream, and as her eyes landed on Rhielle, the woman's cheeks colored in embarrassment.

"Captain on deck!" shouted the woman, rubbing her hands self-consciously across her cheeks.

The "cleaning" stopped suddenly, all women rising and saluting Rhielle sharply. They normally didn't rely on such strict formality, but the women had been caught doing something they shouldn't.

"Back to work," growled Rhielle. "*Actual* work."

As the women scattered across the ship, the monk stepped smoothly to his feet and approached Rhielle. "Good morning, Captain. When will you be handing me over?"

Rhielle crossed her arms. "Are you so willing to be handed over to your unknown captor?"

He shrugged. "You're taking me to Geeni."

"What makes you—"

"A ship full of women pirates? You obviously belong to Geeni."

She clenched her fists at her sides. "This is *my* crew!"

He snorted in dismissal. "You are just one of her many henchwomen. Follow your orders and take me to her."

Her eyes widened as fury sank into her bones. She took a menacing step forward and dropped her voice to a low growl. "Perhaps by not restraining you, I've given you the impression you aren't my prisoner. Well, you are. And I will do with you as I please."

He didn't flinch at her harsh tone, but stood calmly, with his hands clasped behind his back.

Her nostrils flared as she drew a deep breath through her nose. "We are headed to Ravenna, where I will hand you over to a buyer, whoever it is, because it's what *I* want to do. Not because you ordered me to."

The corners of his lips twitched, forming an almost smirk.

She poked her finger sharply at his bare chest. "You didn't win this argument, monk. This was my decision from the very beginning. I knew my decision from the moment I first stepped on your ship." A mostly accurate statement—other than Rhielle not having known her theft was actually a kidnapping.

He matched her low voice and drew closer. "And why do you think it was so easy to abduct me, pirate? Did you not wonder why I was the only one on deck? I'm sure you knew right where to find me, because you heard I slept on deck every night." He chuckled quietly. "Who do you think spread that rumor?"

Yes, she had found it odd he was on deck all alone without a guard in sight, but she would never admit that to him.

Especially when she'd never considered the whole thing was a setup.

This monk had used her in a strange plot to purposefully get abducted. Rhielle lived as a pirate because she refused to be controlled by any laws other than her own, and yet, she had unwittingly become a pawn in the middle of a game where she didn't even know all the players. If they thought Rhielle would blindly follow their orders, they were wrong.

She narrowed her eyes at him. "So, you want me to hand you over to Geeni ... Why?"

"I have my reasons."

His smug tone heated her skin, which was still irritated from the dried rain. "You shouldn't have admitted that to me, monk." She spit out his title like a curse. "Pirates are known for doing the exact opposite of what you want."

He snorted. "Of course you'll take me to her. Geeni appears to have an endless amount of money—Twins only know how she's gained so much wealth. I'm sure she's made you an offer so generous you won't refuse."

Why was he so confident the buyer was Geeni? She wanted to refute him but couldn't come up with any proof to the contrary, especially not with his piercing blue eyes fixated on her face and seeing more than she wanted.

Her lips pulled taut in a grimace. "I don't need to negotiate with people like you or Geeni for money." She leaned in, lowering her voice to a rough growl. "I'm a pirate. I take what I want."

A soft throat-clearing drew her gaze down. Poppy clutched

her hands, trying to hide the bandage covering the wound she'd gained falling out of the rigging. The demure girl didn't meet the monk's eyes, unaware she had stepped into the middle of a fight.

"Yes, Poppy?" Rhielle ground the words out through her clenched teeth.

Poppy looked up at her with an earnest smile on her face. "Your bubble bath is ready, Captain." She curtsied in a very unpiratelike way and bounded off.

Rhielle turned back to find the monk suppressing a smile. "Your bubble bath?" A laugh escaped his mouth. "Are all pirates so fancy, or is it just you?"

She whipped out her dagger and pressed it to his throat. He stumbled back a step, coming up hard against the ship railing.

She glared at him with hard eyes. "This is *my* ship, monk. You will not mock me." She edged the blade closer until he was forced to lift his head and stop looking her in the eyes.

His hands crept toward her arms. "Listen, pirate ..." He shifted his feet, but before he could make a defensive move, two swords suddenly joined her dagger at his throat.

Rhielle stepped back, pleased to see Jazhara and Chysu at her side. At Rhielle's back stood a ring of her crew wielding swords, including the woman who had sighed earlier. Gone was their open-mouthed interest—now they all stood with fierce eyes locked on their target.

Rhielle slammed her dagger into the sheath. "Jazhara, set a course for Isandariyah. We're dumping this false treasure for his own people to handle."

Her first mate raised an eyebrow but didn't object.

The monk clenched his fists. "I demand you take me to her, pirate!"

A dozen boots scraped across the deck as her crew closed in around him.

Rhielle gave him a smug look. "I rule this ship, monk. Your demands mean nothing here."

Jazhara tapped her sword against the monk's shoulder. "What should we do with him while we sail, Captain?"

Rhielle glared at the monk, his anger boiling off him like steam. She bared her teeth in a feral grin. "Put his shirt back on, then chain him to the mast. I'll be in my bubble bath."

6

Rhielle felt much more in control after washing off the rain. The bubbles were just enough to soothe her irritated skin, and pulling on dry clothes felt like donning armor. Her perfectly dry pants fit well, and an airy blouse with a tight vest reminded her of her identity as a pirate.

A pirate under no one's control.

She raised the spyglass to her eye and watched the Resistance ship approach, with Commander Luca Saverio standing proudly on deck. The women in the crew liked to say the man matched his warship—tall, powerful, and handsome. Rhielle agreed with the "tall and powerful" part, but she tried to ignore the man's looks, though she had to admit his ship was stunning.

Rhielle studied the soldiers in bright blue uniforms as the ship drew closer. She hadn't seen a Resistance ship in over a month, and she was eager for news of their ongoing battle with Verkeshe.

"You work for the La Veriddan rebels?" asked the monk. "Does Geeni know you work for them, too?"

Rhielle ground her teeth and whirled to face the monk, who was still tied to the mast. "I work for no one, monk. And those 'rebels' are true patriots of their country, fighting against the occupying Verkeshe army. You should keep your nose out of politics and stick to religion."

He pressed his lips together as if holding back an angry retort.

The corner of her mouth twitched into a sneer. "I'm glad you are learning to hold your tongue. It means I won't have to gag you while I go about my business."

She spun to her first mate. "Jazhara, monitor the horizon for unwanted guests. You know how to signal me."

Rhielle addressed the rest of the crew. "Be prepared to sail as soon as I'm back onboard. If the Resistance has good intel for us, we might find a target to strike on our way to return the monk to Isandariyah."

She spoke to Chysu with an irritated glance at the monk. "Keep a close eye on our 'treasure.'" She smoothed the multicolored feathers on her hat before swinging over the side of the ship and climbing down the rope ladder to the dinghy with a soldier in a blue uniform.

After the soldier rowed her the short distance to the warship, she climbed the ladder and hopped over the rail. Commander Luca Saverio waited confidently on deck with his legs braced wide, shoulders thrown back, and hands clasped behind his back.

"Permission to board, Commander Saverio?" She flourished her feathered hat.

"Lovely to see you, as always, Captain." When he smiled, his eyes crinkled at the corners, the warm brown skin roughened by the hardship of spending over half of his thirty years fighting Verkeshe.

"What news from La Veridda?" she asked. "You know I'm always happy to help your war efforts by diverting valuable resources from the Verkeshian army."

He crossed his arms, his gaze stern. "You mean, happy to steal those resources for yourself, Little Captain?"

She kept her smile plastered on her face despite the extremely condescending nickname. "We both fight against Verkeshe in our own way, Commander. You attack their ships, and I do my best to cripple them financially. It's why we have such a mutually beneficial relationship."

His eyes crinkled again, but this time from squinting to focus intensely on her face. "But I wonder ... is it still so mutual, though?"

She blinked at him several times. "What are you talking about?"

He chewed on the inside of his cheek as he considered her. "I heard a rumor from a reliable source that you are working with the enemy."

The accusation struck her like a blow, and she jerked back. "Are you doubting my commitment to destroying Verkeshe? I've been working with you for five years, since the first time I snuck aboard one of your ships when I was sixteen years old. I have been singularly focused on destroying them for what they did to your country, not to mention what they did to—" She shook off the thought. "Why would you doubt me after all these years?"

"The source is reliable, but I admit I find it hard to believe." His brows squeezed together tightly as he studied her. "Out of respect for the years we've worked together, I am offering you a chance to surrender."

"Surrender." She repeated the word as a flat accusation.

He nodded once, sharply. "Surrender peacefully to me. If you are truly innocent, you have nothing to fear. I will take you to the Resistance leaders, and I'm sure we can get this sorted out."

Heat blossomed in her chest, and words refused to come.

Who might have told him such a rumor? Simmering fury drowned out her rational mind.

"You need not worry about your crew. Until we determine if they were complicit, I promise to treat your lady crew gently."

She choked on his outrageous words—the sound coming out as a laughing cough. "You'll treat my *lady crew gently*?"

"Yes, of course. I'm no monster, Little Captain. The monsters are all from Verkeshe. I thought you believed that, too, but ..." He shook his head sadly. "As long as you surrender peacefully, this will be painless. We will head to meet with the Resistance leaders as soon as my soldiers take control of your ship."

Her boiling anger snapped to ice, and her speculations on the rumor's source changed to mathematical calculations. "You'll take my ship." She spoke the words casually while her mind continued its computations. "I just need to surrender to you."

The commander's shoulders relaxed. "I'm so glad you understand."

"There's only one problem." She plucked a yellow feather out of her hat and tapped it against her lips as if pondering a philosophical thought. "I don't surrender."

His frown was full of pity. "Please be reasonable, Little Captain—"

A dozen arrows thunked into the side of the ship.

A soldier yelled, "We're under attack!"

Commander Saverio's eyes widened as he turned toward the *Lady Tempest*. "How did they know?" He growled and reached for Rhielle, then stumbled as an arrow slammed into his shoulder.

The soldiers who had been subtly prepping to join a boarding crew scrambled to grab their bows, and she used the distraction to sprint to the edge of the ship. An arrow thudded into the railing as she approached, and she ripped off the rope attached to the shaft.

Rhielle jumped onto the railing, wrapping the rope around her wrist. She shook her head at the commander as he tried to staunch the bleeding. "I will not surrender, Commander. Not to you or anyone." She bit the yellow feather in a ferocious grin as she swung from the warship back onto the *Lady Tempest*.

∼

The *Lady Tempest* was already turning by the time her feet hit the deck. Jazhara yelled instructions to the women hauling the ropes to turn the ship, while the rest of the crew loosed arrow after arrow at the Resistance ship.

Chysu lowered her bow as Rhielle approached. "Thanks for the clear signal, Captain."

Rhielle shoved the yellow feather back into her hat as she caught her breath. "You reacted faster than I expected. I thought you might hesitate, considering they're our allies."

"We had a feeling something was wrong. The soldiers on deck were walking around casually ... *Too* casually."

Rhielle nodded her head in appreciation. "I'm impressed you detected that from a distance."

"I didn't." Chysu jerked her head toward the monk behind her. "He did."

Rhielle finally noticed the monk quietly standing nearby. His eyes were wide, following the path she had flown between ships. Rhielle couldn't tell if he was fascinated or horrified. "Who untied him?"

"We were under imminent threat of attack, Captain," said Chysu calmly. "I thought it best if he could defend himself."

"What if he used the chance to escape?"

The monk rolled his eyes, back to his arrogant coolness. "I

have no desire to be taken captive by rebel fighters, pirate. I told you—I need to speak with Geeni, so I'm sticking with you."

Rhielle stabbed a finger at the monk, but stopped before touching his chest. "I do *not* work for Geeni! I—"

"Captain!" Jazhara appeared at Rhielle's side. "We've maneuvered ahead of the warship, but they *will* overtake us. Unless we take *alternative* measures ..." She gave Rhielle a significant look.

Rhielle wanted to defend herself against the monk's accusations, but her first mate was right. "Fine," she growled. "But take the monk below and keep him out of the way."

He shot her an angry glare as Chysu led him away. Rhielle huffed out a breath. She hoped the next stage of their escape made the smug monk seasick.

Rhielle took the helm from an experienced sailor, and the woman melted into the rest of the crew as they prepped the ship for speed. Rhielle's eyes traced the delicate carvings on the inside spokes of the wheel and along the tiller where the ropes from the wheel connected to the rudder below.

She was once again struck by the beauty of her ship. The *Lady Tempest* was truly the most beautiful ship on the entire Dharijian Sea. Her strong masts, her sleek form, her intricate carvings ... The *Lady Tempest* was everything Rhielle would have chosen if she had built the ship herself. As her fingers clutched the wheel, she felt the ship as an extension of herself, skimming through the water. It was nearly enough to make her weep.

Nearly, but not quite.

She tore her eyes away from the carved wheel, and as she looked up at her crew, her gaze landed on Poppy carrying arrows to the archers, who waited to see if the warship would catch up. The girl was determined to fit in as a true pirate, but despite her pirate attire, the girl still looked like she should be in a gown. She delivered the arrows with graceful efficiency, running on tiptoes—a remnant of her lifetime of training to be silent.

As Poppy handed off a fresh quiver of arrows, her eyes met Rhielle's. The girl grinned, then bit her lip as if worried pirates should appear more serious. The wind whipped her hair around her face, obscuring everything but her eyes. Exhilaration—almost a wildness—lurked deep within those lavender eyes.

Memories flooded Rhielle, and with them, a crashing wave of grief. She ducked her head hurriedly, cursing herself for bringing Poppy on board, but begrudgingly grateful the girl had provided what Rhielle needed. She wiped the tears from her eyes and pressed her fingers against the carving at the center of the wheel.

The rune began to glow.

7

Rhielle closed her eyes, even though she was steering. Blocking out everything but the feel of the ship was helpful. With her eyes closed, she could sense beyond the smooth wood of the wheel, beyond the ropes and rudder, all the way to the sea itself.

The sea fought her. It was wild and untamed and didn't like to be controlled, but as Rhielle pitted her strength against the sea, their battle moved the ship ahead. She was never too much for the sea—it welcomed her strength as a worthy foe.

If she believed in prophecy, she would avoid the sea altogether. But despite the ominous prophecy she had received years ago, the clash with the sea exhilarated her. She blocked out everything around her, and the ship shuddered as the sea took hold.

Her battle with the sea sped the *Lady Tempest* through the water.

Keeping her eyes closed had the added benefit of hiding her tears from the rest of the crew. Rhielle hated that her tears were required to activate the rune, but others had tried and failed to make it work. Perhaps the rune only worked for the captain of the ship? Her knowledge of the rune's workings was fairly limited, considering her method of acquiring the ship hadn't lent itself to a full tutorial of its features.

"You can't deny it," growled the monk. "That's one of her runes."

The ship lurched, and Rhielle's eyes shot open with an angry glare. First at the monk, then at Chysu, who had her hand clasped around his arm, trying to lead him away.

"He's sick, Captain. I brought him up to the fresh air to protect us from his retching."

The monk's face was green, though he appeared to be fighting back his nausea just to throw out accusations. "Why are you trying to hide the truth from me? I don't want to hurt your employer. I just want to speak to her."

Thanks to the monk's distraction, Rhielle couldn't sail the ship as fast as when she fully focused, but she kept the ship moving fast enough to draw them steadily away from the Resistance.

She gripped both hands on the wheel as she continued her mental battle with the sea, but faced the monk to start a battle on a different front. "In the past, Geeni offered me good intel, but once I realized she was trying to control me, she went from ally to target."

"Are you saying you stole from her?" His skin turned greener, but she wasn't sure if it was from the continuing acceleration of the ship or that she'd stolen from Geeni.

"I'm a pirate. It's what I do!" She offered him a one-handed bow with a flourish. "Besides, the theft was justified. I love the *Lady Tempest* more than Geeni ever could."

"You stole her *ship*?" He whispered the words, then squeezed his lips together as he swallowed.

"It's *my* ship now, monk. I stole it fair and square." She put both hands on the wheel and flexed her fingers. "And if Geeni didn't want it stolen, she shouldn't have let me sneak aboard to overhear how the rune worked. The *Lady Tempest* is the greatest treasure I've ever stolen. Even more valuable than you, monk."

He opened his mouth, then immediately closed it. He shook off Chysu's hand, sprinted to the edge of the ship, and vomited over the side.

Rhielle scrunched her nose. "Ugh! Remind me to never kidnap a boy again. They have such weak stomachs."

Chysu gave her a flat look. "Captain, we need to discuss our voluntary prisoner. The situation is more complicated than we first thought." Chysu dug in her pocket, pulled out a coin, and flipped it to Rhielle.

The ship lurched as Rhielle snatched the coin out of the air. She closed her eyes and focused on settling into a smooth acceleration, then glanced at the coin.

"An Isandariyan silver," she murmured to Chysu. "What's the problem?"

"Does anything seem familiar to you?"

The ship's speed wavered as Rhielle glanced at the silhouette stamped on the silver piece. "It's one of the seven Isandariyan princes—"

"Yes. Prince Edric. The third-born prince who became a monk."

Rhielle didn't respond, but the ship slowed.

Chysu sighed. "Didn't you study other royal families while you were at court?"

Rhielle turned back to the wheel. "This changes nothing. We're dumping him in Isandariyah, then speeding away to be done with him."

Chysu delicately cleared her throat. "With all due respect, Captain, this changes everything. He's an Isandariyan prince, which makes him a valuable ally or a dangerous enemy. I think it's wise to make him the former."

Rhielle huffed out a breath. "We *kidnapped* him, Chysu. There's no way he will ever be our ally."

Chysu raised an eyebrow. "He will if we can offer what he wants."

"What could we offer a prince? The only thing he wants—" She snapped her mouth shut. "No."

"Captain ..."

"No! I'm not taking him to Geeni. Even if I could find the woman, I don't want to get anywhere near her! And you want to talk about dangerous enemies? How would the Isandariyan queen react if she finds out I dropped her baby boy off with a woman I'm sure is a witch? No. I'm not doing it."

Chysu crossed her arms, a clear sign Rhielle was about to get lectured. "Captain, the Isandariyan queen is likely the one who sent him on this mission. Princes don't just make decisions like that on their own, especially not in Isandariyah. Besides, it's likely the person who arranged the theft of this 'treasure' is Geeni herself. Why not give Geeni and the prince both what they want, while gaining allies in the process?"

Chysu's words were logical, but they grated against Rhielle's instincts. Why shouldn't she just deliver the prince to Geeni? It was what the prince and Geeni wanted. Why not just go along with their plan and get paid to do it?

She clutched the wheel tighter. "They are both using me as a pawn in their game. I won't let them control me."

Chysu's shoulders sagged. "Will you at least talk to the prince and discover why he is looking for Geeni? Maybe that will help you decide what *you* want to do, instead of being swept up in their schemes."

Rhielle considered her words. "You are quite wise, Chysu. I will uncover how this prince's secrets affect me and the rest of the crew. Then I'll decide if we are dumping him back home or selling him to Geeni."

8

At her desk, Rhielle straightened the items that had fallen over during their quick getaway. She propped her flute on its perch and rested her quill squarely beside her ledgers. Once everything was neat, she reclined her head against her sturdy leather chair, as if she didn't have a care in the world. The captain's quarters were her domain, her place of power. Here she could demand answers.

She called out, "Send him in."

Chysu opened the door and ushered the monk inside. The woman gave Rhielle a quietly significant glance, then closed the door, leaving Rhielle alone with the monk.

The prince.

He stood just inside the door, confusion and nausea on his face. He twirled the ring on his finger while he scanned the room.

She beckoned him closer. "Come here, monk. I have something for you."

His face was uncertain, but his footing was steady as he walked to the small chair opposite her desk.

"Have a seat." She pushed a porcelain teacup toward him. "I had Cook prepare a remedy to settle your stomach."

He peered at the teacup for a few moments, but apparently his nausea overrode his suspicion, because he sank into the chair and took a sip. His lashes fluttered as he drew a deep breath, then his eyes opened with a look of gratitude. "Thank you."

She inclined her head in acceptance.

He gulped down the rest of the tea, then lowered the delicate teacup onto its saucer with the practiced grace of a courtier.

She inwardly cursed herself for not realizing his identity sooner. But no matter—she would use that information to gain the upper hand now.

"Tell me, monk ... why are you so determined to find Geeni? What's your business with her?"

His eyes snapped up from his focused study of the teacup and landed on her face. "My business with her is my own, pirate."

Rhielle chuckled as she relaxed against her chair, steepling her fingers. "If you want this ship to ferry you to her, it *is* my business, monk."

He twisted his lips, then muttered, "I have a proposal for her."

She pressed her steepled fingers against her lips. Geeni was powerful—Rhielle knew that for a fact. It would make sense for the prince to seek her out for a political alliance. "So, you plan to propose marriage."

"What?" The word came out as a strangled cough. "Flaming Twins, no! She's my—"

He bit his lip. Did the monk feel guilty for cursing with his goddesses' names?

He drew a breath in through his nose, then said calmly, "A business proposal."

Rhielle raised an eyebrow. Did this prince know what kind of woman Geeni was? Rhielle had sized her up after just a few interactions. The woman had access to a wealth of magical items—Rhielle still didn't know if Geeni made them herself or had a supplier. But the unknown magic stored in the charms on Geeni's neck and wrists was enough to keep Rhielle far away from her. Any proposition this monk would make with Geeni would leave him at a severe disadvantage.

She leaned forward in her chair to study him closer. "Have you met Geeni before, monk? I don't think you realize what kind of woman you are dealing with."

He stared at her with eyes of blue ice. "I know her better than you ever will, pirate."

She thumped back against her chair, intrigued. What was this prince up to? Her curiosity was enough to make her consider delivering him to Geeni. The prince must believe he possessed something Geeni would want, but Rhielle couldn't imagine the woman would ever admit she wanted something she didn't already own.

The prince rested his crossed forearms on the desk as he watched her. "You aren't what I expected, pirate."

Rhielle's hands fisted beneath the desk. "Because I'm a woman?"

He gave her an odd look. "Of course not." He squinted at her bookshelves. "You're obviously well read, with books on a variety of topics in multiple languages." He tapped a finger on the open ledger on her desk. "These look like detailed records of the food on board, which means your crew is well fed, in addition to being well trained and respectful. And that flute ... You probably play for the crew on restless nights ... It's just not what I suspected."

His smile was intrigued, but with just enough smugness to rub Rhielle the wrong way. She had brought him into her quarters to catch him off guard, but instead, he had used the invitation to see into her private life.

She relaxed her face into a blank mask. "You're dismissed, monk."

His smile turned even more smug. He stood smoothly and bowed before heading for the door.

As he reached for the door handle, she called out, "Why you and not one of the others?"

He turned back with a bemused look. "What do you mean?"

She rested both hands flat against her desk as she stared him down. "Why did your mother send *you*, Edric?"

He opened his mouth, then shut it. A thousand lies flitted behind his eyes, but his ultimate answer sounded shockingly like the truth.

"The queen doesn't know," he murmured. "I came on my own."

He pulled the door shut behind him with a soft click.

Rhielle stared at the closed door for several long moments. The prince had set off on a fool's errand without the permission of the queen? His rebellion stirred her begrudging respect. Just because he'd been born into a royal family shouldn't mean he must be confined to a palace for the rest of his life. Maybe his ideas about how to protect his country were better than the ideas proposed by the queen. Why should he be excluded from making decisions simply because of his gender?

What about his brothers? Did they support his decision? Or would they seek him out and try to drag him home?

A prickling shiver ran across the back of her neck, and she shook off the questions. The prince's family dynamics didn't affect her, but they did help her come to a decision.

One, no way would she seek out Geeni. She wouldn't even hand over an enemy to that woman, much less a prince. And two, she didn't hate the prince enough to end his adventure. She wouldn't take him all the way back to Isandariyah, but she needed to be rid of him. She'd drop him off at the next port and send him on his way. If he decided to continue his quest to find Geeni, then it wouldn't be on Rhielle's conscience.

She bent over a map, considering the best port to drop off a sheltered prince. A small port would be safer, but with less travel in and out, he might get stuck there for days or weeks, and he obviously had no coin on him. A larger port would have more options for work and travel to other ports, but that came at the expense of more people who would take advantage of him.

The door opened before she reached a decision. She tapped on the map. "Jazhara, which port—"

"You're needed on deck, Captain." Jazhara held out a spyglass as she caught her breath. "We have visitors."

9

The ship was still far away, but the flag was clear enough to bring a scowl to Rhielle's face. Why did it have to be a ship from Naermore? She would have preferred a Verkeshian ship, so she would have a chance for a fight. But a Naermore ship was complicated.

She returned the spyglass to her first mate with a sigh. "They're drawing closer."

"Yes, Captain," said Jazhara. "How would you like us to handle this?"

Prince Edric edged his way into the conversation. He held out his hand and politely asked Jazhara, "May I?"

She offered him the spyglass with a tight smile.

Rhielle ignored him and asked her first mate, "What are the options if we change course to avoid them?"

"We could head back to where we escaped the Resistance ship, or we could head closer to Verkeshe and take our chances with their navy."

Edric spoke with the spyglass still raised. "Their ship is smaller than yours. Why don't you just fight them?" He gave Rhielle a challenging look. "You *are* pirates, aren't you?"

"The ship is from Naermore, *Prince*." She spit his title like an accusation.

He laughed. "And you are principled pirates who don't attack anyone from Naermore?"

She snatched the spyglass from him and handed it back to her first mate. "Raise the Isandariyan flag and go get Cook."

Jazhara nodded sharply before spinning on her heel and shouting orders to the crew.

"An Isandariyan flag? How dare you use my flag for your pirate schemes!"

She rolled her eyes as she tucked her bright red hair into her hat. "Don't be so dramatic. Our only scheme is to escape with no conflict."

"But why? You're pirates."

"What do you know of Naermore and its place in the war between Verkeshe and La Veridda?"

He huffed dismissively. "Political schemes are my birthright, pirate, but I don't expect you to understand that."

She crossed her arms. "Then tell me, Prince ... How does Naermore still exist as a sovereign kingdom when the power-hungry King Ruzgar of Verkeshe already defeated the much bigger La Veridda during the war?"

He snorted as if the question was too simple. "Because Naermore is no threat to Verkeshe."

"Yes." Though his answer was correct, it still stung. "But Verkeshe controls Merewyn Bay. Why would King Ruzgar allow Naermore ships to sail these seas at all?"

He rubbed his hand across his chin, which had developed dark blond stubble. "I imagine it benefits Verkeshe to keep Naermore a separate kingdom for now, because as long as a king remains in Naermore, his two daughters remain princesses."

She squeezed her lips shut. Though valid, it wasn't the

answer she was looking for. "True," she answered tightly. "Princesses are a valuable commodity."

His expression darkened. "I'm uniquely aware of that fact, pirate."

"Oh ... um, yes, I guess you are." All the other kingdoms waited anxiously for the birth of a prince, but his queendom had a glut of princes and no princesses to secure the succession.

Edric cleared his throat and adopted the tone scholars take when they discuss political marriage, as if real people aren't involved. "Verkeshe expends a lot of resources battling the Resistance and occupying their country. It would be less expensive for King Ruzgar to marry Naermore into his kingdom than to occupy it."

"Very astute, Prince." She regretted the turn of conversation, even though she was to blame for it. She tried to steer the discussion in a less painful direction. "But political alliances aside, King Ruzgar doesn't want to be seen as power hungry. He's rightfully afraid that other countries might finally rouse from their inaction and band together against him. So, for now, he allows Naermore to exist as a sign of his benevolence." She scowled at the thought of a benevolent Verkeshe. "Naermore remains a symbol of a sovereign kingdom in opposition to Verkeshe, so we allow her ships to pass by us freely."

Edric had nodded along to most of her speech, but his head tilted as he fixated on her words. "What do you mean that other countries 'might finally rouse from their inaction'? Do you blame Isandariyah for not stopping Verkeshe from occupying La Veridda?"

She gave him an arch look of accusation.

"I was only eleven when the war started!"

"And your mother?"

He snapped his mouth shut. Lies flitted behind his eyes

again, and this time, he pulled out what must be the most familiar one. "She was busy."

She snorted. "How convenient. I was only five and should have been busy playing with toys, but instead I was scared about what the war would mean for my country."

His eyes narrowed as he studied the single red tendril that had fallen from her hat. "You're from Naermore."

She mentally cursed herself for getting caught up in her past life. "I'm a pirate. I have no country, Prince."

Jazhara interrupted the prince's retort. "Captain, the ship approaches. You should hide now." She looked Edric up and down. "He should probably hide, too. Though he's Isandariyan, he doesn't look it from a distance."

The prince touched his long blond ponytail and scowled at her.

Rhielle jerked her head at the prince. "Come with me."

He crossed his arms like a petulant child. "Why should I?"

"Unless you'd like to abandon your search for Geeni, I suggest you follow me."

He reluctantly dropped his arms and followed.

She led him into a small storage room with a porthole view onto the deck. A burly man climbed from belowdecks and took his place at the helm. The sleeves of his unbuttoned shirt were rolled up to reveal his tattooed brown forearms, and his long dark hair was tied into a thick braid. He looked like an average captain of an Isandariyan merchant ship.

Edric's eyes widened. "There's another man on board? Where's he been?"

"In the kitchen." Rhielle grinned. "That's Cook."

He gave her a flat look. "You keep a man on board to cook for you?"

Her lips curved in a sly smile. "Among other things." She laughed at his open-mouthed shock. "Just watch, and you'll see."

Their porthole didn't face the approaching ship, but it did show the crew's reaction. During the course of her conversation with the prince, all the blond and redheaded pirates had moved belowdecks or had tucked their hair up in wide-brimmed hats.

"Why did everyone change into bulkier clothes?" Edric asked.

"A ship of all women is unusual, even for Isandariyah. Most people just naturally assume sailors are men, so we play along with that assumption so we don't stand out in their mind. We're a simple Isandariyan merchant ship, just passing by."

Cook handed the wheel over to Chysu, who, thanks to her height and a wide-brimmed hat, could pass for a man at a distance.

Cook moved closer to the railing and called out to the other ship, "Lovely day, isn't it?"

The prince's head shot to Rhielle. "He speaks Isandariyan?"

"Of course. He *is* Isandariyan."

His mouth opened and closed several times.

She snorted. "Are you so shocked that one of your citizens would abandon the queendom to come sail the sea with me?"

"Yes!" he hissed.

"Well, it's good for us he did. See?" She pointed at the retreating ship as it passed across their porthole view. "They saw nothing unusual, so they will forget they even saw us. They won't mention us to anyone."

He turned away from the porthole to focus on her. "But ... why?"

She removed her hat and shook her hair until it fell freely around her shoulders once again. "I told you why. Because Naermore is a symbol—"

"No. Why this charade? Why wouldn't you ally with Naermore as you've allied with the Resistance? Since you're originally from Naermore, I'm sure you could befriend them."

She scrambled for a reasonable explanation, but could think of none. "Well, because—"

He stepped closer. "You let someone else pretend they're the captain of this ship. I can't imagine that's a pleasant experience for someone like you. Why couldn't you let that Naermore ship see you as the captain?" He drew closer still. "Who are you afraid they would tell?"

His question sucked all the oxygen out of the tiny storage room. Surely the ship had passed far enough out of view for her to escape, right? She wished desperately that Chysu or Jazhara would knock on the door. Anything that would save her from the prince's piercing blue eyes.

He tipped his head to stare her down, and whispered, "Captain ... what is your name?"

Her name was a lead weight on her tongue. Even if she could bring herself to speak it aloud, her mouth was so dry she couldn't. She searched for a reasonable lie as she wet her lips with her tongue.

The prince's eyes flicked to her mouth.

She sucked in a breath and froze. He was so close. And in a more intimate setting than she had been with any man.

In her former life, she would never have been left alone with a man, especially not in a tiny storage room. After she had taken on the name "pirate," she had lived with a female crew, and though she had teased the prince about Cook, Rhielle would never take advantage of her role as captain to seek a physical relationship with someone in her crew. Other than fighting the Verkeshian military or punching Resistance soldiers in camaraderie, she had never been this close to a man.

She couldn't devise a way to dispel the weighted moment. How could she shift to escape their closeness? She imagined his eyes following her body, and she couldn't find a movement that wouldn't bring a blush to her cheeks.

How had she gotten herself stuck in this situation? She

nt into enemy territory without a carefully planned ape, yet she had stumbled into this battle unprepared. She was suddenly forced to admit the most terrible part. Her battle was not with the prince.

It was with herself.

She was a pirate. She didn't have time to be swooning over princes! If that was what she wanted, she should have never run away.

No, she had made her decision long ago. So no matter what jabs her emotions threw her way, Rhielle was stronger. She wouldn't let a prince make her weak in the knees. Rhielle pulled armor around herself and forced herself to look the prince straight in his eyes.

And found the same battle echoed back.

He was a monk and prince. A lady pirate was a danger to him on all sides. The armor fell into place behind his eyes, the same as it had in hers.

A silent agreement passed between them, and they simultaneously stepped away from each other. In the space of only a few heartbeats, entire cities had dissolved and been rebuilt, and the unspoken words lingered between them.

Rhielle still longed for someone to rescue her from the alarming situation, but as usual, she had to rescue herself. She pushed open the door and ushered him out before her. Then she quickly shut the door, locking all the unsaid words tightly inside.

10

Rhielle stood alone at the bow and watched the approaching shore. After she had snapped at Jazhara to turn the ship to the closest port, the crew had left her unbothered, which suited her fine. Whenever they drew close to land, an itching anxiety clawed at her lungs, and she preferred to deal with that alone.

"Where are we headed?"

She flinched at the monk's low voice. Curse his monk slippers that let him sneak up quietly! Why couldn't he wear loud boots that announced his presence like a considerate pirate?

"Feria," she answered, her hands braced on the railing and her eyes on the shabby buildings in the distance. "It's a small port in La Veridda. We're leaving you here, then we'll be on our way."

He leaned his back against the railing, trying to catch her eyes. "Please, Captain, I need to find Geeni."

His monk's sash fluttered in the wind and brushed across her fingers. She snatched her hands off the rail and gripped them behind her back. "If this is all part of Geeni's plans, like you say, then you'll find her in Ravenna in six days. You don't need me to get there."

"But—"

"It's decided, monk. I refuse to willingly seek out that witch."

"She's not a witch—"

"I've seen her magic with my own eyes. I stole this ship and its rune, but who knows what other magic she has wrapped around her neck and wrists? I will not deliver you to her."

His lips pressed into a thin line. "I'm not afraid of her."

"You should be!" she hissed. "But even so, I will not control you by dragging you back home where you belong."

"Then just take me a little closer. Your ship is fast—"

She smacked her hand on the railing at his back. "I cannot have you on this ship!"

He drew a deep breath to continue his argument as she brushed her swirling hair out of her face and tucked it behind her ear. His chest stopped moving midbreath, and his blue eyes softened into a rippling sea on a calm day.

She was as trapped in his gaze as she had been in the storage room. She couldn't lift her hand and step back because if his eyes followed her ...

He ducked his head, breaking eye contact. "Um ..." He cleared his throat. "I should go, Captain."

Without his eyes on her, she was free to move again. She stepped back and tugged on her vest, though it was still firmly in place. "Yes, well ... I'm glad you agree."

"We've arrived, Captain."

She spun. Jazhara stood at calm attention, her hands clasped behind her back. How much had her first mate heard? "Thank you, Jazhara." She tried to assume her usual commanding tone, but her voice sounded unnatural to her own ears. "Please prepare the dinghy for a trip to shore."

Jazhara's brows were drawn together as if she was piecing

together a puzzle. "Captain, can't this wait until we reach a larger port? If we wait until Terlanna, we can actually dock the ship and pick up supplies. What's the rush to stop now?"

"Thank you for the suggestion, Jazhara," she said tightly. "This is our stop."

"Of course, Captain." Jazhara's eyes slid from Rhielle to the monk, who stood with his head demurely bowed. "Who will row him to shore?"

Rhielle didn't want to deal with the grumbling from the unlucky person she picked for that grueling task. "I'll do it myself."

Jazhara raised her eyebrow slowly, as if testing a solution to her puzzle. "So ... just you and the monk? Alone?"

Edric's eyes shot to Rhielle's, and in them flickered the same panic written in her own. She tore her gaze away before she could get trapped again and cleared her throat calmly. "I don't want to row alone on the way back. Thanks for volunteering."

Jazhara's eyes lit up as if she had discovered a solution, before her mouth turned down. "Volunteering ... Yes, of course, Captain."

～

Rhielle observed the distant port in silence. Edric had offered to row since Jazhara and Rhielle would have to row on the return trip, so he sat by the oars with his back to shore while the two women shared a seat facing land. Rhielle's eyes kept drifting to Edric's powerful forearms, which flexed with each stroke. The rhythmic way his broad shoulders shifted as he leaned forward, then pulled back in tension with the rushing waves ...

Rhielle forced her eyes back to the shoreline. She had never been so relieved to see land.

Jazhara broke the silence. "So, Prince Edric, do you plan on sharing your identity with the people in port?"

His steady rhythm stuttered before evening out. "I ... don't know. I thought spreading the rumor of my location would be too tempting for Geeni to pass up, but why would she trick you into capturing me when she could have sent one of her henchwomen to take me directly to her?" He chewed his lip as he continued rowing. "Maybe it's best to keep my identity a secret until I figure it out."

His uncertainty surprised Rhielle. He had been so confident of his plan, smug even. Should she reassure him? Instead she asked a question that had been nagging at her. "Why did you think Geeni would come after you at all? Other than an easy chance to collect ransom?"

He glanced at Rhielle, then ducked his head back to the oars. "Geeni is my mother's cousin, Ginevere."

"The queen has a cousin?" she gasped. "I thought your grandmother was an only child."

He looked up at her with a question in his eyes, and she winced internally. Did normal pirates know so much about royal bloodlines in other countries?

He shook off the question and answered her instead. "She had a half sister. Some would call her sister illegitimate, being the result of an affair, but in Isandariyah the only thing that matters is the mother."

Rhielle's mouth dropped open. "Geeni is a contender for the Isandariyan throne." She blinked at him. "You plan to kill her."

His hands slipped on the oars. "What? No, of course not!"

She laughed in shock. "Are you handing her the crown, then? Because those seem like the only two options."

"There is another way." He pursed his lips and said no more.

Rhielle's eyes had drifted back to Edric's shoulders when

Jazhara asked, "Why did you become a monk? How can you fulfill your role as prince with your attention split between your country and your goddesses?"

His cold blue eyes snapped up to Jazhara. "The queendom and the Goddesses are one and the same. My vow to one is my vow to the other. I ..." He trailed off as he peered over Jazhara's shoulder. "What does that flag mean?"

Rhielle and Jazhara both spun to inspect the *Lady Tempest*. Someone on deck was waving a large green flag.

"Verkeshe," whispered Jazhara. "It means they've spotted a military ship from Verkeshe."

Rhielle gauged the distance to shore and the distance back to the ship. They were barely a quarter of the way to land. "I'm sure the crew spotted the ship a long way off. We can drop him on shore and still make it back in time."

Jazhara snapped, "Don't be ridiculous! We have to get back now." She glanced at Edric. "It's not that far to shore, Captain. If you're so desperate to be rid of him, push him out and let him swim."

Rhielle gaped at Jazhara's cruel suggestion. How could she —Oh. Her words were a test. She gave her first mate a cool look. "I assume you and I are better swimmers than he is. We can swim the short distance and leave him with the boat."

Jazhara's eyes opened wide. "No, Captain! The prophecy! You can't risk that now!"

She hissed at the woman. Why had she ever mentioned that stupid prophecy to her first mate? She snatched the oars from Edric and handed one to Jazhara. "Fine. We all head back to the ship."

Once Rhielle and Jazhara had fallen into a swift rowing pattern, Edric asked, "The prophecy?"

"Don't worry about it," grumbled Rhielle.

"Prophecies are nothing to be ashamed of, Captain," said Jazhara soothingly. "It's best to talk about prophecies with others. When you keep them to yourself, there's a higher risk of misinterpretation. The Four Gods give prophecies to offer assistance, not anxiety."

"I am not anxious about the prophecy, Jazhara. Just drop it." She kept her eyes firmly on the retreating port over Edric's shoulder.

He shook his head. "I'm surprised you believe in Zaridian mythology."

"Mythology?" Jazhara's voice rose in outrage. "How dare you call my religion 'mythology,' you self-righteous ..." She spewed a mixture of Zaridian and Riddish curses with a few Verkeshian expletives thrown in.

Rhielle chuckled. "Don't take it so seriously, Jazhara. I'm sure he'd call my religion 'mythology' as well."

He arched his brow. "Considering you're from Naermore, I'd actually call your religion 'paganism.'"

Jazhara had stopped her cursing at his mention of Naermore and started an intense study of them both.

Rhielle returned her attention to the shore. "I never said I was from Naermore, monk."

He was silent for a moment, and she turned to look. He was staring over her shoulder. "They are waving the flag even more frantically. Maybe I should row? I'd get us there faster."

His condescending attitude rankled her. "We're doing just fine, monk—"

"Take my spot." Jazhara hopped up and waited by his seat, forcing him to move or risk toppling the boat.

He settled in next to Rhielle, at the precise distance to avoid touching shoulders. She glared at her first mate sitting across from them. Jazhara was the picture of innocence.

Rhielle barked out a command. "Match my speed, monk."

"Yes, Captain." His reply was as smooth as his stroke. She focused on keeping a steady rhythm, but every time his shoulder brushed hers, her oar jerked awkwardly in the water, slowing their movement.

"Captain." Jazhara's voice was unusually tense. "The military ship is very close."

Rhielle had to pretend she was alone on this boat. She blew out her held breath and closed her eyes to block out distractions. There was no monk, no prince, beside her. It was only her and the waves, locked in their ongoing battle. One day, the sea would best her and drag her down to its watery heart, just like the prophecy had foretold. But it wouldn't be today. Today, she would make it back to her ship, and she would flee the Verkeshe until she sought them out again on her terms. Today, she would feel the wind in her hair as the *Lady Tempest* cut through the waves, alone out on the open water, with only her crew at her side.

Her crew and the prince.

"We made it, Captain!"

Her eyes shot open. How were they already back at the ship?

Jazhara grabbed the ladder dangling from the ship and passed it to Rhielle. "The waves worked with us that last stretch, thank the Four Gods." She aimed the loud blessing over her shoulder toward Edric.

He was staring at Rhielle, but she scrambled up the ladder onto the ship, escaping the question in his eyes.

11

Rhielle started barking orders before her feet hit the deck. Most of her crew was prepping the ship for a quick getaway, while a team of women secured the dinghy after Jazhara and Edric made it safely aboard.

She found Chysu giving orders to the helmswoman.

"Report," snapped Rhielle.

Chysu handed her a spyglass even though Rhielle could clearly see the Verkeshian ship headed toward them. "We were flying the Isandariyan flag, so we expected them to pass us by. Instead, they are barreling straight at us with everything they've got."

Rhielle peered through the spyglass to get a closer view of their weapons. This was no simple patrol ship. The massive ship bristled with mounted crossbows, and ranks of soldiers stood poised on deck, ready to release their arrows. If it were night, Rhielle might consider sneaking on board to commit theft or sabotage, and trust in the *Lady Tempest*'s easy maneuverability to get away before the bigger ship could follow. But right now, the warship's sails billowed with a favorable wind, and the strong current swept them directly toward the *Lady Tempest*.

"Get out of here! Now!"

The helmswoman turned the wheel hard, and Jazhara assumed her place by Rhielle's side, shouting orders to turn the sails. Rhielle would need to take her place at the helm once the ship was pointed in the right direction. She searched for Poppy. The girl clutched a quiver of arrows to her chest, gawking at the warship. Her strawberry blond hair swirled slowly, almost as if she were floating underwater ...

"Will you use the rune?" asked the prince.

Rhielle was jerked from her memories. She blinked at Edric, trying to understand his question.

"The rune," he repeated. "I assume you will use it to make the ship sail faster."

Her hands fisted at her sides. "Go somewhere else, monk. I need to focus."

"Doesn't the rune automatically make the ship move? What do you have to focus on?"

She stepped closer and said in a deadly whisper, "Not one more question. Do you understand me?"

"Captain!" Jazhara's barked orders were now aimed at Rhielle. "We need to move faster!"

Rhielle's head snapped toward the approaching ship almost within crossbow range. A half-hearted battle with the sea wouldn't take them far enough fast enough. She needed to focus her full attention on their escape.

She stomped away from the monk with an angry shake of her head and stepped up to the wheel. The helmswoman abandoned her post with a respectful nod, running off to assist elsewhere.

Edric lingered near her shoulder, but the warship loomed even larger in her peripheral vision. She squeezed the wheel tightly and closed her eyes.

She tried to stir the tears by picturing Poppy clutching the arrows, but the girl herself couldn't stir Rhielle's grief. She would have to dive below the surface and retrieve a memory of her own if she wanted the rune to work.

Fractured sunlight through the waves ... strawberry blond hair floating in a halo ... silence as still as the grave ...

She wiped the tears from her eyes with one hand, the other firmly on the wheel. She didn't even open her eyes before pressing her tears against the rune.

The rune would be glowing by now, but it always took time for the magic to kick in. Rhielle imagined a line of magic stretching from the rune down to the rudder, where the press of the sea was the firmest.

She whispered, knowing the sea would hear. "Not today, sea. You won't have me yet. Today, you're *mine*, and you will surrender to me. Carry me away from here, as quickly as you can."

The sea responded with a resounding crash of waves against the stern, and the ship quaked under the sudden pressure. Rhielle kept a firm grip on the wheel, as if the tighter she squeezed, the more obedient the sea. Her arms trembled from the strength of her grip, and her knees weakened at how hard she had to brace herself.

She could no longer hear the shouts of the crew—only the rushing of waves, the rhythm matching the steady pulse of her heart. Time and place faded until all that remained was the sliver of space where her soul touched the sea.

"Captain?" Chysu's soft voice floated on a wave.

A calloused but gentle hand touched hers.

"Captain, we've outrun them."

Rhielle blinked open her eyes. Chysu's hand covered her own, as she clutched the wheel, knuckles white.

"You can let go now." Chysu spoke tenderly, though with

respect. "One of the helmswomen can take over and keep our pace ahead of the warship."

Rhielle loosened her fingers one at a time, though they refused to stay uncurled. How long had she been steering?

"You should eat, Captain. Cook will prepare something for you." Chysu glanced up. "Go with her, monk. Make sure she eats."

Rhielle blinked, her thoughts still fuzzy, and turned her head. The prince waited at her side. He didn't appear to have heard what Chysu had said. All his attention was locked squarely on Rhielle. He stared at her with slack-jawed wonder, barely breathing.

"Prince Edric!"

Chysu's voice snapped his focus, and she repeated her command.

He cleared his throat. "Yes, of course. I'll see that she eats."

Rhielle rubbed her sore fingers, mainly to avoid the prince's eyes. "I don't need a minder, Chysu."

"He hasn't eaten either," said Chysu. "Maybe you are *his* minder."

Rhielle grumbled, "Fine. We'll eat. Call me if the warship gains on us."

She climbed belowdecks, trusting the prince would keep up. Crew members saluted her as she passed, and she smiled at them warmly. It wasn't their fault she felt off-kilter from the close call with the warship.

Yes ... the warship was to blame for the strange tension in her chest.

Cook waved her to a seat in the mess hall and disappeared into the galley. She lowered herself onto the bench, trying to disguise how her legs shook. She placed her hands on the table, stretching her fingers out.

Edric watched her without saying a word. Cook brought bowls of spicy stew and warm ale, along with a slice of bread. It was the bread Rhielle had bought from Olga, the tavern owner who had given her the tip about the prince. Had Olga truly heard the rumor about a red-ribboned treasure? Or was the woman in on it like everyone else?

"Are you the only one who can use the rune?"

Rhielle's spoon stilled halfway to her mouth.

The prince leaned forward, ignoring his food. "Can someone take over for you? Have you ever tried?"

She snorted. "Of course I've tried! It only works for me. I think it's keyed to the captain of the ship." She shrugged and dipped her bread into her stew.

His eyes lit up. "So Geeni keyed it to you with one of your tears? You cried in front of her?"

She opened her mouth to lash him with an angry retort, but she shut it again, unable to answer.

"If you cried for her, it would make sense why the rune will only work for you. Otherwise, there would have to be another explanation ..." He stared at her as if she was a mystery.

Rhielle tossed her spoon into her stew. "Why would Geeni key her ship to me? She didn't give it to me. I stole it from her, remember?"

"Hmm ..." He mindlessly stirred his stew.

"It doesn't matter how it works. It's just magic." She chugged half her ale, which gave the benefit of shading her face from him, so he couldn't see that his words worried her.

"A Spark." Edric continued stirring aimlessly.

"What are you talking about?"

He set his spoon down. "That's what the magic is called—at least that's what we call it in Isandariyah. A Spark. There are those gifted with specific types of magic—controlling wind, speaking to animals, imbuing items with light ... Geeni can harness their Spark and embed it in a rune to be used later. No one knows how she discovered this power ... Maybe making runes is her own Spark?" He shrugged. "But if this ship has the power of superspeed, she must have found someone with that Spark, then coaxed enough tears from them to create that rune. If so, she must be extremely angry you stole such a powerful rune from her."

Rhielle shook her head, trying to get all the new information to fall into place. "So Geeni isn't a witch?"

"I don't know what she is."

"And yet, you want to offer her a business proposal?"

"I have no choice!" he hissed. He controlled himself, and his next words were a calm whisper. "The queendom has no choice."

"And what makes you think Geeni would choose to save the queendom if given a choice?" Rhielle couldn't imagine the woman doing anything that didn't benefit her.

"I think she will take my offer, because it guarantees her what she wants. The Isandariyan throne."

Rhielle's jaw dropped. "You're offering to overthrow your own mother?"

"Of course not!" He rubbed his forehead as if struggling to share his plan with her. He bit his lip. "Even though Geeni has actively tried to kill at least two of my brothers, and planned to kill or capture the queen, I'm offering Geeni a stay of execution. The only caveat is she has to spend the rest of my mother's life under house arrest."

Rhielle laughed. "And why would she take that deal? Especially if she plans to overthrow the queen and take the throne now?"

"Because she will be guaranteed a life of luxury. She will be known in Isandariyah as the future queen. No more scheming or political maneuvering in foreign countries."

"I get the sense Geeni enjoys scheming, Prince. I don't think you'll convince her to give that up."

A muscle flexed in his jaw, but he didn't refute her.

"Besides, why offer this risky proposition now? Why not

wait until Geeni makes her play for the throne and you capture her then?"

"Because she needs to hurry." A hint of pink spread across his cheeks.

"Hurry? To do what?"

"To have a child." He shoveled down a bite of stew.

She leaned back, her fingers again spreading wide on the table. "You mean, to have a daughter and secure the succession."

He gently set down his spoon. "The queen, my mother, is forty-seven years old, and after seven sons, giving birth to a daughter is unlikely ... for many reasons. However, Geeni is only thirty-nine and appears to be in good health. She is of the bloodline of the First Queen, Twice Blessed. She must give birth to a daughter, or Isandariyah will fall."

Rhielle pushed her bowl forward and clasped her hands on the table before her. "Let me get this straight—you plan to make Geeni this appealing offer ... Come with me back to Isandariyah to be willingly locked up and become breeding stock for a future heir."

He shifted uncomfortably. "If the queen dies before Geeni's daughter comes of age, Geeni would become queen herself. That's what Geeni wants—"

"I guarantee you, that offer is *not* what Geeni wants, and when you suggest it, she will either laugh in your face or murder you on the spot."

"She *must* take my offer—"

"Ah ... so it's not truly an offer, but a demand. If you are demanding this of her, you should have brought a fleet of ships with you instead."

He shook his head sharply. "No, it's not a demand. It's just ... this is the only way out, you see? The only answer. If there is no daughter to inherit the First Queen's bloodline, there is no Isandariyah."

"So the success of this plan is based on Geeni's loyalty to Isandariyah and the First Queen?"

"Yes," he whispered.

She wanted to laugh at his ridiculous solution, but he seemed so earnest. And below his strong exterior, Rhielle sensed something fragile. He believed so strongly because he saw no other option that kept his faith in Isandariyah intact.

"Do you believe she will take your offer?" she murmured.

"Yes." His voice was firm. "This is how Isandariyah will survive. The Twin Goddesses blessed the First Queen, and their blessing will live on through Geeni's daughter." He whispered, "It must."

She opened her mouth, unsure if ridicule or sympathy would spill out, when Chysu tapped her on the shoulder.

"I'm sorry to interrupt your meal, Captain, but you're needed on deck." Her shoulders stiffened. "The warship is catching up, and there is another ship heading toward us."

12

Rhielle squinted through the spyglass to identify the ship in the faint light of the setting sun. Getting caught between two Verkeshian military warships would spell disaster. Their soldiers were skilled at complex maneuvers and would trap the *Lady Tempest* between them. The only unknown was if they would destroy the ship with everyone on board or take her crew prisoner.

Neither option would leave her crew alive in the end.

When the Resistance flag fluttered into view, she breathed a sigh of relief. "It's the Resistance. They will square off with the Verkeshe, and we can sail off into the night."

Chysu took the spyglass and frowned as she held it to her eye. "Are you sure, Captain?"

"I'm sure it's the Resistance."

Jazhara crossed her arms and gave Rhielle a serious look. "Are you sure they will chase the Verkeshe ship and not us?"

Her narrow escape from Commander Saverio seemed like a lifetime ago and was still so preposterous her mind refused to believe it had actually happened. "Surely word hasn't reached the entire Resistance fleet."

Chysu spoke in her usual calm tone. "If Commander Saverio received orders to take you captive, it's reasonable to assume the whole fleet has been notified."

Rhielle appreciated the doctor's ability to provide logical advice, but sometimes it really grated on her nerves when Chysu was correct.

Rhielle rubbed a hand across her forehead to relax the muscles still strained from their last getaway, then sighed. "Fine. We head further out to sea and hope the two ships notice each other and don't pay attention as we sneak out of the party."

Jazhara spun on her heel and shouted orders to the crew. Chysu checked the position of the ships one more time in the spyglass, then turned to the helmswoman with directions.

Since it would take time for the ship to turn, Rhielle ducked beneath the overhang that led to her quarters and sagged against the wall. Fighting the sea enough to move the ship was exhausting, and she hadn't recovered from the two times they had already fled today. She prayed desperately to her so-called pagan gods that the ships would ignore the *Lady Tempest* and she could just go to bed.

"Will you use the rune again?" The monk had padded softly to join her in the relatively quiet space outside her door.

"Unless the two ships turn to face off against each other, then yes, I'll have to."

"It tires you." A statement, not a question. Though it seemed obvious, with how she sagged against the wall.

Her pride was too tired to allow her to deny it. "Yes."

He studied her face, his blue eyes shaded in the growing twilight. "It's unusual ... that it tires you."

Her pride awakened enough to send a prickle that unbent her spine. "Unusual? Is that from your experience with other women who control ships with magical runes?"

He had the grace to look abashed. "No, but ... I've met

others who have used Geeni's runes. They've never mentioned it tiring them before. The runes just ... work."

She slumped back against the wall, her slight burst of prideful energy exhausted. "I guess they're stronger than me."

"No ... I don't think that's it." He opened and closed his mouth a few times before he asked the question lurking behind his eyes. "How did you learn about the rune?"

She shrugged. "Just one of my pirate adventures. I knew there was something special about the ship based on the way Geeni had carefully avoided talking about it. One night, I snuck aboard the docked ship and heard two of her henchwomen discussing it. They said pressing a tear against the rune would activate the ship's magic and cause it to sail faster than any other on the sea." She sighed wistfully. "I had to have her."

"They said that exactly? That it was the ship that was magic?"

She gave him a strange look. "Yes, that's what they said. And I knew it was true the first time I tried it. Thanks to that rune, the *Lady Tempest* is magic."

He had seen the ship speeding through the water, so she wasn't sure why he still looked so puzzled.

"It's just ... I heard you before. When you used the rune." He seemed embarrassed to admit he had listened to her. "You ... um ... you didn't talk to the ship, telling it to go faster." His eyes locked on hers. "You commanded the sea."

She tilted her head at the distinction. "Yes, that's true, but it has the same effect. The ship moves faster than it should. I don't think there's a difference."

He clasped his hands behind his back. "I think there's a big difference, Captain."

His calm confidence grated on her, and she prepared to tell him so when Jazhara called, "Captain!"

Rhielle headed onto the deck where Jazhara peered through the spyglass. "They've both turned toward us." Her first mate lowered the spyglass, and her dark eyes held foreboding. "They're coming."

Rhielle blew out her breath, then sucked it in sharply as she faced the crew, who had stilled their preparations to watch her. "Prepare for a long night. We have to head out to open sea to avoid them. Hopefully, we can pass between the ships and leave them both far behind. But just in case I falter, prepare the arrows and sharpen your knives. The Resistance may take prisoners, but Verkeshe surely doesn't."

Her crew saluted and jumped to work around her. A smile tugged at her lips with pride in her crew. Some women like Chysu and Jazhara had been sailing long before they met Rhielle, but many on her crew had been like Poppy, destined for another life when Rhielle brought them on board. And now she would pit her crew against a Verkeshian crew any day.

She spun toward the helm but ran into Edric at her back. She growled, "You need louder shoes, monk."

His lips curved into the first actual smile—other than a smug grin—she had seen from him. The playful smile lit up his face, removing the frown lines between his brows that she'd thought were permanent. His eyes sparkled like the sun glinting off clear water on a calm day. "I'll get some pirate boots at the next port."

An answering smile threatened to break out on her lips, but she pushed it under her looming worry. "If we reach the next port."

He followed her to the helm. "You've outrun warships before."

"Yes, but the Resistance used to be on our side. We could previously lure the Verkeshian ships toward the last location we'd seen a Resistance ship and let them battle it out while we escaped with the goods. Now everyone on the sea is after us."

He smiled hopefully. "The ships from Naermore and Isandariyah will probably leave you alone."

She gave him a flat look. "I kidnapped an Isandariyan prince. I assume your navy will have a few angry words for me."

The helmswoman saluted as she left, and Rhielle placed her hands on the wheel, assuming the responsibility for leading them away from the enemies on either side. She wasn't ready. She already had to cling to the wheel to keep her knees from buckling—how would she battle the sea all night?

What was it the prince had said about how runes were supposed to just "work"? She grunted. That would be nice. Maybe this rune was faulty? She shook the bitter thought out of her head and set about their escape.

13

Rhielle needed tears. Luckily, when she was exhausted, the tears seemed closer to the surface. When she was fully rested and well fed, she could go an entire day without the prickling unease that prefaced her grief. On good days, she could flow from activity to activity with no hint of tears, at least not until her head hit her pillow alone in her quarters at night. The tears found her there, even on the good days.

On bad days, when exhaustion loomed over her, each stirring of anger or frustration or disappointment harbored sadness—a lurking grief that threatened to raise its head at the first sign of weakness. On those days, she couldn't stop moving, even though she was exhausted, because as soon as she stopped, as soon as she stood still for just one moment, a wave of grief broke through the safer emotions, pulling her beneath the surface until she couldn't breathe.

So now, in the midst of her exhaustion, she knew the tears were there. Waiting to take her. To drown her. But she only had time for a few. She couldn't surrender to all the tears lingering below the surface, not and still have the strength to battle the sea. How could she separate a few teardrops from the ocean of grief inside?

"What do you think about to stir your tears?"

Her head whipped to the side, where Edric watched her with a gentle expression. His eyes widened. "I'm sorry. I shouldn't ask you such a personal question, Captain. Forget I asked."

Like she could simply forget he'd asked. Forget he was watching the emotions cross her face. Forget he continually hovered near her shoulder. Forget she found his presence at her side comforting.

Just forget.

"Isn't there something you could do to assist the crew?" she asked.

"Apologies, Captain, but I'm not a sailor. I have no skills to offer them." He edged closer. "But since the rest of your crew is busy, I thought I could stand here and be ready if you need something. Maybe I could bring you water or snacks?"

She blinked slowly. "I'm about to steer a magical ship out into the middle of the sea, but you'll bring me snacks?"

The playful smile lit his face again. "Don't you like snacks, Captain?"

A laugh burst from her throat, surprising her with a strange lightness in the middle of her search for tears. "Yes, I do like snacks, monk. I'm a pirate, but I'm still human."

The amusement in his eyes settled into a contented study of her face. Her fingers itched to brush her fingers through her hair—to straighten it and bring her scruffy state into some kind of order. Instead, she kept her hands firmly on the wheel, reminding herself she was a pirate and had no one to impress. Her unruly appearance only made her more intimidating. She could remain coolly indifferent, even if he watched her all night with his eyes like a calm sea.

She snapped her eyes shut and concentrated on

summoning a tear. The ship had fully turned in their new direction, and it was time to run. She couldn't wait any longer.

Rhielle needed to cry.

She breathed in deeply, seeking her grief on the wind, but instead she scented woodsmoke and spice. Normally smoke on board a ship would be bad, but this was the scent of the monk. The smell of burned prayers offered to his goddesses still permeated his hair, despite days away from his shrine. The scent was eminently comforting. And as she sighed peacefully, an answer sprang to her lips.

"My sister," she whispered. "I think of my sister."

She didn't open her eyes, but she heard his indrawn breath. Woodsmoke and spice filled her nose as he drew closer. "What happened to her?"

Answering was unwise, for many reasons. But the sun had dipped below the horizon, she was exhausted, and she needed the tears anyway.

"I ... um ... just miss her. I haven't seen her in five years."

"Can you not go home and visit her?"

"Going home is ... complicated."

"I'm so sorry, Captain."

Though she could still hear the women of her crew going about their various tasks, his gentle voice cut through the noise as if they were alone.

She had worried even sharing that much would drown her in tears, but instead, a manageable few rose to the surface. As she wiped them from her eyes, these tears didn't feel as bleak as usual.

Still sad ... yet somehow different, from being shared with someone else.

With eyes closed, she touched the tears to the rune. She waited for the magic to travel the length of the ship until she sensed the sea. Usually she just felt the portion of the sea near the rudder, but tonight she also sensed the sea streaming along the sides of the ship as it cut through the waves under the power of the wind.

She focused on each individual wave and whispered to them all at once. "Listen to me, sea. I know you'd like nothing more than to pull me down to the depths tonight, but you can't take me yet. Carry me and my crew away from here. Faster than you've ever carried us before. Do what I say. Do it now."

The ship shot forward, so quickly Rhielle's fingers almost slipped off the wheel. She wrapped her forearms around the handles, holding the wheel in a tight embrace. She would not release the wheel and let the sea win. It would submit to her. There was no choice.

Cries and rustles echoed over the waves as people and cargo slid across the deck, but she didn't open her eyes. She had to trust the crew would look out for each other while she focused on their escape.

There was nothing but Rhielle and the sea.

Rhielle and the sea ...

Rhielle and the sea ...

A drop of rain landed on her cheek and burned a path across her skin.

Her eyes shot open, and the ship lurched.

The monk tumbled into view and clutched the wheel at her side. "Are you okay?"

Rhielle's head swam, like she had drank an ocean full of ale, and she couldn't get her bearings. The sea was dark, with only a sliver of a moon shining amid a swathe of stars. The waves battered the side of the ship, but she couldn't command them anymore. The rune was dark and would require another tear, but she could barely stand, much less battle the sea again.

"Did we escape? Are we out of their range?" A raindrop landed on her hand, and she hissed, wiping it on her pants before it could blister her skin. The rain had awakened her from steering the ship. She rubbed her fingers across her tender cheek.

The prince studied her with confused concern. A few drops of rain speckled his tunic, but he didn't notice.

Of course he didn't notice. Rain did not affect normal people. Some found rain irritating and some found it whimsical, but she knew no one else whose skin burned at its touch. The affliction wasn't normal. It wasn't normal even for her, considering it had only started five years ago. But no matter how many times she told herself it must be inside her head, she couldn't stop the prickling pain every time a drop touched her skin.

Another drop landed on her neck and trickled down her collarbone. She scraped her nails across her skin and yelled, "Get Jazhara! Now!"

Jazhara was assisting the crew, who had almost been swept overboard when the magic crashed to a halt, but the monk jumped and dragged the first mate to Rhielle's side.

Jazhara took one look at Rhielle, then glanced up at a dark cloud that passed across the moon. "Four Gods, a storm ... Poppy! Find Captain's hat. Now!"

The monk stepped back and let Jazhara take his place at Rhielle's side. The petite woman murmured, "Listen to me, Captain. We've shot between them, but we can't keep heading out into the open sea. We need to circle back around and find a safe port to wait this out. If we wait until morning to head toward land, they will spot us and figure out which way we headed. I hate to say this, but we need to move faster than the wind will carry us. Are you strong enough?"

Battle the sea again already? Exhausted tears welled in her eyes. She almost choked them down out of habit, but instead, she let them flow down her cheeks as she nodded slowly.

Jazhara patted her cheek fondly, careful to not disrupt any tears. "You're a good captain." Her first mate turned to Edric and shook him out of his confusion. "Listen to me, monk. Your job is to stand here and make sure she doesn't fall. Hold her hands against the wheel yourself if you must, but do *not* let her fall, got it?"

"Yes ... yes, of course," he stammered, assuming his place at Rhielle's side.

Poppy ran up with Rhielle's hat in hand. "Captain?"

Rhielle scraped a trickling drop off her forehead and accepted the feathered hat gratefully. The feathers were more waterproof than she was. "Thank you, Poppy." Rhielle pulled her hat on securely and buttoned her jacket with shaking fingers.

"Are you sure about this, Captain?" Even in the faint moonlight, Edric's eyes flashed a blue that reminded her of a summer day.

"Don't let me fall," she rasped as she wiped the tears from her eyes and pressed them against the rune. Then she slammed her mind into the sea, praying she would survive the battle.

14

Rhielle woke from the fight, crushed between the ship's wheel and a warm boulder. Her hands gripped the wheel, locked tight, and her eyes were squeezed shut. She only kept her feet thanks to the pressure against her back. She twitched her little finger, just to see if she could, and the warm boulder shifted.

"Captain?" The monk babbled in a frantic whisper. "Are you awake? ... Conscious? ... Back in this plane of reality? I'm not sure where you go ..."

He had so many questions, and she had no energy to answer. Her brain was sluggish and her senses muted. The only crystal clear sensation was his warm breath against her neck.

She wanted him to speak again, so she asked, "Are we out of danger?"

"Yes." His deep voice rumbled against her back, both soothing her and rousing her. "Jazhara came by a moment ago and said we were safe, but to let you wake on your own."

The prideful part of her mind said she should shake him off and stand, but another part of her didn't want to move—and it wasn't just because her knees would buckle if she did.

She took the first step to reclaiming her dignity and opened her eyes. The sun was peeking over the horizon. "We sailed all night?"

"*You* sailed all night. The rest of us just tried to hold on." He chuckled quietly, and the vibration sent a tingling warmth racing across her skin.

She cleared her throat. "I should probably attempt to stand on my own two feet, monk."

"Oh ... yes, of course, Captain." He shifted, and instead of his chest holding her up, he gripped her around the waist with a strong arm, giving her time to push herself away from the wheel.

It wasn't until he moved that she felt his calloused hands slide off hers. She looked up at him while he still supported her around the waist. "You held my hands to the wheel?"

He ducked his head as if ashamed. "Jazhara said to not let you fall, and ... well, the rain irritated your skin, and you refused to wear gloves ..."

Gloves hindered her ability to feel the sea through the wheel. But instead of an explanation, she whispered, "You covered my hands with yours to protect me from the rain?"

His jaw worked as if he was confused about what answer to give.

She found the strength to pull one hand off the wheel, and she slipped her hat off her head. The hat was in terrible shape —the brim had been crushed just as she had been between the wheel and a boulder.

She sighed as she examined the ragged feathers. "I bet I look as rough as my hat."

He smiled softly. "You look like a woman who saved her crew." His eyes focused on her cheek. "Your eyeliner smeared." He brushed a thumb beneath her eye and froze.

A familiar weighted moment slid into place around them. The moment when they both realized their foolishness. It was bad enough she was being an idiot, but to see him mentally scolding himself was embarrassing in an entirely different way.

She positioned her legs fully underneath herself to stand at the same time he stepped back. She searched for words to shift the conversation in a safer direction, but she couldn't find a single one.

"Captain! You're awake."

Edric's sigh of relief at Jazhara's approach was as clear as her own.

Rhielle asked, "Where are we?"

"We're almost to Ravenna, Captain."

"Ravenna! We're days away from Ravenna!"

"No, Captain. We are only a few hours away. Not only did you steer us away from danger last night, you brought us all the way to Ravenna. You sailed faster than you ever have before. Perhaps we should bring the monk on every trip." She winked and slapped him on the back.

The pride that had escaped her earlier now prickled up her spine. "That's unnecessary—"

"I can't stay—" said the monk.

They both cut off their words and avoided the other's eyes.

Jazhara sighed dramatically. "Well, we only have a few hours until we reach Ravenna, Captain. I had Poppy draw a bubble bath for you, and you can steal a few hours' sleep while someone else steers the ship in the more traditional way."

The monk shifted his feet, perhaps uncomfortable with the discussion of Rhielle's bubble bath. "Um ... I should get to my morning prayers."

He turned to walk away, but Jazhara called after him. "Do your prayers on the port side this morning, monk." She elbowed Rhielle in the ribs. "It needs a good scrubbing, right, Captain?"

He gave her a confused look but headed to the port side as

commanded. Rhielle didn't wait for him to begin his salutations before she stumbled to her quarters alone.

∼

Though she only slept a few hours, when she woke, the sky outside her window was dark. She shook off the disorientation and dressed in a long emerald jacket with various sheaths hidden underneath. She tucked an extra blade into her boot and strapped on her sword. The soap from her bubble bath had soothed the irritation caused by the pure rainwater, and she hoped the weapons would counteract her lingering vulnerability.

Her crew saluted as she stepped on deck. Their awe was endearing, but it stirred a strange loneliness that brushed too close to weakness. She nodded sharply in acceptance, which sent them scattering back to their tasks.

She looked around at the cause of the darkness. The ship was tucked into the secret cove they had discovered on a previous trip to Ravenna. Rhielle had noticed a strange pattern in the ocean's current, and when they pressed beyond the hidden entrance, they had sailed into an open cavern wide enough for the ship. Sunlight filtered through the trees clinging to the side of the cave walls. The ship rocked gently in the waves from the sea pouring in on one side and from a tumbling waterfall on the other.

Jazhara was taking stock of their current supplies. Her first mate frowned. "We lost some of our water overboard last night. And we should stock up on food while we are here. Who knows how long it will take to sort out this nonsense with the Resistance? We need to be prepared for long stretches at sea."

"But members of the Resistance are always hanging around Ravenna. If they spot us—"

Jazhara gave her a sharp look. "If they spot *you*. The rest of us aren't as recognizable by the Resistance and can sneak into town to pick up the supplies we need. Besides, women pirates are rare enough that if we put on dresses and look like local barmaids, we can hide in plain sight."

"Fine. Just keep plenty of weapons in those dresses, okay?"

Her first mate's expression said Rhielle was an idiot for thinking the warning necessary.

Rhielle pulled a scarf out of her pocket and wrapped it around her hair. At Jazhara's confused head tilt, Rhielle said, "It's my attempt at a disguise. I won't be wearing a dress."

"Captain, you shouldn't—"

"I'll avoid anyone who gives off the slightest hint of being a Resistance soldier and strictly stick to pirates."

Jazhara merely crossed her arms and stared her down.

"My contacts here are the best chance I have to discover the rumors the Resistance heard about me. I need to clear my name, or else we'll be on the run for the foreseeable future."

"Yes, but—"

"And we are a few days early for our meeting with the mysterious contact who offered to pay for our treasured prince. If it was Geeni who made the offer, I need to find out now so we can escape before she arrives."

Jazhara dropped her arms with a huff. "Fine. But respectfully, Captain, you will not be going alone."

"Chysu can come—"

"Take the monk."

Rhielle gave her a flat stare. "The monk? You think I can remain inconspicuous while dragging a monk through the streets of the pirate city?"

"That's been handled. I sent him to see Cook."

"What does Cook—" Rhielle stopped talking when Edric stepped on deck.

His leather boots clicked loudly as he approached. He didn't look up as he fidgeted with his long-sleeve white shirt, unusual on him since his arms were always bared with his tunic. The laces at the neck had been left casually untied, revealing his muscular chest. His flowing red trousers had been replaced with tight leather pants, and he wore a sword sheathed low at his hip.

When his eyes finally flicked up and met hers, she noticed they were smeared with dark liner. It made his eyes even more blue, if that was possible. His hair, typically tied back neatly, had been shaken into careless waves. A single small braid lay on his shoulder.

He lifted the braid when he caught her staring at it. "Poppy suggested it. Do you think the beads are too much?"

Rhielle opened her mouth slowly, fascinated with his kohl-rimmed eyes. "No ... It's just right."

His face lit in that playful grin. "Listen ..." He stomped a booted foot. "I can't accidentally sneak up on you."

She shook her head, picturing him back in his usual clothes. "I'm surprised you would change from your monk garb so easily."

"They're just clothes. I'm still a monk without them." He shrugged. "But this is more clothing than I've worn in a long time! I'm usually shirtless while I work in the shrine, tending to the flame."

Rhielle's eyebrow rose up her forehead unbidden. Clever Twin Goddesses ... If Rhielle were a goddess, she might require her monks to serve her shirtless as well.

Jazhara cleared her throat, and Rhielle jumped, having forgotten her first mate was still there. "You two look perfectly dressed for a jaunt around Ravenna. Captain, I'd tell you to bring our monk home before dark, but as you know, nighttime in Ravenna is when the fun starts." She kicked them off the boat before they could object.

15

After climbing out of the cove and traipsing through a stretch of forest, Rhielle and Edric arrived at the outskirts of Ravenna. She kept him at the edge of her vision because the sight of him in pirate gear was still too startling. He strode confidently, his hand casually resting near his sword, his eyes slightly disdainful.

"You walk like a pirate." She hastily averted her eyes, afraid she had said the phrase a little too awestruck.

"I wasn't trying—" He chuckled softly. "I guess a pirate walks the same as a prince."

Her lips curled in a rueful grin. "Most pirate captains do rule over their crew as if they were a prince."

"Or a princess." He paused to give her an ironic swashbuckling bow.

Her heart stuttered before she laughed awkwardly at his joke. She kept walking, and he scrambled to catch up.

The pirate city at noon was much the same as most other bustling centers of trade. Shopkeepers advertised their wares, and food carts wove through the crowd. The city contained the same sort of taverns and inns and brothels as any city. But Ravenna was notable in a few specific ways.

One difference was the number of bouncers and brutes and security guards. Ravenna was known as the pirate city, but it also boasted another name. The Free City of Ravenna. Since there was no government, each pirate was a law unto him or herself. Which meant each pirate merchant needed their own brute squad. The sheer amount of muscle in Ravenna was staggering. But with everyone overprotected, the power equalized, creating an uneasy peace. If the pirates turned on each other, the city would crumble into chaos, but since it was financially beneficial to keep the peace, they usually did.

Usually.

The other difference in Ravenna was the type of goods sold. In other cities, you could find a shady character in a back room, willing to sell you whatever illegal or dangerous item your heart desired. But in Ravenna, stolen artifacts were sold next to fresh bread, and poison was sold next to smuggled booze. You could find anything you wanted in Ravenna, available for coin or trade, with no questions asked.

Rhielle scanned the crowd quickly before stopping at a food cart and purchasing two orders of flatbread with spicy goat meat and crumbled cheese. She offered one to Edric. "It's good you know someone with coin, because for a prince you arrived shockingly low on funds. All you have is that ring, and I don't think that will get you much."

His eyes darted to his ring before he gave her a pointed look. "Well, considering I 'arrived' courtesy of a kidnapping, I'll count myself lucky to have kept the ring."

She grinned as she took a bite of flatbread, savoring the freshness of the meat and cheese. They hadn't restocked supplies on the ship for a long time, and though Cook was great in the kitchen, he could only do so much with the food on board.

Edric smiled as Rhielle wiped the grease from the corner of her mouth.

"What?" she asked. "I'm a pirate. Did you expect me to eat like a proper lady?"

"You were eating with your pinkies up. You *did* look like a proper lady." His laughter settled into a fond smile. "It was cute."

She narrowed her eyes. "Pirates are not *cute*."

"You're right," he said very seriously, before changing the subject. "So what sort of 'pirate activity' are we here to do?"

"We're keeping our eyes out for anyone in a bright blue uniform. The Resistance soldiers are welcome in Ravenna, since Verkeshe considers them pirates anyway. I have to avoid them until I can find someone who will tell me what charges they've brought against me."

"That bothers you, doesn't it? Why not add the Resistance to your list of targets?"

"Even pirates need allies sometimes," she said ruefully. "And I'm angry someone has spread a rumor I'm working with Verkeshe. It's absolutely ridiculous to anyone who knows me."

"It's probably a misunderstanding. I'm sure you can clear it up." He scanned the crowd. "Who do you trust here?"

"Trust? No one. But I've traded secrets for coin with a few contacts here. I think I can pay them for the info I need."

He saluted her. "Then lead on, Captain."

She narrowed her eyes, but he seemed sincere, so she led him into the tavern to wait for her contact to arrive. Unlike Olga's tavern, this one was filthy, and there was no fresh bread, but people were always willing to spill secrets.

"What are we doing here?" he asked.

"Drinking." She picked a booth at the edge of the room and signaled the serving girl. "You aren't a true pirate until you smell like rum."

He leaned closer. "Um ... I don't drink."

She rolled her eyes. "I didn't say you needed to actually drink. I said you need to *smell* like rum. Can you accomplish that inconspicuously?"

"Oh ... um ... yes, I can manage that."

After Rhielle paid for their rum, Edric lifted the smudged glass and took a clearly faked sip. Rhielle sighed, then tossed back her own glass before slamming it back on the table. She turned in her seat so she could survey the room but also keep an eye on the monk across from her.

Edric looked like the epitome of a pirate, except by now, she knew him well enough to detect his discomfort. He absently rubbed a finger across the old lipstick on his glass, and his eyes would occasionally shoot to the mirror behind the bar before anxiously peering down at his drink. He must find his appearance as startling as she did.

"Did you always want to be a mon—um ... a pirate?" She blurted the question before considering the fact there was more than one way to blow his disguise.

Confusion flashed across his face, then he dropped his eyes back to his rum with a gentle smile. "I was a very headstrong child, and someone had the bright idea to send me to study with the mon—the *pirates* who maintain the Twins' volcanic shrines ..." He bit his lip and glanced around, but other than a noisy card game at the table beside them, no one was nearby.

She tapped her fingers on her empty glass. "I'm surprised your mother allowed you to become a pirate. Most mothers *like yours* would prefer to see their sons married and producing lots of grandchildren."

His shoulders tensed as he tightly squeezed his full glass. "Children are not an option for me. They're too dangerous."

"Dangerous?" she laughed. "Most children I've met are noisy and tedious, but I wouldn't call them dangerous."

He leaned across the table, and the pirate faded away, his serious countenance all prince. "If I had a daughter, there are those who would try to put her on the throne, disregarding the Goddesses' blessing passing from mother to daughter. It would invalidate everything I believe in." His eyes locked on hers, willing her to understand.

And suddenly she did.

"Being a monk sworn to celibacy means that you could avoid the risk of ever having a child. You became a monk to run away."

"What? No, I—"

Rhielle's eyes shot to the door. "There she is." The woman scanned the room for the easiest payout, and when her eyes settled on Rhielle, they gleamed. She shimmied to their table. "Hello, Captain. It's a pleasure to see you."

"You mean, 'a pleasure to see such a good tipper.'"

The woman laughed as pleasantly as a courtier, though she was clearly no such thing. She turned her head, her attention finally landing on Edric, and her eyes took on a predatory shine. "Hello, stranger. I'm Delia." She slid into the booth to sit at his side and flipped her caramel curls across her shoulder, drawing attention to her low-cut dress. "Where did you come from, sweetheart?"

"Isandariyah."

Rhielle wanted to slap her forehead. She didn't care if he was a monk. He needed to learn to lie.

"Isandariyah," purred Delia. "What a lovely country!" She carefully lifted a strand of his hair and wound it around her finger. "But your blond hair isn't typical for Isandariyans."

"My father was from Verkeshe."

Rhielle swiped her hand across her throat to signal him to stop talking, but he seemed content to continue his chat with Delia.

The woman rested her hand next to his on the table. "An Isandariyan woman taking a Verkeshian lover. How romantic."

He shrugged as if it was no big deal. "She's actually had many lovers in her life. None of my brothers look the same."

Delia laughed brightly. "How delightful! A woman after my own heart."

Rhielle slapped her hand on the table, drawing Delia and Edric's attention. "It's been lovely chatting, Delia, but I need some information." When she lifted her hand, a coin remained on the table.

Delia shifted her hand, scooping up the coin with deft fingers. "What do you need to know?"

"What rumor did the Resistance hear about me? And who spread it?"

Delia leaned back against the seat. "The rumor is you don't sneak onto Verkeshe's ships to steal, but that their military willingly hands you coin in exchange for information. I heard you've been selling them information for the last four years. It's how you got enough money to pay for your ship."

Fury built in Rhielle until she exploded. "I'll have you know I *stole* that ship—thank you very much." The thought of buying her ship with blood money from the Verkeshe military sickened her. "Who dares accuse me of this? I've been working with the Resistance for over five years. How could they believe an accusation like this?"

"I heard it was a direct order from the general to bring you in."

Rhielle dug her nails into the table like claws. "So no matter what I say, I won't change their minds."

Delia shrugged her shoulders delicately. "You could turn yourself in and explain it to the corporals yourself. I'm sure they are reasonable, especially if you surrender directly to them."

"I will *not* surrender to them, Delia, but thank you for the advice." She slid her hand across the table, and three coins peeked out underneath. "I understand if you need to sell the information about my whereabouts, but I would appreciate it if this buys me a little time."

Delia's lips curved in a smirk. "I'm quite busy tonight, so I'm sure I won't have time to chat with any friends until late tomorrow morning."

Rhielle lifted her fingers, and the coins disappeared into Delia's hand. "A pleasure doing business with you, Captain." She turned back to Edric. "And a pleasure just sitting next to you, Isandariyan. I'll be across the street at the Lotus tonight. Stop by and see me if you want to experience *everything* Ravenna has to offer."

Edric watched Delia leave. "What's the Lotus?"

Rhielle stared at him for several moments. Was he messing with her? Or was he really as clueless as he seemed? Either way, she didn't feel like giving him an answer.

"We have to go," she said.

"You don't trust her?"

"Absolutely not." She reached for Edric's rum and drank it all at once. "The corporals of the Resistance have deeper pockets than mine. She'll sell my whereabouts to them before the night is over."

Rhielle led him quickly to the front door, hoping to get at least an hour's head start. But outside, across the street at the Lotus, Delia pointed at the tavern, and two Resistance soldiers ran right for them.

16

Rhielle grabbed Edric's hand and yanked him back inside the tavern, shoving people out of their way as they headed out the rear door into the alley. She had been to Ravenna many times, but now she wished she had spent more time in the back alleys. She knew a secluded way out of town, but in full daylight they'd be easily spotted, and she refused to lead the soldiers to her ship.

"We have to hide. Come on!" She tugged his hand and pulled him down the alley at her side.

Edric kept pace with her, so she started to drop his hand, but he readjusted his grip to hold her more firmly. "Which way?"

The soldiers finally made it through the tavern and slammed open the back door as Rhielle pulled Edric to their left. They sprinted together past a shady apothecary and two weapons dealers. The brutes outside the shops raised eyebrows as the pair ran by, but didn't move to stop them since they offered no threat to their employers' goods.

At the next intersection, they barreled through a cluster of very drunk pirates singing bawdy songs. The pirates shouted lewd comments after them, but were otherwise too drunk to follow. After they rounded the next corner, they jumped a fence into a quiet alley filled only with rats picking through the trash.

"Did we lose them?" Edric whispered. He was as out of breath as she was, but he didn't appear scared.

He still held her hand.

"We should hide," she said.

Rats scurried as the two Resistance soldiers rounded the building at the other end of the alley. "Don't bother hiding, Captain."

Rhielle let go of Edric and held up both hands to show she was unarmed. "Listen, guys, there's been a mistake."

The taller soldier snorted. "They always say that. But it doesn't matter to us—we're just lowly grunts. You're wanted by the higher-ups."

"Surely we can come to an agreement amongst ourselves." She moved closer, to give her more room from the fence at her back. If she distracted them, maybe Edric could get away to warn the others. She wasn't sure how to communicate that plan, though. He didn't know the codes she had taught her crew.

The thicker soldier looked her up and down. "Ah, I see ... What kind of bribe are we talking about here? Financial or physical?" He waggled his eyebrows.

Edric drew his sword and pointed it at the man. "I intended to leave you both only mildly injured, but you've caused me to reconsider."

She inwardly groaned. It would have been so much easier to disarm them if they thought she would willingly bribe them. Instead, they both drew their swords and glared at Edric like they would enjoy slicing him to bits.

Honestly, did the man think he was protecting her honor? She was a pirate. Protecting her honor was ridiculous.

And ... sweet.

She drew her own sword with a sigh. Did monks even know how to fight? "I guess I'll find out," she murmured to herself as she waved the men closer. "Let's get on with it."

The soldiers rushed forward, both aiming for Edric. She nearly pouted at their rudeness in dismissing her, but she harnessed her outrage as she sliced her sword across the taller one's hamstring.

He screamed, then turned to her and shouted a profanity specific to her gender.

Rhielle rolled her eyes. "How original, sir." She aimed a blow at his head, but he caught it with his sword, even as he hopped on one foot.

She spared a glance at Edric and gaped. He was good. Very good. She was so distracted by his lunge, she almost missed her opponent's sword racing toward her midsection. As she spun to block the strike, Edric squared up at her back.

His presence behind her in a fight was even more comforting than when he had been at her back while she sailed the ship. Her opponent was injured, and honestly not very skilled, but she was reluctant to end the fight. And she got the wild sense Edric was just as hesitant.

Her opponent tripped and howled, and she cursed under her breath. His cry would surely draw other soldiers. "Time to end this." She stalked to her fallen opponent and knocked him across the head before he could yell again. By the time she turned, Edric's unconscious opponent slipped to the ground.

She slammed her sword back into the sheath and crossed her arms. "You should have told me you were such a good fighter. We could have faced them several blocks earlier."

He crossed his arms to mimic her. "You should have told me *you* were such a good fighter, because I would have let you take them both."

Her lips curved in a satisfied smile. "Much as I'd enjoy

fighting a platoon with you, I think we should lie low until it gets dark."

He saluted sharply. "Aye, Captain. Lead the way."

∼

Rhielle paced to the mouth of the small cave, checked the position of the sun, then paced to the back. Did the sun set slower in Ravenna than anywhere else in the world?

"You should rest while you can." Edric sat on the damp cave floor, legs crossed and eyes closed—the picture of a serene monk except for his pirate clothes.

"I can't rest. What if the Resistance discovered my crew picking up supplies? What if they found the ship? By now, the entire crew might be captured." Or worse.

His eyes opened. "Your plan to wait until dark to escape is good. If you lead the Resistance to your ship, you'll never forgive yourself."

If the Resistance had already captured her crew, Rhielle wouldn't forgive herself for that either.

The monk unfolded himself smoothly and stood. "What is this place? Looks like it's been abandoned for a long time."

She recognized his attempt to distract her, but went along with it. "An old distillery. A pirate captain brewed his personal blend here, but as Ravenna grew, so did his brewery, and he moved it into town." She nudged a broken jug with her foot, and stagnant water sloshed onto her boot. "This cave is close to the secret cove, but we have to climb a rocky hillside, and I don't want to risk it until dark." She paced back to the cave entrance and stared at the sun, which refused to touch the horizon. "Will the sun never set?"

He leaned against a rickety table, careful not to disturb the partially filled glasses strewn on the surface. He watched her pace into the gloomy interior before heading back to the entrance. "Have you really worked with the Resistance for five years?"

She once again allowed herself to fall into his distraction and slid down the cave wall, extending her legs before her. "Yes, I joined the Resistance when I turned sixteen and served on a warship until I grew tired of living in a strict military structure. At eighteen, I stole a small ship from a Verkeshian noble and gathered my own crew, then I finally acquired the *Lady Tempest*."

"What convinced you to join the Resistance when you were so young? Especially since you are from Naermore and not tied to La Veridda?"

She frowned, but there was no reason to keep denying she was from Naermore. "Even after Verkeshe overthrew the La Veriddan king and occupied the capital, the country's soldiers have continued to fight for over fifteen years. If they had just surrendered to King Ruzgar all those years ago, Verkeshe would have not only swallowed up La Veridda, they would have turned on Naermore, and possibly your queendom as well. The Resistance is the only power keeping Verkeshe in check."

"That's why it's so important to clear your name with them. You respect them and want them to respect you in return."

"Yes. The Resistance soldiers are like my family. Other than my crew, they're all I have left."

"But what about your sister?"

Rhielle went deathly still. "What about her?"

"She's still your family, even if you haven't seen her in years. Is there truly no one else?"

She chewed on her lip, weighing her words. "My mother died three years ago while I was at sea. We never saw eye to eye—I wasn't the ideal daughter, and she always preferred my sister. My father remarried soon after my mother died and has since had a son. Now that he has what he always wanted, I doubt he thinks of me at all."

The cave was silent, with only a soft drip of water somewhere in the depths.

She finally raised her head. The sky had darkened so much she could barely make out Edric's face in the dim cave. She hopped up and looked outside. "Soon it will be dark enough to sneak back to the ship and leave Ravenna until this all blows over."

"I'm not leaving Ravenna."

She spun to face him. "What do you mean?"

He straightened from his perch on the table. "I'll make sure you escape safely, but I'm staying here in Ravenna. I'm waiting for Geeni."

She stomped closer to him. "You can't still be considering this ridiculous plan! Geeni will never—"

"I have to try. There is no other option for Isandariyah. I'll convince her. I must."

"You won't convince her to give up her plans! And if she says she'll come meekly with you back to Isandariyah, she'll be lying."

He stood straight, clasping his hands behind his back. "I'll know if she's lying."

"At the tavern, you didn't even realize Delia was flirting with you, so how will you know if Geeni is lying?"

He started to answer, then shook his head, as if confused by the turn of the conversation. "Delia wasn't flirting with me. I'm a monk."

She growled. "No ... you're a *pirate*, remember?"

He looked down at his clothes, then scratched his head. "Huh, that's interesting ..."

She rammed a finger into his chest. "Listen to me, monk. You *will* get back on board the *Lady Tempest* and escape with me and the rest of my crew. I'll drop you off anywhere in Isandariyah you want, but I will *not* sail off and leave you here."

He put his hands on his hips and pulled himself to his full

height. "I'll remind you I am not under your command, *pirate*. So you will get on your ship and sail off into the sunset, because what I do is none of your concern."

"You'll get yourself killed before Geeni even arrives!" she hissed.

A glowing light illuminated the cave entrance. "Lucky for you both, I'm here early," drawled Geeni.

17

Rhielle immediately unsheathed her sword and pointed it at Geeni. The woman looked like a perfect pirate tonight: tight red pants, shiny black boots, and only a few strands of her pink hair peeking out from underneath her pirate hat. Gold necklaces covered the neckline of her tight vest, and bangles clinked on her wrist, while armbands wound around her biceps. Rhielle didn't know which rune Geeni had activated, but she held a lantern that glowed with a flameless light.

Rhielle looked at Edric, irritated he hadn't drawn his sword. Even if Isandariyah gave magic the pretty name "Spark," this woman was clearly a witch.

Edric rubbed a hand across his cheek, then clasped his hands behind his back. "Hello, Ginevere."

"No need to be so formal, dear. You can call me Geeni." She smirked. "Or Auntie Geeni, if you prefer."

"Geeni." Edric said the name carefully. "I have an offer for you."

She laughed lightly. "You get right down to business, don't you, dear? Well, I do appreciate it when a man doesn't waste my time with niceties." She glanced at Rhielle out of the corner of her eye as she continued her conversation with him. "Though you might tell your pirate friend it's rude to point a sword during political negotiations." Geeni gave Edric a knowing look. "Not everyone is taught the proper ways of royalty."

Rhielle ground her teeth but didn't lower her sword.

Geeni disregarded her, leaning against the cave entrance as if she was having a cozy chat. She held the glowing lantern casually and used it to make a speed it up gesture. "Let's get on with it, then. What do you have to offer me?"

"Come with me peacefully, submit yourself to house arrest for the rest of the queen's life, and you will be afforded every luxury. You can choose your own consort, but time is of the essence for you to produce an heir. This is your opportunity to honor the blood of the First Queen running through your veins by providing an heir and future queen of Isandariyah."

Rhielle was glad she was holding a sword because it kept her from slapping a hand to her forehead.

Geeni stared at him for a full five seconds without moving, then her lips curled in a slow smile. "Aren't you such an earnest young man? I do believe if someone offered you the chance to serve your Goddesses that way, you would take it. Which is truly precious. The problem is you and I are nothing alike. I don't think you can even fathom a game on the level I am playing."

Though Rhielle had anticipated Geeni's response, Edric's stricken face still pierced her heart.

Geeni pouted with exaggerated pity. "It's not your fault, dear. You're a prince, sheltered from the bigger world around you. I blame your mother, of course. She purposefully keeps you in the dark because she's afraid one of you will grasp for her throne like her dear old daddy did."

Edric didn't shift from his rigid posture with his hands

clasped behind him, but at this last accusation, he cocked his head as if suspicious.

Geeni tapped her lip as she considered him. "The question remains, what should I do with you? If you were a princess, I might keep you close ... It's always good to have a couple spare princesses when you need them." She chuckled at a secret joke, then tapped her lip again. "Princes are a lot easier to come by, but you are all tedious to a fault. Why can't you let me be?"

"Let you be?" Edric snorted in disbelief. "You tried to kill both Jaemin and Hawthorne."

"Only after they interfered with my business. If you boys would have stayed tucked inside the palace, I wouldn't have considered you at all. Frankly, you're irrelevant to me."

Though he held his stiff position, he fidgeted with the ring behind his back. "You're telling the truth."

Geeni raised an eyebrow. "I'm glad you realize that. It will hopefully save us some time. As of this moment, Prince, you've done nothing more than amuse me with your naivete. As long as you do nothing further to hinder me, you're free to stay here in Ravenna and play. Or sail back to Isandariyah and continue with whatever it is princes do to occupy themselves. What you do is irrelevant to my plans, so if you leave me alone, I'll leave you alone."

He drew a sharp breath. "That's true ..." His eyes flicked to Rhielle, then back to Geeni. "But what about the pirate?"

Geeni pressed her hand against her chest fondly. "To show such concern for a common pirate! Isandariyan princes really are quite darling." Her eyes finally turned to Rhielle. "The 'pirate' is coming with me."

Rhielle's sword hadn't faltered since she first aimed it at Geeni's arrival. "I will *not*—"

Geeni moved faster than Rhielle could comprehend. The light shifted as Geeni darted forward while unsheathing her sword and knocking Rhielle's sword out of her hand at the same time. Edric barely even had time to turn his head before Geeni had stepped back with her sword resheathed.

A deadly calm replaced Geeni's playful condescension. "You are coming with me."

Edric clasped his hands near his chest and anxiously twirled his ring. His focus shot between Geeni and Rhielle as he tried not to miss anything else.

Rhielle shook her head sharply. "You will not take me without a fight."

Geeni raised an eyebrow. "Your crew said much the same when my guards claimed the *Lady Tempest.*"

Fire blossomed in Rhielle's chest at the thought of her crew under attack without her at their side. Edric was fiercely shaking his head, but Rhielle knew he was in denial. Geeni had found the ship.

"Most of them survived," said Geeni casually. "I'm not a monster, you know. I'll give them a chance to serve on my crew. But that depends on your good behavior."

Edric shook his head more vigorously, but Rhielle refused to take her eyes off Geeni. "If you hurt them, I swear—"

"Come with me peacefully, and I promise your remaining crew will be safe."

Edric abandoned his head shaking and grabbed Rhielle's arm. "She doesn't have your crew! She's lying."

Geeni's head swiveled slowly back to Edric, and she glanced at his hand. "The truth-seeking magistrate ... You have the ring with his Spark."

Rhielle looked between the two of them, trying to understand what Geeni's words meant.

His lip curled. "True."

Geeni held out her hand, palm up. "Give it to me now." When he didn't move, her eyes narrowed. "You know I told the truth earlier when I said you were irrelevant to me and could go on your way. So listen to me closely now ... Naughty princes who steal my runes are very relevant to me, and I can just as easily pull that ring off your corpse. Does the ring think I'm lying?"

A muscle in his jaw twitched, revealing the truth of Geeni's statement, but he still didn't move.

Geeni sighed dramatically and stepped toward him, but Rhielle ran to tackle her. Geeni blocked her with an elbow. The woman barely exerted herself, yet Rhielle flew across the cave into a pile of broken pottery. Her hand landed inside a jug full of stagnant water, and she hissed, drawing her hand to her chest.

Geeni froze, her eyes flicking between Rhielle and the spilled water. The woman actually seemed concerned, but why would she care? Geeni looked into Rhielle's eyes, like she was ... waiting.

This would be the perfect opportunity for Edric to disarm her, but his gaze darted over Rhielle as he checked for injuries.

Before he could react, Geeni had a dagger in her hand, aimed at his finger. "Slide off that ring, or I'll remove the finger along with it."

He reflexively covered his finger with his other hand and twirled the ring.

Rhielle shouted, "Just give her the ring, Edric! It's not worth it."

Geeni nodded appreciatively. "Listen to her, Prince. Rhielle's a clever girl who knows how to save her own skin."

He slid the ring over the first knuckle, then paused with his head cocked. "Rhielle?" He blinked as if trying to place the name.

"Oh, you really didn't know!" Geeni laughed loudly. "Each prince has his own lying woman close by. And this time, I'm not even the one who convinced her to lie!"

Edric looked down at his hand, as if the ring had told him

the truth of Geeni's statement. Then he turned to Rhielle. She didn't need a magical ring to tell her the truth.

He knew who she was.

The fact he knew sent her past life crashing over her. Everything she had run away from dropped squarely back on her.

And Geeni was to blame.

Rhielle slammed her hands down, and she didn't even care that one hand splashed into the stagnant water.

Let the water burn her skin.

Let the water drown her as it had her sister.

Let the water rise and claim them all, as long as it swept Geeni out to sea, never to return.

A glass of water vibrated on the table. Geeni and Edric both turned at the sound, and watched as the glass wobbled closer and closer to the edge before it crashed to the ground. Geeni hopped back as glass shards landed on her boots. She stared in horror as two more glasses started shaking.

The ground quaked, and Geeni and Edric stumbled, but Rhielle remained firmly rooted to the ground with her hand burning inside the water. Though she felt the flesh melting off her hand, her skin was unaffected inside the jug of trembling water.

Geeni stepped backward toward the cave entrance, and cast her eyes over her wrists, then her neck, but she seemed at a loss for what rune could handle whatever was happening.

Rhielle wasn't exactly sure what was happening herself. But somehow she knew that, hidden in the deep heart of this cave, an opening led out to the sea.

And the sea was coming.

18

Water flooded the cave, dragging debris from deep within the hideout. The old still tipped over, crashing into the water before a wave slammed it into a wall. Edric braced himself against the table, but even that started sliding as the water rose. The glowing light disappeared as Geeni stumbled, barely catching herself against the cave wall as broken pottery and seaweed tangled around her feet.

Rhielle stood slowly, dragging her burning hand through the seawater. The salty water didn't feel pleasant, but it was better than fresh water—the salt diluted the pain into a prickling irritation more than a burn. The water rushed past her, streaming toward the entrance in ever rising waves. Her thoughts felt sluggish, similar to when she steered the ship with Geeni's rune. But that didn't make sense ... Rhielle obviously hadn't touched one of Geeni's runes.

Rhielle shook off her drowsiness. Geeni must have activated a rune herself, and Rhielle planned to take advantage of it.

She scooped her sword out of the water and sheathed it before sloshing closer to Edric. The waist-high waves had flipped the table, pressing him against the wall, but when she took his hand, he slipped free and staggered to her side.

Rhielle turned to Geeni, who had clawed her way to the cave entrance. The waves were fiercer there as they battled their way out of the cave and spilled onto the rocky ground beyond. Geeni clutched the rough cave wall with one hand as her other fumbled with the necklaces around her throat. Rhielle had no idea what other chaos magic the woman wanted to call, but she didn't intend to find out.

Rhielle grabbed the edge of the table, and with a scream, she pried it away from the wall and shoved it toward Geeni. The end of the table caught Geeni in the gut, knocking the wind out of her. The table formed a partial dam against the entrance, and the broken still and pottery stacked up against it, pressing her tighter.

Edric stumbled, but Rhielle caught his hand and pulled him through the water. "Time to go."

Geeni tried to seize them as they scrambled over the table dam, but her hand slipped on the flotsam battering against her. They slid off the table in a wave that dragged them out into the night across the rocky ground.

Rhielle gained her feet first and hauled Edric up. "Hurry. We have to find the crew."

He planted his feet, though he wobbled on the shifting wet rocks. "Your crew is safe. She doesn't have them." He raised their clasped hands to show her the ring. "She was lying."

Rhielle didn't want to remember any of the conversations from the cave, so she shook off his hand. "We hid in the cave because of the Resistance, not Geeni, remember? We have to go. Now."

Edric glanced back at the dark cave, where crashing and curses echoed. He clenched his jaw. "Fine. Quickly, though."

Rhielle snorted. Obviously quickly. She sprinted up the rocky hillside but slowed when she realized Edric could barely keep his footing on the slick rocks. She urged him forward, sick with dread they might be too late.

When he finally spoke, his voice was hesitant. "Are you ... okay?"

"I'm fine." Rhielle avoided meeting his eyes, but the ring on his finger probably told him her statement was less than accurate.

"You're soaked ... with water."

Of all the things weighing on her, that one hardly made the list. "It's salt water. It's not pleasant, but it doesn't burn like fresh water."

He hummed quietly in understanding. "Ah ... The salt mutes the effect. That explains the bubble baths."

She shot him a look, then focused on the way ahead without answering.

They made it up the rocky hillside without being spotted, and then wiggled through an overgrown cleft in the rock, toward rushing water. They emerged into a grassy area between two streams—one running through the trees to the city below and the other splitting off into a waterfall.

Nearing the stream where it crashed over the side of the cliff, she lowered onto her stomach and peeked over the edge. The *Lady Tempest* bobbed gently in the cove below. She had imagined the sails on fire and her crew screaming while being led away, but the ship was just as she had left it. The cliff was tall enough to cover the very top of the ship's sails, but not so tall that she couldn't see her crew moving around on deck.

"They're safe," she breathed.

"I'm glad to hear that. You should leave Ravenna immediately. It's not safe for you here."

She jerked to her feet. "Why are you saying it like that? You're coming with us."

"No. I'm going back for Geeni."

She gaped at him. "Edric, she laughed in your face. You won't convince her—"

"The time for convincing is over. She's coming to Isandariyah whether she wants to or not. She has a responsibility to produce the future queen."

She placed her hands on her hips. "So you'll actually *force* her to breed for the sake of your Goddesses, monk? Sounds like the queendom is just as awful to its women as the kingdoms are."

He went deathly still. "I guess you would know best, *Princess*."

"I'm not a princess!" she hissed.

"No, you ran away to become a pirate." He barked a harsh laugh. "And you accused me of running away by becoming a monk. At least I didn't abandon my people to go play at sea."

"This is no game to me, monk. I became a pirate to fight Verkeshe in a way princesses are not allowed to fight. I will not surrender to Verkeshe or the Resistance or Geeni or anyone."

His eyes narrowed. "So you run. Surrendering yourself to the sea."

His words startled her, but then she laughed bitterly. "You unknowingly quote the Zaridian prophecy given to me. How very blasphemous of you. Yes, I'll eventually surrender to the waves when they drag me down into the heart of the sea. But until the day the sea takes me, I'll continue to fight."

"I'm not interested in how you rationalize it, Princess." He growled the title like a curse.

She poked a finger at his chest. "You have no right to judge me for any of my decisions, monk. I fight anyone who seeks to control me, but you're happy being controlled by Goddesses who would force a woman to breed for them."

"How dare you belittle the Goddesses!" he hissed. "They do not control me. I *chose* to become a monk and follow them of my own accord."

"You became a monk so you could avoid having a family and, as a result, avoid heirs that would disrupt your Goddesses' very particular rules about inheritance."

A muscle twitched in his jaw. "I don't need you to understand. Go back to Naermore or out to sea—it makes no difference to me. I'll find Geeni and make sure she fulfills her responsibility to the queendom one way or the other."

Before he could turn, she gripped his shirt in her fist. It had already dried, though her own shirt was still sopping wet, the salt water prickling as it crawled across her skin. She channeled the irritation into her voice. "You can't go back there. You saw what Geeni did with all that water. Who knows what else she's capable of?"

His eyes widened as he stared at her. "What *Geeni* did? Are you serious?"

She shook his shirt out of her hand. "Fine. What Geeni's *runes* did. Haven't you seen how many she wears?"

He glanced at the ring on his finger as he snorted a laugh. "I'd have to offer the ring another tear to find out if you're lying to me or if you're in such denial you believe that's true." He shook his head. "I don't have time to sort your denial from your lies. I've waited too long as it is. Goodbye, Princess."

Edric headed toward the hidden cleft in the rock, but she blocked his path. "You aren't going back there, monk."

"Oh really? And how do you plan on stopping me?"

She unsheathed her sword. "By whatever means necessary."

He gave her an incredulous look. "So to *protect* me from Geeni, you'll injure me?"

"I won't injure you so bad that Chysu can't stitch you back up."

He tried to step around her but couldn't get past her sword to reach the path. "I will not fight you, Princess."

She curled her lip in disgust. "Because I'm a girl?"

He rolled his eyes. "I spar with women in Isandariyah all the time."

"Good. Then spar with me now. If you win, you're free to kill yourself by going after Geeni. But if I win, you'll come back to the *Lady Tempest* with me."

He looked at her suspiciously, then glanced at his ring, but he didn't offer it another tear. "You're trying to delay me so she's long gone by the time I get there."

"Then you better win this match quickly, monk. Unless you're scared I'll win?"

Edric unsheathed his sword.

19

A feral grin spread across her lips at the sight of his bared sword. She needed a good fight. Despite her relief at finding her crew safe, the confrontation with Geeni had left her on edge. Her saltwater-soaked clothes clung to her, and the prickling made her want to claw off her skin. She needed the distraction of a rush of adrenaline from either a fight or sailing away on her ship.

And since she couldn't sail off until he was on the ship, she had to fight first.

A quiet internal voice wondered why sailing off without him wasn't an option, but she smothered that question with the heavy pulse thundering in her ears. She would win the fight, drag him back to the ship, then sail into the night. After that, the painful knot in her chest would unwind.

Where had that painful knot even come from?

Edric watched her carefully, waiting for her to make the first move. Possibly his usual sword-fighting strategy, but she got the aggravating sense it was more chivalrous than strategic.

"I'm quite content for this fight to last all night, monk," she taunted. "You're the one with somewhere to go."

He huffed angrily, then lunged at her.

She twirled out of his reach. He made a few more lunging strikes and a couple of careful parries before Rhielle realized he wasn't fighting to win quickly. Not like they had extended the fight with the Resistance soldiers. No, this time his fighting seemed almost ...

Polite.

How dare he disrespect her by fighting *politely*! She had spent her childhood sneaking out of embroidery lessons to train with the grizzled members of her father's army who found a fierce little redhead amusing. She had earned her spot in the Resistance after working up through their ranks, then eventually got her own ship on her own merit. Would her crew follow a captain who only fought *polite* opponents?

Her desire to defeat him magnified as her focus on him narrowed. Edric was bigger and stronger, and if they fought a polite match following all the rules of conduct, he would defeat her.

Of course, she had no intention of following the rules.

When he sparred back in Isandariyah, he probably wore his monk uniform and soft slippers. He hadn't adjusted to heavy boots, especially not boots still soggy with seawater. So she edged their fight onto the smooth, flat stones surrounding the stream.

Edric politely followed her. She lured him even further with a few gasping breaths and a stumble that was quite realistic, if she said so herself.

He pressed closer, trapping her between his broad chest before her and the stream behind. The fresh water prickled heat up her spine, and her gasps became more real than fake. She saw the moment he decided to stop playing with her. He pressed forward with several quick slices, until their blades scraped together, the swords locking hilt to hilt between them.

He didn't release the pressure of his sword against hers, and his voice rumbled through her hands. "I could dump you in this stream right now, Princess. Do you surrender?"

"I don't surrender, monk," she growled, pushing him back.

He only slid half a foot before he straightened, frowning at her. He blew out a breath as if irritated he would have to defeat her properly.

She knew he would use one of two moves to win. Both would put him in a position to deliver the deadly blow that would declare him the winner, but without actually injuring her. If she believed for a moment he would actually hurt her, she wouldn't risk it. But once he lifted his sword, showing her which of the two moves he'd chosen, she moved.

The wrong way.

His sword skimmed her arm, and she gasped, clapping her hand against the wound as he jumped back in surprise. Her sloppy movement had been totally unexpected with the skill she had shown him.

She hunched her shoulders, biting her lip as she whimpered.

"Rhielle! I'm so sorry!" He dropped his sword on the ground and rushed toward her, his heavy boots sliding awkwardly on the wet stones.

She grabbed his arm and ducked, flipping him over her back into the stream.

He flailed in the shallows until he could sit up, spluttering. A few drops of fresh water splattered her skin, but she refused to let an unintentional whimper escape her lips. As he wiped the water out of his eyes, she walked calmly and picked up his dropped sword. She slid her sword into her sheath and pointed his sword at his neck, her boots carefully planted on the rocks.

With his blond hair plastered to his face, he looked like a cat left out in the rain. He glared at her. "You cheated."

"I'm a pirate. Of course I cheated." She lowered his sword

and rested it point down against the rocks. "But I won, and now you're coming with me."

"I can't—"

She clicked her tongue. "I expected a monk to honor his word. Unless you're no better than a pirate?" She dropped his sword and offered him her hand.

He hesitated, perhaps wondering if she would trick him again. Guilt nagged at her for using his honor to defeat him. Because even now she felt no hesitation in offering her hand— he would never pull her in.

Edric eventually let her help him up—probably deciding it was more honorable than refusing a lady's hand. She had to strain to pull him out of the stream, considering he was now a waterlogged boulder.

He didn't immediately release her hand, instead pulling her closer to examine her arm. "You're bleeding."

She ground her teeth. "Honestly, the fresh water on your hand is more painful than that scratch."

His fingers sprang apart, but before she could lower her hand, he seized it again.

"What are you doing? I just said—"

"Does this always happen?" He shifted their hands closer to her face.

"Do I always end up holding hands with my bested opponent? No."

He raised their hands higher. "No, look at the water. Does it always do that?"

She stared at the water beading on her skin. Where it lingered, it burned, but she breathed through the pain so he wouldn't see. "Does it always burn? For the last five years, yes."

He shook his head. "No, I mean the way it beads on your skin without dripping. It's very odd."

"Usually I brush it off before it sits too long. Have I mentioned how unpleasant it is?"

He kept hold of her hand. "And look at the water on my hand. Is this ... normal ... for you?"

The question irritated her, but not as much as the water. It dripped from his long blond strands, splashing on his hand.

Then the water *moved*.

Not dripped. It moved across Edric's skin, slithering like a crystal snake.

Until it beaded against her own.

She shook him off and wiped her hand against her jacket, though she couldn't wipe away the sting.

Edric reached for the sleeve of her uninjured arm and squeezed the fabric. "You're still soaked from the cave? Why haven't you dried off?"

She brushed his hand away from her arm. "Why does it matter to you? Looking for a sign of weakness?"

He sighed in exasperation. "Rhielle, you have a Spark. Just admit it."

"A Spark? You mean magic?" She laughed. "Water clings to me and burns my skin ... What kind of cursed magic is that?"

"You summoned the water that flooded the whole cave!"

"I summoned it? How could I unintentionally summon water?"

"I don't know, but—"

"And if I have some kind of magical control over water, why can't I control it the opposite direction—getting it off me?"

"Well, maybe—"

"Just stop, Edric. It's a curse. Or maybe a disease. But definitely not a Spark."

"Listen to me. Sparks are blessings, Rhielle. You owe it to the Goddesses to—"

"I owe your Goddesses nothing, monk!"

His nostrils flared as he drew a breath. "You can't run away from your magic like you ran away from your family."

"How dare you!" She pushed him, expecting a boulder's

worth of resistance, but his boots slipped, and he tumbled off the bank, into deeper water than before.

He plunged fully underwater, and when his head bobbed up, he coughed swallowed water, blinking with a dazed expression as he tried to stand. She groaned, searching for a long branch to pull him out without wading in herself. If her boots filled with fresh water, she'd have to climb down the cliff barefoot to get to the ship.

"Come on, monk!" she called from the bank. "Focus on my voice. Swim this way, and I'll pull you out."

He shook his head as if shaking off a trance, then gave her a sheepish look, embarrassed about falling into the water again, even though she had pushed him both times. He got his feet under him and stood, smearing his eyeliner as he brushed his hair away from his face.

The water trickled between his fingers and slid down his neck, nestling in his thin shirt clinging to his chest. Moonlit water sparkled on his lashes and grazed the bristly stubble on his cheeks. A single droplet kissed his bottom lip and refused to move from its shimmering perch.

He turned his head upstream, blinking quickly and scattering the glittering drops from his lashes. She followed his gaze.

A single wave rippled across the steady stream and crashed into Edric, pulling him under, before dragging him over the edge of the cliff.

Rhielle froze in shock for a full heartbeat before diving after him.

20

Rhielle burned before her body even hit the water. Her dive followed the path of the waterfall, and the splashing water prickled violently against her skin the entire way down. But the stinging droplets were nothing compared to the moment her body struck the water below.

She crashed into the churning waves and had to squeeze her mouth shut to keep from screaming. The fresh water scalded her exposed skin and washed the seawater off her clothes, scalding the skin underneath. She hadn't immersed herself completely in fresh water in five years—other than bubble baths with enough soap to dilute the water. She hadn't been prepared for the overwhelming pain.

The water clung to her, threatening to drag her deeper. She unfastened her sword belt with trembling fingers, but didn't waste time unbuckling her boots. She had to find Edric quickly, for his sake and her own.

Rhielle cracked open her eyelids, then immediately shut them. Not a hint of moonlight filtered through the dark waves, and now her eyes burned worse than in salt water. If she couldn't see him, she would just have to swim until she ran into him.

But the cove was big enough to fit two ships the size of the *Lady Tempest* ... How could she find one monk in that much water? The sheer impossibility threatened to unnerve her, but she blocked out the part of her mind that could do math and swam deeper.

He would have sunk further than her. The man really did resemble a boulder. Rigid, hardheaded, unyielding ... steady ... constant ... faithful ...

She swam deeper.

Fresh water and seawater swirled together inside the cove, patches of burning fire alternating with prickling irritation. As she sank further, she reached the heavier seawater lurking below. The stinging pain on her skin lessened except for the wound on her arm caused by Edric's sword.

The monk had only fallen off the cliff because of her. If she hadn't pushed him ... if she had let him run off after Geeni ... if she had never kidnapped him in the first place ...

How could she find him in this unending blackness? She wasn't even completely sure which way was up, other than a vague sense of the painful fresh water looming over her. He was here somewhere, maybe floating right next to her, and she would never know.

She imagined him—not in his pirate clothes, but as a monk—his red garments billowing around him ... his blond hair floating ...

Like a halo ... Just like her sister's hair had floated when the sea took her ...

Aliyabeth ... beautiful, firstborn princess, Aliyabeth.

Dead beneath the waves for five years.

As Rhielle sank deeper into the water, the undulating waves loosened her scarf, and as it drifted away, her hair floated around her head. The tendrils brushed her cheeks like gentle fingers, compelling her to relax.

Begging her to surrender.

Was this it? The day the sea would take her for its own? The prophecy given to her by the Zaridian prophet beckoned: *You will surrender to the waves and let them drag you down to the heart of the sea.* Maybe it was time to give in. She had lost her sister and now Edric to the sea. Maybe she should just let it take her, too.

But she wanted to see her crew again. She wanted to sail her ship. Wanted the wind in her hair, the kiss of the sun on her cheeks, the songs of her crew at night.

She wanted to live.

And so she fought.

She kicked as hard as she could, aiming in the direction she hoped was *up*. She passed beyond the safety of seawater into the burning fire of fresh water. The pain sped her on, and she kicked faster in her struggle to reach the surface. Her lungs begged for the chance to draw a breath, but she hit a boulder, driving the last air from her lungs.

Edric's hair tangled around her fingers, and she grasped his shirt, dragging him with her. The memory of dragging her sister's dead body flooded back, but she pushed it down, not willing to admit he was dead until she saw it with her own eyes.

She burst above the water's surface, sucking in a desperate breath. The splashing water burned her mouth and lungs, but it burned less than the lack of oxygen. She wiped water out of her eyes and swam toward the closest rocky ledge, with Edric floating lifelessly in her grip.

Rhielle climbed onto the rock, heaving Edric until he lay flat. She smoothed his hair away from his face to see if he was breathing. "Edric! Can you hear me? Wake up!"

His stillness sent a shiver through her. She clasped her

hands and began chest compressions. His body was cold, but so was the water, though her skin still burned like fire.

"Please, Edric! Wake up! I'm sorry it took me so long to find you." Tears rolled down her cheeks, leaving salty trails in their wake.

He had been submerged too long, his lungs surely full of water. She pressed harder. "Cough up that water now, monk! Do you hear me? I'm the captain, and I order you to breathe!"

Edric reflexively contracted and coughed up water. She turned him on his side, sagging in relief against his shoulder. "You're breathing! Thank the Spirits, you're breathing."

After he finished coughing up half the sea, she helped him sit up. He wiped the water off his face, smearing the remaining eyeliner, and looked at her with eyes as blue as the sea on a clear day. "You saved my life," he rasped.

Her breathing was ragged, from lack of oxygen, from pain, and from something else she couldn't name. "I'm the one who almost killed you."

He turned to look at the waterfall. "You dove off a cliff ... to save me."

"I ..."

His eyes widened suddenly. "You're soaked! With water!"

She would have laughed at the ridiculous statement, but she was in too much pain.

"You need to dry off." He started unbuckling her boots. "Take off your jacket."

A blush rose unbidden to her cheeks. "I'm not removing all my clothes, monk."

His shocked eyes shot to hers, then flashed back to her boot as he slid it off her foot. "Just your boots and jacket so you dry faster. It will take a moment for your crew to row a boat over here to pick us up."

Shouts came from the direction of the ship—someone had noticed them plunging off the cliff. Rhielle cleared her throat, willing the blush away. "Yes, of course." She struggled to peel off the wet jacket, and once it was gone, the skin on her arms and back burned slightly less.

He pulled off her other boot and set it beside them on the narrow ledge. "I guess that's all you can remove for now." A faint blush rose to his cheeks, but she ignored it, hoping her own wouldn't follow. He leaned forward. "Thank you. For saving my life."

She opened her mouth, searching for a flippant remark, but nothing came.

"You're soaked. Do you never dry on your own?" He shook his head with a bemused smile. "The water clings like it can't bear to be separated from you." He reached for a red strand hanging heavily near her cheek. He pinched it between his thumb and forefinger, gently wringing out the water.

The drops landed on her legs and sizzled as they sank through her pants, but she didn't flinch. Didn't move. She couldn't even draw a breath.

He held the strand next to her cheek, his body as still as hers. How did she keep falling into moments like this with him? Was he so inexperienced with women that he didn't realize the intimacy of his gentle touch? Maybe she was like Delia—someone he accidentally flirted with.

Though he hadn't looked at Delia like he looked at her now.

He looked at Rhielle like she was beautiful. Like he truly saw her, flaws and all, and found her fascinating. Like he wanted to lean closer.

Like he wanted to know what her lips tasted like.

She couldn't move, because her thoughts raced along a similar path. What would it feel like if that boulder crushed her against his chest? His fingers slipping from the single strand, weaving into her hair ... His lips stealing the breath from her lungs, drowning her in a kiss ...

Rhielle surrendered to the current as an imaginary tide swept them so close their breath mingled.

Edric's voice was barely more than an exhale. "You're dangerous."

Her breath finally escaped in a whisper. "Because I almost killed you?"

"No."

The single word doused her with cold water, and suddenly she saw it. A monk only a heartbeat away from kissing a pirate. Would he forsake his vows and give up his life as a monk? Would he risk falling in love, even if it meant producing a daughter that put the queendom at risk? Would he abandon his mother and brothers, running away with a pirate?

But danger for her lurked inside his blue eyes too. Would she give up her life at sea to become a princess for him? Wear gowns and dainty slippers? Speak demurely and take up lady-like hobbies?

Would she never sail the sea again?

The danger simmered between them, a tangible heat more painful than the water clawing at her skin. The thought of never sailing again was even more terrifying than the sea dragging her to its watery heart. She couldn't spend the rest of her life on land. She should shift—lean back and break the weight of the moment. Let him run after Geeni while she sailed away.

But Edric's lips were so close. It would only take the slightest movement, a mere softening of her spine, to lean close enough to press her lips against his. And despite the risk, she wanted to bend, if only for a moment. Could she bend without it breaking her?

"Captain."

Chysu's calm voice startled them both, and they scooted away from each other.

The ship's doctor floated in the dinghy, close to their narrow ledge. She stared carefully ahead, pretending not to notice their guilty expressions. "You should come quickly, Captain. We've heard a rumor that Resistance ships are circling the island, looking for us. The crew has returned from gathering supplies, and now we need to get back out to sea."

Rhielle tugged her wet shirt, trying to look more put together than she felt. "Thank you, Chysu." She picked up her discarded boots and threw them into the dinghy, before hopping neatly inside. "Come on, monk. Time to go." She offered him her hand.

Edric stared as if her hand might bite him, as if the danger Rhielle presented had suddenly caught up to him. He didn't take her hand, but lowered himself shakily into the boat on his own.

Rhielle shot him an irritated look, but took her seat at Chysu's side and rowed toward the ship.

He kept his head down and stared at his hands, spinning the ring on his finger. She was glad a single tear only held so much magic, or he might have detected her ruse atop the cliff.

Or maybe he would have run toward her, even if he knew she was lying.

The sound of her crew grew louder as she approached. Jazhara yelled commands, and cargo being stowed scraped and rattled. The familiar sounds soothed her sensitive nerves. Soon they would escape out to sea and hide in the dark, while she took a bubble bath and scraped off the lingering fresh water. She would be out on the waves, and all would be well.

"I'm keeping this boat, Rhielle."

Her head snapped up. "What are you talking about, monk?"

"Once we get you to the ship, I'm taking this boat to find Geeni."

Rhielle growled, her hands clenching on the oar. "I beat you—"

"I can't go with you!" he shouted. He looked away as if embarrassed by his dramatic outburst, then he lowered his voice, though it still held a tremble of panic. "I'm *not* going with you, Princess."

Rhielle stared at him, silently taking her anger out on the waves beneath her oar. Chysu glanced between the two of them, mouth pinched shut, not asking how Edric had discovered Rhielle's true identity.

They pulled alongside the *Lady Tempest*, and the crew threw down ropes to secure the dinghy and a ladder to climb up.

Rhielle addressed Chysu while glaring at Edric. "Go ahead, Chysu. Tell Jazhara to set sail as soon as my feet hit the deck."

Chysu's eyes shot to Edric, then drifted slowly back to Rhielle. "Aye, Captain."

Edric didn't watch her climb, but kept his blue eyes locked on Rhielle. "Don't try to change my mind."

"I won't," she said tightly. "Though I will say, I can't believe you're running off to get yourself killed so soon after I saved your life."

He had the grace to look guilty. "I have to go. But ... I wish you well, Princess."

The title grated on her already overstimulated senses. She rubbed a hand beneath her collar to unstick it from her neck, but it seemed permanently burned into her skin. Her hair hung heavy against her back, the water searing her shoulder blades.

"Are you okay, Princess?" He stood, reaching toward her, but hesitated before touching her.

"I'm fine," she snapped. She grabbed her soaked boots and gritted her teeth as she tucked them under her arm. "I don't need your help, monk. I knew the pain I'd suffer when I jumped in after you."

He chewed on his lip as if unsure what to say, guilt written clearly on his face.

She stepped onto the first rung and awkwardly swayed into the side of the ship, her boots dropping back into the dinghy.

Edric picked them up and held them out to her, but she clung to the ladder, swallowing deeply. "Forget the boots. I don't need them."

She raised an arm to the next rung and bit her lip on a moan. She pressed her hand against her wounded arm and pulled it back bloody. "I guess I lost more blood than I thought ..."

Edric stepped up behind her. "Rhielle? Are you well enough to climb?"

"Yes ... I'm ..." Her bloody hand slipped off the rung.

"Rhielle!" Edric grabbed her under the arms as her eyes fluttered shut.

21

Edric carried Rhielle up the ladder, and as he carefully lifted her over the railing, he yelled for the ship's doctor. "Chysu! Come quickly!" Carrying Rhielle's limp body up the ladder hadn't affected his steady breathing, but his heartbeat thundered in his chest.

Guilt popped Rhielle's eyes open. "You can put me down, monk."

"You're awake!" He pressed her closer to his chest to support her wounded arm. "Let Chysu look at your arm."

Chysu approached calmly and stared at Rhielle, a hint of judgment in her dark eyes.

Rhielle cleared her throat. "Put me down. Now."

Edric gingerly lowered her legs while supporting her back. "You should sit, Princess."

The moment her feet touched the deck, Jazhara yelled, "All hands to stations! Cut loose the dinghy! Step lively now!"

Edric's hand slipped from Rhielle's back as he rushed to intercept Jazhara and the sailors who cut loose the dinghy. "No, wait! I'm leaving."

Jazhara gave him a pitying look. "Sorry, Prince. The order was to leave the moment Captain's feet hit the deck."

Rhielle darted to the helm. She didn't intend to take the wheel herself yet, but it helped her avoid Edric. The betrayal in his eyes unsettled her more than she'd expected.

"Rhielle?"

She ignored his question and spoke to her crew. "As soon as we exit the cove, be ready for me to activate the rune. I expect we'll have Resistance ships hot on our heels."

He stepped in front of her, blocking her view out of the cove. "You tricked me?"

Her lip curled in a wry smile. "The 'swooning maiden' act is distasteful, but I can't deny its effectiveness."

He crossed his arms over his broad chest. "Have you ever heard of the little girl who cried wolf?"

"Don't worry, monk. If a big bad wolf comes after me, I won't call for you. I'll kill it myself." She strode around him toward the front of the ship and rested her hands on the rail as they glided out of the cove.

She sensed the boulder at her back before he spoke. "The supposed ransom for me was just Geeni's trick," he growled. "So ... why are you kidnapping me again?"

Rhielle spun to face him and hissed, "Because you'll get yourself killed!"

He smacked his hand against the railing. "Let me! Isandariyah has plenty of princes to spare."

She ground her teeth as she searched for an answer, but the truth was, she had none. At least not one she wanted to admit.

She turned away from him and called, "Chysu!"

"Yes, Captain?" The woman appeared at her side. Chysu had probably been watching Rhielle closely in case she really was wounded.

Or in case another sword fight broke out.

"Doctor, the monk is hysterical. Understandable since he

was recently dead before I revived him. Please examine him for injuries and have Cook brew him some tea. I'm sure he'll need it once I activate the rune."

Rhielle didn't drop her commanding expression as Chysu led him away. Once Edric's furious glare dipped belowdecks, Rhielle's shoulders sagged, and she signaled to Poppy.

The girl skipped up to her with full arms. "Your dry clothes, Captain! Chysu told me to hold on to them until you were ready."

Rhielle immediately started stripping out of her wet clothing. "Spirits bless that woman for taking care of me, even if she doesn't agree with my decision."

Poppy blinked in confusion and handed Rhielle a thick scarf to tie up her soaked hair.

As Rhielle tugged on her dry boots, Jazhara approached, and her furious expression sent Poppy scampering off.

"What in the Four Gods' names happened back in Ravenna?"

Rhielle focused on buckling her boots. "It's a long story."

"And we're kidnapping the prince. Again." It was an accusation, not a question.

Rhielle stood, trying to let her height offset her shame. "I had to. He was going to get himself killed."

The *Lady Tempest* pulled out of the shadowed cove into the waters surrounding Ravenna.

And three Resistance ships promptly greeted them.

Jazhara glared at Rhielle in accusation. "He might have lived longer if he stayed behind." Then she sprinted toward the crew, shouting, "All hands to battle stations!"

The crew had already been prepared for a quick getaway, but Jazhara's command spurred them on. They readied the sails the traditional way as they prepared the ship for Rhielle to activate the rune. They just had to get the ship pointed in the right direction, and she would take it from there.

She squeezed the thick scarf around her hair one more time, tossed it into the pile of her wet clothes, and hopped over to the helm. Their bearing was close enough, and it was time to go. The helmswoman yielded her place at the wheel, and Rhielle closed her eyes, trying to recall her sister.

The only image that came to her mind was Edric, cold and lifeless after tumbling off the cliff. The image prompted a strange sadness, heavily shaded with guilt. She blinked rapidly, and a single tear formed on her lashes. She sighed, pressing the tear against the rune until it glowed, then she reached for the sea.

And nothing happened.

She opened her eyes, watching the rune's glow fade. Maybe it hadn't been a proper tear? Maybe—

She flinched as an arrow thunked into the deck of the ship.

Jazhara yelled, "Take cover! Archers, stand by to shoot on my command!"

Rhielle glanced up as Poppy ducked behind the longboats strapped to the hull of the ship. What if the girl got struck by an arrow? Got tossed overboard? Was killed by the Resistance as they boarded the ship? No matter how many traumatic scenarios Rhielle imagined, she couldn't prompt another tear.

Chysu bounded up from belowdecks, her medical bag in one hand, the other clasping the prince, who was dressed once more as a monk. "Captain, I'm needed here in case of injuries. Permission to let the prince go?"

Edric gaped at the three approaching ships and ducked as an arrow zoomed by. "Why are we still here?" He glanced at the unglowing rune and her dry eyes. "Did you break it?"

"I did not break it!" She spun to glare at Chysu. "And no, you do not have permission to let the prince go. Tie him to the mast so he doesn't get in our way."

Chysu pinched her lips together, but she complied with her captain's orders. Edric stepped calmly to the mast, unwilling to take his anger out on Chysu, instead saving his evil glare for Rhielle.

He could glare all he wanted as long as he didn't stupidly injure himself.

A giant crossbow bolt zipped overhead, ripping straight through two sails.

"Captain!" yelled Jazhara from her place near the archers. "We have to get out of here. Now!"

Rhielle growled, snapping her eyes shut.

Her sister ... Aliyabeth ... Taken too soon ... But her father didn't want to lose his negotiating power of two marriageable princesses, so no one could know she was gone. Rhielle had needed to bury that sadness deep within. So deep, she couldn't always find it. She couldn't even picture her sister's body right now. All she could picture was ...

Edric ... lifeless on a rock ... Or leaving him behind to face Geeni on his own, never seeing him again ...

"Rhielle!" he screamed. "You need to hurry!"

Her eyes popped open, and she found him. Alive. Tied to the mast. Furious at her.

"What are you waiting for? Look what they're doing!"

The ships were circling, surrounding the *Lady Tempest* on all sides. They loosed arrow after arrow at her crew, while steadily ripping through her sails with massive crossbow bolts.

Chysu finished patching up a woman who'd been shot in the shoulder and looked up at the ripped sails. "The Resistance is known for shooting flaming bolts at a ship's sails to destroy it quicker."

Rhielle's focus sharpened on the rune carved into the ship's wheel. "They don't want to destroy the *Lady Tempest*," she said with dead certainty. "They want to take her."

The thought of someone stealing her ship brought tears closer to the surface, but her blind rage choked them out. How dare they even *think* about taking her ship? After all she had done for the Resistance over the years? How could they turn on her like this?

Chysu stepped close to Rhielle's side. "Captain ... we may have to surrender."

Rhielle glared at her. "We do not surrender! We'll get out of this."

Chysu didn't back down. "Our sails are almost completely shredded. Without a working rune, this ship is dead in the water. They will board at any moment. If we surrender now, they may have mercy on the crew."

Rhielle's stomach churned at the thought of the Resistance swarming the ship and injuring her crew. As pirates they were skilled at stealthy missions and sneaky tricks, not close combat with three ships' worth of soldiers. At the end of the fight, would she have any crew left standing?

Chysu lifted a spyglass and studied each ship. "One ship belongs to Captain Saverio. You said he promised to treat the crew fairly before. We should surrender now—"

"He said he'd treat my lady crew *gently*, Chysu! I will *not* surrender to that condescending—"

"Listen to me, Captain!" hissed Chysu. "Poppy can't even hold a sword!"

Rhielle narrowed her eyes and said coldly, "Then give her a dagger. Do you understand, Doctor?"

Chysu flinched as if stung. She straightened her shoulders, hands locked behind her back. "Aye, Captain. I understand."

Rhielle watched Chysu walk away, but her eyes snagged on the monk silently watching her.

Silently judging her.

She would prove there was no need for surrender. She could still fix this. All she needed was a single tear.

A single tear that would not come.

She tried cheating by squeezing her wounded arm. Tears from pain wouldn't work on the rune, but maybe they would lure out the true tears. But no matter how hard she squeezed her arm, she only drew more blood, no tears.

She smacked her hand against the rune, screaming at it and, by extension, the sea itself. "So this is it? This is when you'll take me, dragging me below? Well, I won't surrender. I will fight you to the bitter end."

Rhielle grabbed a sword and walked to the railing facing Saverio's approaching ship, but aimed her voice at the sea. "You will not have me."

Her crew lined up on either side of her, and though they stared down the approaching ships, unease passed through the ranks.

They were not ready for this fight.

But Rhielle had no choice. Surrendering was not an option.

"Captain?" Jazhara's loud commands had dropped into a strangely soft tone.

"I told you, I will not—"

"Look!" She shoved a spyglass into Rhielle's hand.

Rhielle turned the glass on the Resistance ships. The soldiers were all staring the opposite direction. She followed their focus to the horizon.

Five ships approached.

"Who is it?" whispered Rhielle frantically. "More Resistance?"

Jazhara took the spyglass back and held still while she searched for some clue to identify the ships. Then she lowered the glass, sketching a shape in the air with her fingers, blessing her gods.

"Captain, the ships are from Isandariyah."

The Resistance ships had reached the same conclusion, and turned away, leaving the *Lady Tempest* floating useless in the water.

22

Her crew sagged in relief as the Resistance ships departed, but Rhielle yelled at them to stay focused. "We aren't safe yet! Isandariyah will not just let us go. I kidnapped their prince, remember? Multiple times. They will not just let us sail away."

Jazhara said, "We are no match for the Isandariyan crossbows, Captain. With the rune not working and the ship dead in the water, we have to hand over the prince and surrender."

The word sent icy fear racing down her spine. The Isandariyans would take her ship and lock her up. Being trapped on land in a prison cell was the worst fate she could imagine. She jerked to her full height and let her voice ring out across the ship. "I wouldn't surrender to the Resistance, and I won't surrender to Isandariyah. Prepare for a fight."

Edric strained against his bonds. "Rhielle, just let me go. I'll tell them to let you escape."

"Do you think I'm an idiot?" she snapped. "They won't just let us go on our way. We have to fight."

"Do you want your crew to die? Some of them are just young girls."

She stormed closer to him and hissed, "They're pirates, no matter their age. They knew what they were in for."

He dropped his voice to a low growl. "Even if you are content to die at sea, Rhielle, it doesn't mean the rest of them are."

She choked down the bile rising in her throat. There was no escape. No way out. Surrender was the only option. The thought was so terrible, a part of her just wanted to let the ship burn down around her.

But her crew …

"Surrender," he whispered. "I promise you, your crew will not be harmed."

She closed her eyes and released her held breath. "Untie him."

A collective sigh rose from her crew, which filled her with equal parts guilt and disappointment. Edric massaged his chafed wrists, then walked to the railing and raised his hands to wave at the lead Isandariyan ship.

How long would it take for them to recognize the blond man in red was their own? Jazhara handed him a spyglass so he could answer that question for them.

"My brothers are on that ship … two of them … Strange, but that explains why they were so aggressive."

"Will they attack?" asked Jazhara.

"They've recognized me. They won't destroy the ship."

Rhielle squinted at the ship. "They still have soldiers with bows raised."

He lifted a brow. "So do you, Captain."

Rhielle's nails dug into her palms as she gave the order that went against her very nature. "Stand down."

Chysu lowered her bow, and every archer on board followed suit.

"They've lowered their weapons." He handed Rhielle the spyglass.

She spotted the two princes on the deck of the lead ship. One wore a dark blue uniform, the other a fashionable jacket, unbuttoned a little too far.

Two women stood tucked into a line of soldiers—one with black hair, one blonde—both dressed in sumptuous gowns highly impractical at sea.

"Who are the women?"

"My brothers' wives." His brows drew together. "Their elaborate weddings were a terrific waste of money that will inevitably lead to a daughter who will destroy the queendom."

She snorted. "With that attitude, I'm surprised they invited you to the weddings at all."

He gave her a flat look.

The uniformed prince cupped his hands and yelled, "Brother! Are you well?"

Edric turned to the quickly approaching ship and shouted, "I'm fine, Jaemin. The soldiers can relax."

Prince Jaemin warily scanned the *Lady Tempest*. "I'm hesitant to believe you aren't speaking under duress, Edric."

"I told you, I'm fine. What are you doing out here?"

The other prince replied, "We have an urgent meeting with Prince Niklys in New Khazburg." He scanned the ship, but much differently than Jaemin had. "Brother, are you on a ship of all women?"

Edric replied in a clipped tone. "Yes, Hawthorne."

Prince Hawthorne grinned wickedly. "Such a wasted treasure on a monk!"

The princes' two wives exchanged very unladylike eye rolls.

Jaemin didn't smile at his brother's playful words, his eyes still wary. "Join us on our ship, Edric." He signaled his soldiers to prepare the dinghy. "You'll come with us to New Khazburg."

"No." Rhielle's voice was firm.

Everyone's eyes shot to her, but Jaemin spoke first. "Excuse me?"

"Edric will stay with us," Rhielle said calmly.

The two princes on the other ship started speaking over one another, but the low voice of the prince on her own ship drowned them out. "Let me go to them—"

"Without you here, they have no reason to not set fire to my ship. You're staying."

The archers on both ships grew twitchy. A battle at this close range wouldn't end any better for her crew than them being shot full of flaming arrows, but by holding on to the prince, she maintained a semblance of control.

"Fine," he whispered harshly. "I will tell them what they need to know to leave your ship alone."

"There's nothing—"

"Brothers!" he yelled cheerfully. "You don't understand. I'm on my own diplomatic mission here." He lifted a hand, gesturing to Rhielle. "Let me introduce you to Princess Rhielle Everglenn of Naermore."

Her mouth dropped open as her head swiveled to glare at him. She would murder him. Being blown out of the water soon after would be worth it.

The princes and their wives stared incredulously at Rhielle, who looked rough, even for a pirate. She had to admit, their disbelief was justified.

Edric realized his claim was hard to swallow. "I can prove it! Rhielle and I will come over there. I'll let you wear the magistrate's ring while she tells you the truth herself."

She hissed, "I said I'm not letting you go over there!"

"Do you think my brothers are stupid enough to blow up a princess's ship? Just come with me, tell them your identity, and they will let you go on your way."

From the expressions on the other ship, the only way they would believe she was a princess was with magical proof. "Fine," she huffed. "We'll do it quickly."

Jaemin signaled his crew to send the dinghy across to the

Lady Tempest. Edric took Rhielle's hand like he was a proper courtier about to assist her over the railing.

She smacked his hand away. "Knock it off!"

He chuckled softly as he followed her down the ladder to the dinghy.

When they made it up the ladder onto the massive Isandariyan ship, soldiers surrounded the oldest prince in formation, while the women and other prince had moved safely below deck. Jaemin and the soldiers stood at ease, but they didn't fool Rhielle. Jaemin was prepared for a trick, waiting for her to attack.

Finally, a flattering response!

Edric pulled the ring off his finger and handed it to his brother. Jaemin turned around—Rhielle assumed he didn't want to shed a tear in front of her. When he turned back, he promptly asked, "Who are you?"

The words were difficult to say. Her crew had discovered her identity early on and spread the word to one another over the years, privately, when she wasn't around. But she hadn't said the words out loud for over five years.

"I'm Princess Rhielle Everglenn, second-born daughter of King Merrick Everglenn of Naermore."

Jaemin's eyes widened, and he stared at her in continued disbelief.

"Well, brother?" asked Edric. "I assume you will treat the princess with the courtesy due her?"

Jaemin cleared his throat and bowed, his manners finally catching up to him. "Welcome aboard our ship, Princess Rhielle. It is an honor to meet you."

She pulled herself into a haughty stance. Though it was the posture of a captain, she hoped he read it as that of a princess. "Thank you for your courtesy, Prince Jaemin. I will head back to my ship now."

"Wait!" said Edric. "You can't leave yet, Princess."

She ground her teeth. "And why is that, *Prince*?"

"You're a representative of Naermore. An ally. What kind of allies would we be if we left you on a ship in need of repair?"

"We will do just fine—"

"I insist! You must stay on our ship and enjoy dinner with us. It's only proper."

"*Proper?*" she growled.

A ruthless fire burned behind his perfectly polite eyes. "While we enjoy a dignified dinner, our soldiers can assist your crew in making enough repairs that your ship can follow us into port."

"Why would we follow—"

"Obviously you will want to meet Prince Niklys as well, Princess."

"Prince Niklys? If I ever meet Prince Niklys, I'll—"

"Naermore is an ally of Verkeshe, correct? I assumed you'd want to pay your respects. It's what a true princess would do, of course." He blinked innocently.

If she threw the man overboard, how long would her crew survive? Not long, but it might still be worth it.

"Is everything okay?" Jaemin looked between the two of them, twirling the ring on his finger as if trying to uncover the truth.

The truth was definitely more complicated than a ring could explain.

"Everything is as it should be, brother. Truly." Edric smiled warmly, and Jaemin nodded. The ring apparently convinced him.

"Excellent. I'll send some soldiers to your ship to assist with repairs, Princess. I look forward to getting to know you over dinner." Jaemin bowed respectfully and left them alone.

She spun on Edric the moment Jaemin was out of earshot. "What do you think you're doing? I am not going to New

Khazburg as some kind of diplomat! I'm a pirate, not a princess."

He whispered darkly, "You made your choice when you claimed the title of 'princess' to save your crew's life. So you're going to New Khazburg to follow it through. Your crew requires it, do you understand?"

The threat was only barely veiled. "Why are you doing this? You could leave me here and go on your way."

His lips curved in a vicious grin as he leaned forward, his breath hot against her ear. "Because this time, Princess, I'm the one kidnapping *you*."

PART II

23

Rhielle sat in her bubble bath, plotting Edric's death. He'd personally escorted her to the quarters reserved for royalty on the Isandariyan ship and gleefully told the royal servants Rhielle required the finest soaps and oils for her bath. She would have gone without just to spite him, except her skin still burned from her dive into the cove. The ungrateful man would pay for kidnapping her.

Just as soon as her bathwater cooled.

A polite knock accompanied a voice outside the door. "Princess Rhielle? Your lady's maid is here."

"My lady's maid?" she asked incredulously. "What in the Spirits' names—"

Poppy scampered inside, her arms full of ruffled satin. She melted into a perfect curtsy. "I'm sorry for disturbing your bath, Your Highness. I'm here as your lady's maid."

Rhielle's hands clenched on the side of the tub, and she attacked Poppy with a menacing glare. "What did you call me?"

The girl's eyes widened in terror. "I ... um ... Jazhara thought ... I'm sorry, Captain. I—"

Rhielle smacked her hand on the water. "Jazhara is encouraging this? Why would she think I need a lady's maid?"

Poppy's mouth opened and closed, the girl weighing if it was wiser to remain silent or to answer the question. "Um ... Captain ... Jazhara sent me because I'm from Naermore, and because I know what is expected of what she called 'fancy people.'"

Rhielle couldn't deny that fact. Most days, the girl still curtsied instead of saluting.

Poppy ducked her head, almost hiding behind the satin in her arms. "Jazhara also said she didn't want you to be alone on this ship until we determined if the Isandariyans were dangerous."

"And she thought to send the youngest member of the crew as my unarmed bodyguard?"

Poppy swallowed, gathering her courage. "With all due respect, Captain, 'fancy people' are more dangerous in ballrooms than on battlefields."

Rhielle gave her an appraising look. "Hmmm ... Point taken. And what skills do you have to offer in these ballroom battles with fancy people?"

"I can prepare your armor." Her cheeks glowed as she laid the satin gently on the bed. "We raided the ship for the nicest clothes we could find. It's not what a princess from Naermore would normally wear, but we gave the excuse that the trunks with your clothes were ruined during the battle. But once I style your hair, I think you'll look like a proper princess."

"A proper princess?"

Poppy focused on fluffing out the satin, distinctly avoiding Rhielle's glare. "I also suggested makeup, but Chysu said if I tried to apply anything other than eyeliner, you'd break my fingers."

At least Chysu was sensible. Rhielle sank into the water up to her shoulders. She just needed to play the part of princess until her ship was repaired, then she'd find a way to get back to her crew and escape.

Of course, she'd also need to figure out why the rune wasn't working. It was likely just the stress of her burned skin after rescuing the prince. Now that she had taken a soothing bath, she felt much better. She could probably make the rune work right now if she tried.

Tonight, when the sea was dark, she'd grab Poppy and sneak back onto the *Lady Tempest*, toss the soldiers overboard, and escape into the night.

The only unknown variable was Edric. She'd prefer to kidnap him again, to pay him back for this whole "princess" stunt, but she couldn't think of a way to kidnap him without endangering Poppy or her crew.

She would have to leave him. Maybe after a fight where she let him have it. No polite sword fight. A quick and furious clash of blades, where she left him on his knees, breathless, watching as she sailed across to her ship, Poppy clutched in her arms.

The dramatic scene pleased her until she remembered the number of soldiers on board. They wouldn't stand still while she got into a one-on-one fight with the prince. A showdown would never work. She needed to sneak away.

She would have to leave without saying goodbye.

Pain stabbed through her at the thought. Obviously, the pain was from not getting to see his face when she defeated him.

Obviously.

She would just have to imagine his face when he realized she was gone. She imagined him standing on deck, staring off into the distance. Hands behind his back, as if unaffected, but his face tortured, his blond hair fluttering around his cheeks ...

Yes, that would have to be enough.

Poppy dressed, styled, and primped her, yet Rhielle still didn't feel like a "proper princess." That was one reason she'd run away in the first place—nothing about Rhielle was proper. She could barely restrain filthy curses from springing to her lips as she hobbled in tight shoes behind the royal servant to dinner in the captain's quarters.

Rhielle had no idea which of her pirate crew had loaned her the delicate heels, but they were not even close to the right size. The satin dress was a nauseating pink, both too tight and too ... fluffy. She tugged at the neckline—could it be called a neckline if it didn't reach her neck? The dress bared her shoulders and dipped so low she was forced to keep a princess's good posture or she'd spill out of the top. Even though Poppy called it "armor," Rhielle felt disturbingly unarmed.

The royal servant ushered her toward the captain's quarters, but Rhielle hovered in the doorway before stepping in. The two eldest princes and their wives stood in a tight circle, talking quietly, while Edric stood off to the side, drinking a glass of water and pointedly ignoring them. He had shaved his rough stubble, tied his blond hair back in a neat braid, and either found a clean monk uniform on board or a servant had pressed his. He looked as fresh as if he had just stepped into a shrine, ready for a day of worshipping his Goddesses. No one could guess he had spent the last few days kidnapped by pirates.

Edric glanced up, his gaze almost passing over her before he blinked once, slowly, eyes locking on her. A jolt went through her at the sudden connection of their eyes. She clenched her fingers on her skirt to keep them from floating up to tug on her neckline. Touching her dress would only draw attention to the flush that had spread from her chest up her neck.

He stared at her, his lips slightly parted, body poised as if ready for attack, though she couldn't tell if he felt more like predator or prey. She straightened her bare shoulders, summoning the commanding posture of a ship's captain. She refused to let the man make her feel bad about this ridiculous charade, especially when it was completely his fault.

"Princess Rhielle!" The black-haired woman glided toward her and took her hand warmly. The woman's dress was even more low-cut than Rhielle's, yet she wore it with a confident grace. "I'm Alanna, Jaemin's wife. I would have waited for a proper introduction from Edric, but he seems unable to close his mouth."

Edric snapped his jaw shut and glared at Alanna as a hint of color rose to his cheeks. Rhielle didn't have time to respond before Alanna pulled her closer to the others. "You met Jaemin earlier, and his brother Hawthorne, and this is his lovely wife, Elliya."

The young blond woman was lucky enough to have a dress that covered her shoulders, though Rhielle itched just looking at the lacy sleeves. Elliya dipped into a pretty curtsy. "A pleasure to meet you, Princess."

Rhielle hadn't been among "proper" folk for over five years and struggled to find the correct response. "Yes, um … likewise."

Alanna didn't allow the conversation to stutter, but took Rhielle's hand and led her to a seat at the head of the table. "Let's sit and chat. I'm curious to know how you met Edric. He's remarkably tight-lipped about the whole situation." Her eyes shot to him, but he purposefully avoided looking at her.

Rhielle took her seat at the head of the table, with Alanna to her right and Elliya to her left. The princes sat next to their wives, with Edric between them at the other end. Alanna leaned closer to Rhielle as if the three women might whisper secrets like girls. "So tell me, where did you find our dear monk prince?"

It clearly wasn't a question for just the girls because the princes perked up, waiting for her response. Edric finally met her eyes from the other end of the table, and in them she detected a slight threat. To protect her crew, she needed to remain a princess, which meant she needed a reasonable excuse for him to end up on her ship. And since he had dodged the responsibility of coming up with a cover story, it now fell to her. He was waiting for her to move first, just like when they had sparred on the cliff.

Well, he'd lost then, and he would lose again.

She quickly scanned everyone's fingers, and thankfully didn't see the truth-telling ring, but she stuck to a vague version of the truth, just to be safe. "Edric was captured by pirates. Lucky for him, I saved his life." She sipped her wine, watching him as the first blow landed.

"Pirates!" Hawthorne shook his head, his dark waves brushing his shoulders. "You get captured by pirates, then rescued by a ship of lady sailors? That sounds like a story from my youth, not yours, brother." His wife bit her lip on a giggle, apparently unthreatened by Hawthorne's previous exploits.

Edric stared at Rhielle, irritation pinching his brows, though perhaps it was irritation at himself for letting her get the upper hand. "Yes, pirates ... Nasty creatures. Faithless anarchists, full of trickery. You can't trust a word they say."

She raised an eyebrow. "True, but I've known princes who could lie just as easily as pirates."

He merely glared at her, unmoving.

Prince Jaemin cleared his throat. "I'm glad you came to his rescue, Princess. He is lucky you were there."

"Yes," she said coolly. "He is quite lucky I saved his life."

A servant deposited a plate in front of Edric, which he conveniently used to escape from admitting the truth. Rhielle turned to her own food, grateful for the distraction. The roast duck and curry rice were delicious. Even though Cook was a skilled chef, when they were out at sea for long stretches, he didn't have access to fresh meat or milk and was forced to get creative. She was one moment away from using her finger to scoop the remaining cream sauce off her plate when she looked up—the others were only halfway finished.

Smug laughter twinkled in Edric's eyes as he took a slow bite. She picked up her fork and considered stabbing him with it. Instead, she held it as daintily as she could manage and gathered the few grains of rice she had left.

Alanna leaned toward her. "How's your sister?"

Rhielle's fork clattered onto her plate. "My sister?"

"Princess Aliyabeth, right?" Alanna laughed lightly. "Though I've never met your sister, I feel like I know her well."

"What do you know about Aliyabeth?" Her throat clenched at her sister's name. She hadn't said it aloud for years.

Jaemin adjusted his uniform and said primly, "Perhaps we shouldn't tell that story, dear, as it involves a certain ... complicated ... family relationship."

"Rhielle is familiar with Geeni," said Edric calmly. "Very familiar." His eyes were more accusatory than was warranted, considering the woman had tried killing Rhielle at their last meeting.

The quiet blond woman spoke up. "Interesting ... Considering your station and your cleverness, I guess you either worked for her or were almost murdered by her."

"Or both," mumbled Alanna.

Rhielle had no response to that, other than, "Uh ..."

Alanna patted her hand. "Don't blame yourself. Geeni has taken advantage of us all."

Elliya's blue eyes hardened. "Geeni takes advantage of people when they are most vulnerable. She doesn't care who gets injured in her quest for power."

Rhielle looked up at Edric while she spoke to everyone. "Is there no reasoning with her? Maybe if the offer was good enough?"

Hawthorne snorted a laugh. "Making a deal with Geeni is

like making a deal with an open flame. You might think you'll keep warm, but invariably she will burn you."

Edric ground his teeth but stayed silent. He clearly disagreed with everyone else at the table.

"Since the princess knows Geeni, there's no harm in telling the story," said Alanna. "I'm one of the unfortunate souls who worked for Geeni without understanding the ramifications. My job was to steal a book from the palace, and Geeni decided the easiest way to get me inside was to give me the identity of a princess." She winked at Rhielle. "Princess Aliyabeth."

Rhielle's heart stuttered to a stop. "You impersonated my sister?" She tried to imagine this playful woman performing the role of her sister and failed.

Her sister had been soft-spoken and wise. Even at seventeen, she could sway a room to do as she wished with a quiet suggestion. Who would she have grown into? What could she have done for Naermore? For the world? All that potential, gone in a single moment.

Elliya whispered, "Princess? Are you okay?" She looked reproachfully at Alanna. "It might have been politically unwise to admit why you feel acquainted with Princess Aliyabeth."

Alanna chewed her lip. "Perhaps you're right. I apologize for speaking flippantly, Princess. I have nothing but the highest respect for you and your sister. And someday, when I meet Aliyabeth, I will tell her the same thing."

"When you meet her ..."

Rhielle occasionally heard news about the royal family in Naermore—stories about her mother's passing, her father's remarriage, and the newborn prince. News about Rhielle and her sister was more rare. The two princesses were both assumed to be quiet women waiting around for the right marriage proposal. Idle gossip from people who had no stake in their lives.

But Alanna and the others spoke about her sister as if she

would someday join them for dinner, like they'd sit around a table together, discussing their countries' politics and enjoying the companionship of peers. Aliyabeth should have been the one at the table, not her.

She stood abruptly. "I've got to go."

As she fled, the discussion switched to how Alanna caused an international incident, but Rhielle focused more on blinking back her tears.

24

Rhielle already wore her pirate clothes when she woke Poppy at midnight. The girl blinked groggily but obediently followed Rhielle. Poppy's pirate clothes were back on the *Lady Tempest*, but she glided silently in her simple dress and slippers as a proper lady should.

Even though Rhielle was sacrificing her chance to see defeat on Edric's face, she had to leave immediately. She couldn't get through another conversation about her sister. Not when one of them might wear the truth-detecting rune. And not when the tears threatened to burst out of her neatly constructed dam at the mere mention of her sister's name.

At least she had plenty of tears at her disposal for their escape.

Rhielle listened to the conversations on deck before she risked peeking around the corner. There were more voices than she'd expected for this time of night, but as long as her crew was watching for her sign, it wouldn't matter. They would see her, shoot an arrow with a rope, and she'd swing back home. She'd done it many times, and Poppy was light enough that Rhielle could manage them both.

She took the girl's hand to keep her close during this most dangerous part of the escape. Poppy looked at her with complete trust—her lavender eyes wide with exhilaration. Familiar grief crushed Rhielle. The girl looked so much like Aliyabeth had in her youth. Had she lived, Aliyabeth would be twenty-three, but this was the way Rhielle remembered her—young and so full of life. She tucked the emotion away, saving the tears to power the rune, and slid around the corner.

And ran directly into Edric.

"Good evening, Princess."

She wanted to slap the smug look off his face. "Let us go, Edric!" she whispered harshly. "You have no reason to keep us here and continue this charade."

"No more reason than you had to kidnap me."

"I was saving your life! Geeni would have killed you."

"And the Resistance wants to kill you. You'd already be dead if our fleet hadn't shown up."

She couldn't dispute the point. Although if she could get the ship's rune to work again, the Resistance would never catch them.

Rhielle shook away the logical arguments. "This has nothing to do with saving my life. You just want to punish me for tricking you. Admit it."

"Perhaps." His lips curved into a wicked grin. "Maybe I'll tie you to the mast as you tied me." He raised a beckoning hand, but instead of a soldier with a rope, a servant with a tray glided over. Edric handed her one of the delicate teacups.

She squinted at the steaming liquid. "Poison?"

The servant blinked in shock, but Edric calmly took another teacup and handed it to Poppy. The girl hadn't moved from her position tucked at Rhielle's back and watched them both with wide eyes.

"It's chai." He spoke gently to Poppy. "You can take it back to your room, if you wish. There will be no escape tonight."

Poppy swallowed and looked up at Rhielle with pleading eyes. The girl was waiting for permission from her captain to depart ... or perhaps from her princess. Rhielle contained the irritated grumble rising in her throat and nodded a sharp dismissal. Poppy's shoulders sagged in relief, and she dipped into a curtsy before scurrying to her room, her teacup carefully balanced.

Edric sipped his own cup of chai, his eyes locked on Rhielle over the rim. She raised her cup and sniffed. While she didn't think Edric would poison Poppy, she wouldn't be surprised if he handed Rhielle a cup with a sedative to ensure she didn't attempt another escape later. She couldn't detect any hint of poison, though it would be difficult to smell anything unusual over the warm spices. Since her escape attempt for the night had been foiled already, she risked a sip.

Her eyes drifted shut as the spiced tea and milk blossomed on her tongue. The creamy warmth brought back memories of drinking hot chocolate on a snowy day as a child. The velvety chai set her at ease and soothed her irritation at Edric.

Her eyes popped open. Edric watched her with a contented smile.

She swallowed the tea and cleared her throat. "This is how you'll tie me to the mast? With your country's delicacies?"

His smile turned roguish. "I thought you might have tied yourself willingly after tasting our curry at dinner."

Her stomach was still contentedly warm after the delicious meal, so the accusation hit home. She stabbed a finger at his chest. "I'm only here because you're holding my crew hostage. I'm not interested in anything your country has to offer."

He glared at her finger with an eyebrow raised. "I hope you are more diplomatic when we meet Prince Niklys, Princess."

"I'm not—"

"Yes, you *will* meet Prince Niklys. To protect your crew,

you've committed yourself to the role of princess, and I intend to see you follow it through."

The teacup rattled as her hands shook with fury. "Listen here, monk—"

A chill wind blew through her hair and wrapped icy tendrils around her neck. She shivered at the same time Edric rubbed a hand across the back of his neck.

"Sorry about that!" called Alanna. "That one got away from me."

Rhielle had been so focused on Edric she hadn't noticed Alanna on deck amid the rest of the crew. The dark-haired woman stood at the ship's stern, her attention on the *Lady Tempest* behind them. She raised a hand and curled her finger as if beckoning the ship to follow.

The ship moved.

Rhielle shoved her teacup into Edric's hands and ran to Alanna's side. "You're controlling my ship?" Had she figured out a way to operate the rune at a distance?

Alanna shook her head. "I have no control over the ship itself, but I convinced the wind to assist, despite the unfortunate state of your sails."

Even though Rhielle's crew and the Isandariyan soldiers had spent the evening repairing the sails, they were still too shredded to work properly. But instead of passing straight through the tears, the wind pushed steadily against the scraps of untorn fabric, moving the ship forward.

"That's impossible!" said Rhielle. "Wind doesn't work that way."

"Wind only works that way if you ask *very nicely*." Alanna swirled a finger near her cheek, and a soft breeze fluttered through her hair. "The wind happens to be very fond of me."

"A Spark," Rhielle said flatly. "Edric told me that's the name for magic like yours." She looked up. He stood next to the ship's captain, ordering the crew to set their own sails in the traditional way. "Why don't you just order the wind to move this ship, too?"

Alanna laughed lightly as she stayed focused on the *Lady Tempest*. "I don't order the wind. I told you, I talk nicely to it. Besides, it takes a lot of concentration to convince each individual breeze to focus on the sails in exactly the right spot. I'd much rather be sipping chai, snuggled up with a handsome prince." She winked at Rhielle before turning back to the ship.

Rhielle had assumed she meant drinking tea with her husband until the wink. "I wasn't snuggled up with Edric."

"No ... you seemed upset with him. Good thing that icy wind cooled you both down." Her gaze stayed locked on Rhielle's ship.

Rhielle narrowed her eyes. "How convenient that a single breeze escaped the control you have on all the rest of that." She waved a hand toward the *Lady Tempest*'s strangely full sails.

Alanna's lips twitched in amusement. "Yes, very convenient. Perhaps next time it will be a sultry breeze that escapes. I'm curious if that would prompt a different reaction between the two of you."

Rhielle imagined a tropical breeze flowing around her and Edric ... their shallow breaths mingling with the heat ... steamy air tingling her skin ... a drop of sweat trickling down his temple ...

Alanna's lips curved in a smug grin, and she didn't turn as Rhielle snapped her jaw shut, then stormed away.

Before Rhielle made it belowdecks, she paused near Elliya leaning over the ship's railing. The Isandariyans pretended to be so civilized, yet they left the poor girl puking all alone? She would give Edric a piece of her mind after she took the girl to find some tea.

She placed a gentle hand on the woman's shoulder. "Elliya, are you okay?"

Elliya spun, startled. "I'm sorry I didn't hear you approach, Princess. And yes, thank you, I'm well."

"You aren't seasick?"

Elliya covered her lips with her hand, but to hide a timid grin. "Oh, I see why you ... No, I was talking to the dolphins. See?" She pointed at the pod of dolphins racing alongside their ship.

"You were talking ..." Rhielle sighed. "That's your Spark." Did all the women in their queendom have some sort of magic?

"Yes, though it still feels strange to admit it out loud. But Alanna and I have discussed it with the princes, and we think it's time to stop keeping magic a secret. Secrecy allowed Geeni to take advantage of people who had a Spark but didn't even know what it was."

Anything that could diminish Geeni's power was fine by Rhielle. "Can you talk to all animals?"

"Yes, um ... except in very unique circumstances."

By the way Elliya avoided her eyes, Rhielle suspected there were still some secrets unrevealed.

Elliya glanced at the dolphins and smiled softly. "I was glad to hear the dolphins chattering. It's so quiet on board. There are a few ship cats, who are nice in their own catlike way, but thanks to them, there isn't a single rat or mouse on board." She frowned as if disappointed by a ratless ship.

Was everyone with a Spark so odd, or did the princes only fall for strange girls?

Elliya looked up at Alanna still curling her finger—beckoning the wind to do as she wanted. "Alanna didn't even bring Bibi on this trip." Her lips curved in a pout, but her eyes twinkled. "We could have managed one monkey on the ship, but not a whole litter of babies."

Rhielle opened her mouth to ask a question, but immediately closed it, unsure where to start.

Elliya giggled awkwardly. "Look at me, dominating the

conversation. I used to be so quiet, but I've been encouraged to speak up more."

Her eyes drifted to Hawthorne, who had joined Edric near the ship's captain. Hawthorne watched Elliya with an intensity Rhielle assumed would leave the timid woman shrinking, but instead, Elliya stood taller. "So tell me, Princess Rhielle, how did you rescue Edric from pirates?"

Her bold question caught Rhielle off guard. "Um ... we stole him off the pirate ship and ... um ... escaped."

Elliya's eyes narrowed, the woman clearly not buying the weak explanation. "You just escaped?"

Rhielle might as well offer a partial truth. "The *Lady Tempest* is faster than other ships because it has one of Geeni's runes."

The admission dispelled all suspicion from Elliya's eyes, replacing it immediately with wide-eyed fascination. "A rune? Is it permanently built into the ship? What is it crafted out of? Most of her runes have been gold, except for the slippers, of course, and I've wondered if different materials provide different results. Does it create a continuous effect until you disable it, or does the magic fade away and require a new tear to power it?"

Rhielle blinked, trying to process the onslaught of questions. "Um ... I have no idea how it works. In fact, it's currently broken."

"Broken?" Elliya's face fell. "You must have already burned through the tears Geeni stole to create the rune. The good news is Geeni probably only had limited tears from the person with that Spark. To steal more tears, she would either need to hold that person prisoner or manipulate them for their entire life." A fierce anger shimmered behind Elliya's blue eyes. Had Rhielle underestimated her?

Elliya sighed. "Dead runes are still useful for study, but I would have liked to see the rune work for myself."

Rhielle wanted to see the rune work more than Elliya did. "I don't think it's completely dead. The last time I pressed a tear against it, the rune still glowed, but the ship didn't move like it used to."

"It still glows? Maybe it isn't dead yet." Elliya's eyes lit up again. "Can I come see it? Maybe I can figure out how it's different from the other runes I've seen."

A new plan began forming in Rhielle's mind. "Of course you can see it! We can go right now. I'll get Poppy—"

"We can't go now, as much as I'd love to! It's important we speak to Prince Niklys quickly, and we shouldn't slow the ships for us to travel back and forth. But once we reach New Khazburg, I'm sure I can sneak away to look at the rune."

Rhielle didn't want to wait until they made it to New Khazburg, but other than Geeni, Elliya seemed to be the person most familiar with runes. If anyone could fix the *Lady Tempest*, it would be her. Once Elliya got the rune working, Rhielle could dump all Edric's "helpful" soldiers overboard and escape.

"You're right," said Rhielle. "I'm sure we can sneak out of a boring dinner to study the rune, just the two of us." She winked, and Elliya's face lit with the excitement of a new discovery.

Guilt twinged inside her, considering she'd have to dump Elliya overboard too before they escaped. Well, as long as there were dolphins nearby, the nice girl would probably be fine.

25

The next morning Rhielle watched New Khazburg approach with a sense of impending doom. She had to find a way back to her ship before Edric pulled her deeper into his bizarre revenge. But as the navy's flagship pulled into the harbor, her hopes for a quick getaway sank like a stone. Her smaller ship was diverted to a remote dock while she was stuck on a ship headed directly for a caravan of carriages waiting to take the Isandariyans to the castle.

And unless she could escape into the crowd, she would get swept along with them.

Poppy waited at her side like a proper lady's maid, though the girl's open-mouthed stare wasn't as dignified as might be expected of a noble. As a sheltered young girl from Naermore, Poppy wouldn't have seen a city as large as the occupied capital of La Veridda.

Rhielle pulled her close. "Stay sharp, Poppy. Be ready to move on my signal."

Poppy's spine straightened. "Yes, Captain."

Rhielle nodded, pleased at the girl's automatic response.

Even though Rhielle once again wore the ridiculous pink dress, at least someone remembered her correct title.

She scanned the crowd, counting the soldiers. Though they were technically all from Verkeshe, they wore black and gold uniforms—different from the Verkeshian military's green. Did they believe themselves separate from Verkeshe? Some of them might have been in La Veridda since the war ended fifteen years ago, so maybe they viewed themselves as something different after all this time.

The La Veriddan soldiers didn't appear nervous receiving the Isandariyan dignitaries, but very curious. Isandariyah was famously removed from most of the world's politics. The queendom welcomed refugees from wars in other countries, but rarely got involved itself, so this envoy was highly unusual.

Unloading their ship took much longer than the *Lady Tempest* ever did. When Rhielle's pirate ship docked, she could be one of the first to jump off and be on her way. But on this ship, she was caught between the servants disembarking first to prepare the carriages and the Isandariyan nobles. She clenched her poofy dress, anxious to move … to run … to escape.

But she was trapped in satin and tight shoes.

She would kill that monk.

She didn't see him with his brothers and their wives, so he must have snuck off the ship with the first servants. Who would stop an Isandariyan religious man? He could move as freely as he wanted, because he had abandoned his role as prince, yet he forced her to wear the title she had shed long ago.

His would be a slow death.

Rhielle took her place in the line to disembark, silently cursing her delicate shoes. She wanted to stomp angrily off the ship, but she had to take tiny steps down the ramp. After making her way off the dock, she headed straight for an empty carriage and pulled Poppy inside.

The girl examined the inside of the luxurious carriage, then whispered, "I thought we were going to escape."

Rhielle thumped back against the padded seat and crossed her arms. "Of course we're going to escape. But we'll wait until the procession to the castle starts and jump out of the carriage when there aren't as many eyes on us. I'm counting on Jazhara to create a distraction." Rhielle was confident she could kick off her shoes and run, but getting Poppy away unseen would be easier with a diversion.

A soft smile lit Poppy's face at the idea of an adventure, and she leaned forward to whisper, "I'll be ready, Captain."

The carriage door opened, and Rhielle prepared to use her princess voice to say she and her lady's maid would ride alone, when Jazhara hopped inside.

Poppy slid over, letting Jazhara sit next to her. "Is this it?" whispered Poppy. "The distraction?"

Jazhara only said "Captain ..." as her eyes directed Rhielle to look at the open door.

Edric followed her inside. "Hello, Princess."

The big man took the seat at Rhielle's side, forcing her to gather her fluffy skirts and scoot out of his way. "What are you up to, monk?"

"I thought you would want a report from the captain of your ship." He sat comfortably beside her, unconcerned by how much space he took up, despite his lack of irritating petticoats.

She hugged her skirt closer, not wanting to touch him at all. "That's the story you told your brothers, but what are you really up to?"

He twisted, resting his elbow on the back of their seat. "I thought Jazhara could talk some sense into you."

She huffed out a laugh. "You think Jazhara will take your side in this? My first mate is just as anxious as I am to end this farce and get back to sea." When Rhielle finally turned to look at Jazhara, the woman's expression was one of apology, not agreement.

Rhielle's eyes narrowed. "Jazhara ..."

Her first mate didn't react to her threatening tone, other than by speaking very calmly. "Captain, it's beneficial for us to stay here while we finish our repairs and purchase the supplies we couldn't procure in Ravenna. So long as we remain in New Khazburg, the *Lady Tempest* is protected from the Resistance by both the Isandariyans and the local military."

"So you're asking me to play the princess, too?"

Jazhara lifted her hands in surrender. "Just for a few days, Captain."

"A few *days*?" Rhielle hissed.

"Don't upset yourself, Princess." Edric's eyes twinkled with mischievous condescension. "Jazhara is free to walk around the city so she can pick up some more fancy dresses for you. I know you'll want to be dressed appropriately for all the parties you'll be attending."

She flew at him, trying to clasp her hands around his throat, but the tight quarters and even tighter corset limited her reach. He leaned away with a soft chuckle.

"Captain, please ..." said Jazhara calmly. "For your crew."

Rhielle spit out the words through clenched teeth. "Fine. For the crew." She threw her first mate a sharp look. "I expect you to stock my quarters full of treasure for my return."

Edric smiled innocently. "I'm sure Jazhara will buy you the most luxurious soap for a bubble bath she can find."

As Jazhara exited the carriage, Rhielle strangled the satin in her lap, imagining it was Edric's throat.

∽

The carriage ride through the city was silent. Rhielle had no breath for words, suffocated by thick satin and a burning rage.

Edric sat next to her, in his lightweight monk clothes, legs relaxed as he lounged in the seat, but she couldn't find a comfortable position. Whenever she moved, the ridiculous layers of fabric seemed to multiply and would land on Edric's lap. She would have been happy drowning him under the heavy fabric, except every time the satin brushed his hand, a smug grin spread across his lips.

He was reveling in her misery.

She'd finished plotting his murder in a dozen different ways by the time they arrived at the castle. Edric offered his hand to assist her out of the carriage, and she snapped her teeth at him. He shrugged and helped Poppy out instead, letting Rhielle stumble out of the carriage on her own.

They met up with the princes and their wives inside the castle. A servant wearing Prince Niklys's colors of black and gold bowed deeply. "Allow me to show you to your rooms so you can relax before dinner." Curious—he spoke in Riddish, the traditional language of La Veridda, not the language of Verkeshe.

Prince Jaemin stepped forward. "We are here on a matter of urgent business with Prince Niklys. We require a private audience with him at his earliest convenience."

The servant's eyes widened at the unexpected request. "Wait here, Your Highness. I will notify Prince Niklys of your need for haste."

As the man hurried off, Jaemin turned back to the others, his eyes catching on Rhielle. "I apologize, Princess. I should have told him you would want to head to your own room."

"I can speak for myself, Prince," she said through a smile that was mainly just bared teeth.

Alanna touched Jaemin's arm. "Perhaps she should join us for this meeting."

He glanced sharply at his wife. "This is a highly personal

matter, Alanna. Prince Niklys will probably be upset that we know what we do—he won't want the information to spread any further than us."

Rhielle had been planning an escape to her room and then out of the castle, but she perked up at this intriguing information. They knew a secret involving Prince Niklys? Perhaps she should remain quiet like a proper princess and listen.

Elliya stepped closer, Hawthorne trailing her. "Yes, it is a private matter." The blond woman clutched a battered book against her chest. "However, Rhielle should be told. Considering why she is visiting Prince Niklys in the first place."

"Why I'm visiting?" Rhielle snapped her jaw shut. So much for being a quiet princess. She glanced at Edric, who was just as confused. She faced off with the two women. "What do you know about why I'm here?"

Elliya's cheeks reddened, and she ducked her head, but Alanna didn't flinch. She met Rhielle's eyes matter-of-factly. "Because Prince Niklys has finally finished his mourning period after the loss of his wife."

Rhielle swiveled her head between the two women, hunting for an answer. "What does that have to do—"

"She's not marrying Prince Niklys," growled Edric.

Rhielle spun. Edric loomed at her back, hands fisted at his sides. He glared at Alanna, but the woman merely quirked an eyebrow, as if intrigued by his vehement reaction. He turned his glare on his two brothers, who both seemed confused by the entire situation.

The servant reappeared and waved his hand to usher them forward. "Prince Niklys will see you in his private office."

The three princes and two women faced Rhielle. She had no idea what was going on, but she knew one thing: Edric did not want anyone under the illusion she sought a marriage with Prince Niklys.

Which made her choice clear.

"I didn't realize my intentions were so obvious. But now there are no secrets between us." She dipped her head demurely. "I can't wait to finally meet Prince Niklys." She fluttered her lashes wildly, but it didn't obscure her view of Edric's fury.

26

Prince Niklys was more welcoming than Rhielle had expected. When she traveled to Verkeshe five years ago, she had been introduced to King Ruzgar and his second-born son, but Prince Niklys had been in La Veridda for the last fifteen years and had rarely returned home. She didn't notice a strong family resemblance other than the golden blond hair common in Verkeshe. He wore his hair longer than the Verkeshian soldiers, opting for a style closer to a traditional La Veriddan one.

Overall, he was quite an attractive man, though he was close to twice her age. The wrinkles at the corners of his eyes proved he smiled often, and he held himself with a confident grace without appearing cocky. As she curtsied, her eyes roved over him appreciatively.

Edric's scowl proved he noticed.

She ducked her head to hide her grin.

"Welcome to New Khazburg!" Prince Niklys spoke in formal Riddish, like his servant had. "I'm pleased you've come, though I admit I'm concerned about the sudden nature of your visit."

Jaemin made the required introductions of Alanna, Elliya,

and his brothers before indicating Rhielle. "And this is Princess Rhielle of Naermore. We rescued her ship from the Resistance and escorted her the rest of the way here."

Niklys took Rhielle's hand and brushed a delicate kiss across her knuckles. "Princess Rhielle ... I wish I had known you were on your way. I would have arranged an escort."

She didn't release his hand. "That's generous of you, Prince Niklys. Such kindness from someone so recently out of mourning."

It wasn't subtle.

But Rhielle rarely was.

Niklys raised an eyebrow at her overt hint. Then his face beamed as he covered her hand with his own. "I have the deepest respect for your father, King Merrick, so you will be my honored guest at dinner tonight."

A muscle twitched in Edric's jaw, but he kept his attention strictly ahead.

She forced herself to giggle softly as she drew back her hand. The sound was even more distasteful than pretending to faint, but a pirate always did what had to be done.

Niklys shifted his focus back to Jaemin. "I assume this urgent matter is about more than escorting the princess." He ushered them toward two long sofas near his desk. The two couples joined each other on one, which left Rhielle to sit beside either Edric or Niklys.

She smiled demurely as she lowered herself onto the cushion next to Niklys.

Jaemin appeared not to notice the fury radiating off Edric, but Alanna's eyes narrowed shrewdly. Rhielle ignored her, staring up at Niklys adoringly.

Jaemin cleared his throat. "Prince Niklys, I'm sure you know the challenging position Isandariyah is in regarding the succession."

Niklys nodded thoughtfully. "Yes, the rest of the world

places such importance on sons, yet the queendom is in want of a princess."

"Exactly. My brothers and I have been desperately seeking ways to track bloodlines, so we can prove if a child has the blood of the First Queen without them being born directly of the queen." He swallowed as if to slow his words. "That study led us to a discovery we didn't expect." He glanced at Elliya to rescue him.

Elliya looked like she would rather hide than speak to Niklys, until Hawthorne smiled encouragingly at her. She drew a deep breath, lowered her clutched book to her lap, and rubbed her hand reverently across the cover. "Many years ago, you knew my mother. Yulia Zaleska."

Niklys's face lit up, though he looked a little confused at the apparent change in topic. "Yes, I knew her in school, though I lost track of her at some point. She was a brilliant student. I assume by now she must be an equally brilliant scholar."

Elliya's smile turned sad. "Unfortunately, she died giving birth to me, but her scholarship remains. That's what we are here to discuss with you." She squeezed the book with both hands. "Her journal details the results of her experiments on how to determine blood types. It's not precise enough to prove who *is* related, but it can definitively prove who *isn't*."

Suspicion simmered behind the man's dark blue eyes. "There have been rumors about my illegitimacy since I was born, but it hasn't stopped me from ruling this country as a true prince. So if this is some kind of threat—"

"A threat?" squeaked Elliya. "No, definitely not!"

Rhielle leaned back to get a better view of the uneasy prince at her side. Perhaps this peaceful discussion would end in bloodshed.

"We offer you no threat, Your Highness," said Jaemin. "We only desired to warn you there are those who would try to steal this knowledge for their own gain, and we want you to be prepared."

"Why warn me at all? How is my bloodline any of your concern?"

Hawthorne squeezed Elliya's shaking hand and faced Niklys. "It's our concern because the person trying to steal this proof is from our family. Her name is Geeni, but when she went to school with you, she went by Ginevere."

Niklys slapped a hand over his mouth, covering a ... smile? "Geeni is *trying* to steal proof I am illegitimate? Meaning, she doesn't have it already?"

"This is the only proof." Elliya clutched the journal to her chest. "She suspects what it says, but she's never seen it."

Niklys's eyes widened as he processed this information.

Then he threw his head back and laughed.

When Rhielle maneuvered herself into this meeting, she hadn't known what kind of secret they would reveal, but this conversation was nothing like she'd expected. She glanced at the other princes, Alanna, and Elliya, but none of them appeared to have a clue why Niklys was laughing.

He laughed so hard, tears came to his eyes. As he wiped them away, he said, "I apologize for my outburst. You don't know how ironic it is that you would bring this to me now."

"No ..." said Jaemin slowly. "We honestly don't know ..."

Niklys wiped the last tear from his eye and leaned forward, resting his forearms on his thighs. "I thought Geeni already had this proof. That's how she's been blackmailing me for the last twenty years."

No one moved, beyond dropping their jaws.

Niklys rubbed his hands through his golden blond hair, setting it wildly askew. "This whole time ... she's been bluffing. If only you'd come sooner, I could have saved so much money."

Rhielle glanced at Alanna and Elliya. This was why they thought she should be in the room. If she hadn't been faking her interest in Niklys, this knowledge would have definitely affected her decision to seek an alliance with him.

What would happen if someone could prove the older prince wasn't the true son of the King of Verkeshe? What would that mean for the future of La Veridda? Would Verkeshe just abandon the country? Would the younger brother come take over?

Would there be another war?

Niklys spoke again, since no one else knew what to say. "So tell me, is there proof?"

Elliya shrank in on herself like she wanted to sink into the couch. "You really want to know?" She glanced at Rhielle before looking down at her mother's journal.

Her meaning was obvious ... *Do you actually want me to tell you in front of a woman you might want to marry?*

"Yes," he said firmly. "I want the truth. No matter what it is."

Elliya swallowed. "My mother has detailed notes about testing the blood of two brothers and their father, though she doesn't say who they were. But Geeni gathered the blood, probably by bribing someone close to you. After my mother realized who the blood belonged to, she fled Verkeshe, seeking asylum in Isandariyah and changing her name." Elliya swallowed slowly, uncomfortable delivering such awful news. "Though my mother doesn't name you or your brother in her journal, Geeni admitted it was your blood. And my mother gives precise notes on how to recreate the test which proved that the younger son might be a true son, but the older son surely is not."

Niklys leaned back against the couch with a deep sigh. "Honestly, it's a relief to know the truth. Geeni said she had proof ... but I couldn't trust what she had was actually the truth, just something that enough people would believe was the truth. Knowing I'm not the king's son sets me free in a way I hadn't expected ..." His eyes took on a faraway look.

"Prince Niklys ..." said Jaemin hesitantly. "How would you like us to proceed?"

Niklys shook himself out of his thoughts and smiled at Jaemin. "Tonight, we'll enjoy a lavish dinner together, and then tomorrow night, I'm throwing a ball to celebrate."

"To celebrate?" Rhielle couldn't imagine what the man would possibly want to celebrate.

Niklys spread his arms wide. "I want to express my gratitude for your kindness in bringing this information to my attention. We will celebrate Isandariyah, a true ally." He turned to Rhielle and took her hand, caressing it more than was strictly necessary. "And Naermore, a country as full of grace and dignity as her princess."

Edric snorted a laugh.

Rhielle shot him a glare, then simpered at Prince Niklys as he kissed her hand.

A pirate did what she had to do.

27

Rhielle tugged on the neckline of her dress as she strode down the hallway to dinner. Poppy had acquired the traditional La Veriddan dress from someone in the castle, and without the girl's help, Rhielle would never have gotten herself into it. The silk was a single sheet of fabric cunningly wrapped around her body. Poppy had draped the fabric over Rhielle's shoulders and around her waist, leaving the end of the long skirt to trail behind her.

Thankfully this new dress covered her shoulders, though it was still lower cut than she preferred. How could you properly fight if you were constantly worried you'd slip out of your dress? Poppy had reassured her she wouldn't need to fight anyone at dinner, but Rhielle wasn't so sure.

Though she had played along with the assumption she was courting the newly eligible Niklys, she had no illusion he was an ally of Naermore. The soldiers in Niklys's castle might wear different uniforms from the Verkeshe military, but they served King Ruzgar. She was in enemy territory.

And she was wearing a silk dress.

Poppy glided quietly at her side, glancing at Rhielle out of the corner of her eye, ready in case she was needed by her captain.

Or her princess.

Rhielle couldn't blame the girl for being confused. Poppy had been extremely resilient, considering the strange circumstances.

Rhielle spared her one last look before heading in for dinner. "Poppy, I'm proud of how you've handled yourself." The girl's face lit up, and Rhielle squeezed her arm comfortingly. "Thanks for helping me get dressed. You were quite clever to find me a new dress on such short notice."

Poppy's pale cheeks colored a soft pink. "Oh ... well, I didn't do that myself. A servant girl delivered it courtesy of the prince."

Rhielle cocked her head. Niklys was already offering her gifts? Receiving presents was a new method of stealing from her enemies, but as long as she was trapped as a princess, she might as well use her time to acquire treasure.

"Be ready to leave at a moment's notice. I don't know when the opportunity to escape will present itself, but I need you to be ready the instant I say it's time. Can you do that, sailor?"

"Yes, Your High— Cap— Yes, of course." She dipped into a curtsy, before scurrying to the kitchen with the other servants.

Rhielle pushed open the door to the dining hall and strode inside. Her steps began as she usually walked: confident and powerful. But her footsteps stuttered at the reactions of the people standing around the table.

Elliya and the two older Isandariyan princes smiled politely, but Alanna nodded appreciatively, as if to a peer. Edric's eyes were unreadable, but they followed each of her steps across the long marble hall.

However, the look in Niklys's eyes almost caused her to lose her nerve and go change. He watched her hungrily, as if she were an offering from her country being delivered into his hands. He saw a princess surrendering her heritage by dressing in the garb of her future husband's country, losing herself completely to him.

Rhielle, a pirate, was dressed as an obedient wife, chained to a life in a castle, never to sail again.

The thought closed her throat, and her footsteps slowed as she struggled to breathe. Rhielle yearned to spin on her heel and flee the room, but she couldn't run without appearing weak. She had to fight—to kick her way to the surface before she drowned in the fear.

Her next step was intentional, followed by the next, until she made it to the table, chin held high.

At the head of the table, Niklys set down his glass and pulled out a chair to his right. "You look beautiful, Princess."

She nearly choked on the sourness of wine on his breath, but accepted her seat without betraying her shaking knees. "Thank you, Prince." She hated the softness of her voice, but she couldn't speak louder without revealing how out of breath she was.

Edric's eyes never left her as he sat down across from her, though protocol suggested it should be the eldest prince to Niklys's left. Instead, the two couples took the next seats.

Jaemin looked at the empty seats at the long table. "Is it just us tonight?"

Niklys signaled a servant to refill his wineglass. "At the ball tomorrow, I'll introduce you to the rest of the court, but tonight I thought an intimate dinner would be best." He gulped down half his glass. "Learning the truth of my illegitimacy has left me in an odd mood."

The truth had left him sloshed. He must have been drinking nonstop since the moment they told him.

Elliya unfolded and refolded her napkin in her lap. "I apologize for bringing you such distressing news, Prince."

"You do not need to apologize. You are faithful allies to

share this information with me, instead of using it to your advantage."

If Rhielle had known this secret earlier, she would definitely have used it to her advantage. But as Niklys's eyes landed on her, she just smiled awkwardly, as if accepting the compliment herself.

Alanna beamed, full of sparkling charm. "Thank you for welcoming us so kindly, despite this distressing news. I admit, La Veridda is not what I expected. I thought the country would have adopted more Verkeshian culture after all this time, but it looks much as I remember from my childhood."

Niklys leaned forward excitedly, splashing wine on the elegant tablecloth. "You're originally from La Veridda?"

"Yes, I was born here. After my father died in the war, my mother fled with me to Isandariyah." Her enchanting smile never faltered, but sadness lurked behind the words.

Nostalgia tinged Niklys's face. "I remember La Veridda before the war ... a country of knowledge and enterprise, with a navy that rivaled any on the sea ... The war destroyed so much we haven't been able to regain in the last fifteen years."

Rhielle stared at him open-mouthed. "La Veridda wouldn't have to rebuild if your country hadn't destroyed it in the first place."

Edric's sharp glance speared her, and the others sighed or rolled their eyes at her undiplomatic words, but only regret touched Niklys's eyes. "I was only twenty-five when we invaded on my father's order. I wish the La Veriddan king would have surrendered immediately ... He should have been the only one to suffer, since he started the war."

Rhielle ignored Edric's kick under the table and the pleading looks of the others, leveling her full attention at Niklys. "La Veridda started the war? Your country was the aggressor! You attacked La Veridda because they threatened your dominance."

Niklys faced her, curiosity sparking in his eyes. "I would have expected your father to tell you the real reason behind the war. Few people know the truth, but your father is one."

"What does my father have to do with this?"

"We warned him he should be careful with you and your sister, or you might be kidnapped as our young princess was."

Rhielle smacked her hands on the table. "Your princess? Your country kidnapped the La Veriddan princess! That's what started the war. There is no princess in Verkeshe."

He merely stared at her, a deep well of grief lurking in his dark blue eyes.

Rhielle blinked, trying to process this strange onslaught of information.

Hawthorne softly cleared his throat. "Prince Niklys, are you saying La Veridda started the war by kidnapping your sister?"

Niklys finished the rest of his wine with a gulp. "We had different mothers. She was the daughter of our father's second wife ... Our father—" His voice cracked, and he signaled for more wine. "Well, I guess she wasn't truly my sister after all."

"Why has her kidnapping been kept a secret?" asked Jaemin. "It would have surely given you more justification for the war. You would have gained allies."

Niklys raised a single brow. "Do you mean Isandariyah would have come to our aid if we had revealed La Veridda stole our princess?"

The Isandariyan princes exchanged guilty looks, which answered his question. Rhielle sensed their guilt was also tinged with sadness, though she wasn't sure why.

Niklys chuckled darkly. "My father—The king didn't want to appear weak and admit his child was stolen from his own fortress. And the king of La Veridda never took credit for the kidnapping. He denied the accusation, saying we stole *his* daughter instead." Niklys shook his head. "He was mad by the end of the war. It's why he died so soon after surrendering. If he had lived, we would have made him swear fealty to Verkeshe and set La Veridda up as a colony instead." His face turned wistful as he swigged his wine.

His easy talk about colonization and surrender rankled Rhielle. Prince Niklys might not be the natural-born child of King Ruzgar, but he was surely his son. They believed themselves supremely gifted to control everyone else. Kings and princes were all the same.

Edric sipped his water, his eyes locked on hers, disapproval and judgment written plain.

Yes, kings and princes were all the same.

The conversation lulled as servants brought out the first course. The food smelled so delicious Rhielle wanted to stuff herself, yet her stomach churned. She was trapped at a table full of royals in a castle too far inland for her comfort, with her ship docked at an unknown location. Her flimsy dress threatened to choke her, and even her skin felt too tight. Rhielle had to clench her hands in her lap to keep from clawing anxiously at her skin for escape.

Niklys leaned toward her suddenly, whispering, "There's nothing to worry about, Princess."

She flinched, then immediately reprimanded herself. Rhielle was not a woman who flinched at the sudden movement of drunk princes. She gritted her teeth. "I'm not worried."

He leaned closer, to not be heard above the conversation of the Isandariyans. "I know it's not the most convenient time for this revelation about my illegitimacy, but even if the secret gets out, the king will deny it. He won't surrender this country, and there's no way my younger brother will give up his pampered life in Verkeshe to take over the job." He cleared his voice of the bitterness that had crept in. "So there's no need to worry. My position as a prince of Verkeshe and leader of La Veridda is secure."

It was laughable he could imagine his uncertain status as prince caused her even a moment's worry.

Before she could tell him so, he took her hand clenched in her lap. "A union between our countries would be very beneficial to us both, Princess."

She froze like a trapped animal. A part of her screamed to wake up, that she was not prey, she was a fighter. But her body refused to move. Her title pressed down on her, choking out reasonable thought.

"What about Princess Aliyabeth?" asked Edric.

Rhielle gasped, the question splashing over her like cold water. Niklys's hand still clasped hers, but it was no longer a concern worth mentioning. She could barely find the breath to speak. "What did you say?"

Edric folded his napkin precisely in his lap and focused on Niklys. "It isn't appropriate to court a younger daughter while the older is unmarried."

The friendly conversation between the married couples halted, and they turned with open mouths toward Edric. Niklys blinked at him in confusion.

A powerful mix of fury and sadness washed over Rhielle. She pulled her hand away from Niklys, shoved down the ever-present grief, and grabbed her anger with both hands. "You self-righteous hypocrite. How dare you comment on the proper timing for a woman to be married! I don't believe in your Goddesses, and I don't intend to follow their archaic rules."

Alanna crossed her arms and stared disapprovingly at Edric. "Though he's dressed like a monk, you should know the Goddesses say nothing about when it's 'appropriate' for a woman to marry. Any archaic opinions he has on the matter are his own."

A muscle in Edric's jaw twitched, but he didn't dispute her.

Niklys frowned, then shook his head as if to clear away his

drunkenness. "Well, the older daughter marrying first actually *is* tradition in Verkeshe."

Rhielle stared at him but didn't reply. She refused to admit the same was true in Naermore.

Her fingers clamped her dinner knife as she glared at Edric, who sat unmoving, rage boiling off him like steam.

Niklys glanced at the monk, then turned to Rhielle, placing a gentle hand atop hers. "Perhaps this is a conversation best had in private."

Rhielle wanted to fling off his hand and stab the knife into the table to demonstrate she didn't respond well to condescending suggestions from princes of any country. But much as she would like to stab Niklys, it was nothing compared to her desire to battle Edric.

Instead of stabbing Niklys, she released the knife and turned her hand to clasp his. "Yes, Prince, I think this is a conversation we should have in *private*." She fluttered her lashes, then glanced at Edric. "Somewhere very, *very* private."

Alanna and Hawthorne exchanged raised eyebrows, though both of their spouses appeared confused by the entire situation.

Niklys's eyes flashed with a hungry delight—he understood clear enough. "Tomorrow after the ball," he whispered, the wine still strong on his breath. "We'll talk. In private." He lifted her hand and brushed his lips across her knuckles.

She suppressed the revulsion at being kissed by one of her sworn enemies and instead focused on the enemy dressed as a monk. "I'm so glad the Isandariyans rescued my ship," she said innocently. "Why, if it wasn't for Prince Edric, I wouldn't be here at all."

She laughed, trying to keep the sound playful, not strangled.

Edric didn't say a word.

28

After a dinner that lasted an eternity, Rhielle couldn't bear the confinement of her small room, so she escaped to the roof. And since the guards didn't see her as a threat or an escape risk, they let her go.

As a girl in Naermore, she had escaped to the castle's roof often. The icy mountain air had cooled her furious thoughts and settled the anxiety clawing at her skin. But the capital of Naermore was deep within the mountains, far from the Dharijian Sea or the Great Ocean on the other side. That air had been cold and dead, but the air tonight was alive.

The moon hid behind heavy clouds, casting the rooftop garden into deep shadow, so she could only see a few steps in front of her as she walked along the winding path. A fountain splashed nearby, and though the sound was soothing, she gave the spraying water a wide berth.

The thick scent of roses floated on the breeze, but it couldn't overpower the brine of the sea. Beyond the warm glow of the city prowled a blackness untouched by the hidden moon. Her soul longed to be out there—gliding across the smooth waves, the wind in her hair, her crew at her side with no expectations she be anything other than what she was ...

A captain.

A pirate.

Free.

She moved closer to the edge of the roof, stepped over the delicate ironwork railing that was the original La Veriddan architecture, and climbed the thick barricade the Verkeshe had added. An ugly addition to be sure, but considering the Verkeshe had invaded the castle, a worthwhile precaution.

Rhielle peeked over the barricade and studied the exterior of the castle. Well-placed balconies ... Decorative stone carvings ... Plenty of handholds all the way down ...

"I'm sure you could descend the wall, Princess, but bringing Poppy would be impossible."

Rhielle squeezed the barricade, taking her anger out on the rough stone instead of spinning around in shock and giving Edric the chance to gloat at having startled her.

Especially since he'd said exactly what she had been thinking.

She lowered herself slowly down the barricade and climbed back over the railing, careful not to let her cleverly draped dress expose her legs. She cursed herself for not changing in her room first. The La Veriddan silk was cooler than the thick satin monstrosity, but still highly impractical.

Rhielle smoothed the fabric into place as she approached him. "Perhaps I'll leave the girl here and run off alone."

"You'd never abandon your crew." He crossed his arms over his thick chest, an unmoving boulder, confident of his declaration.

Obviously, he was right. Which was why she suspected Jazhara had sent the girl to keep Rhielle in the castle while her crew finished repairs.

Being a pirate with morals was highly inconvenient.

She mirrored his stance. "Fine. If you know I'm not leaving without Poppy, why did you follow me up here when I didn't bring her with me?"

A muscle in his jaw tensed before he ground out, "You can't marry him. He's twice your age."

A laugh burst from her throat. "That's what princesses do, monk. They marry someone too old for them for the sake of their country."

His eyes were more fierce than she had ever seen them, even during their battle atop the cliff. "You can't marry him, Rhielle."

The man deserved to be slapped, but instead she batted her lashes sweetly. "I had forgotten how much I love being a princess! Thanks for kidnapping me and forcing me to remember."

"You can't—"

"Stop it, Edric! You're being an idiot! Do you seriously think I changed everything about myself, suddenly deciding to marry a prince like a proper princess should?"

A hint of doubt crept into his fierce eyes, but he didn't answer her.

"If I wanted to marry Prince Niklys, I could have married him five years ago when he was looking for a wife. I was only sixteen back then, but my father would have agreed to an arranged marriage with Niklys for either of us."

It would have been her sister, of course. But somehow Aliyabeth had wound up at the bottom of the sea, and left Rhielle with Niklys kissing her hand.

She shook away the melancholy thoughts. "But I'm a pirate, not a princess, remember? And you knew what I was when you brought me here. If you're so concerned I'll take advantage of Niklys and marry him, you shouldn't have brought me here in the first place."

He blinked, confusion replacing some of his anger. "I'm not worried you'll take advantage of him."

"Of course I'll take advantage of him! It's what I do. Maybe I'll get him to escort me through his military headquarters, where I'll be so overwhelmed, I'll faint and need to rest so I can spend the day spying on him."

He snorted a bitter laugh. "You're quite skilled at tricking stupid men with that 'fainting maiden' act."

She couldn't use it as often as she'd like. It only worked when the man you fainted on was trustworthy enough to take care of you, not take advantage of you.

"You knew what I was from the moment we met. It's not my fault you forgot." She lifted her arms to show off her silk dress. "I may be dressed as a princess, but make no mistake—I'm still a pirate, and I have no issues using Prince Niklys to get what I want."

The fury returned to his eyes. "Even if it means marrying him?"

She shrugged casually. "Perhaps." Rhielle refused to admit she would never allow it to get that far. She would be long gone before Niklys could even propose.

His voice dropped back to a low growl. "You can't marry him."

"Oh, I definitely can," she purred.

He took a single step closer, looming above her. "You won't."

A thrill raced through her—she had stirred the boulder to move! She matched the fire in his eyes with her own. "You have no control over me, monk. I'll do as I wish."

He was close enough she could see his body trembling with restrained anger. He drew a deep breath through his nose. "Spar with me."

She blinked, trying to put his words into context. "Spar with you? Now?"

"Until first blood. If you win, I'll buy you a fleet of ships as your wedding gift. But if I win, you decline Niklys's proposal."

The premise itself was ridiculous. As if she'd ever marry Niklys! Which meant there was no risk in losing, other than how much she hated to lose. But if she won, would he really give her a fleet? The queen might have something to say about her son gifting a pirate a fleet of her ships.

Well, that would be his problem to solve.

She accepted before he could rescind the offer. "Deal. What weapons will we use?"

He narrowed his eyes in a shrewd look. "Are you telling me you came to dinner unarmed?"

Her lips curved into a slow grin. She pulled her weapon from the sheath under her dress as he drew his own dagger.

29

Rhielle huffed out an irritated breath. "It's supremely unfair how much easier it is for you to conceal a weapon under your clothes. Do you know how hard it was to hide this dagger under this flimsy dress Niklys gave me?"

"The dress is from me," he said calmly.

"From you?" While she considered Poppy's nonspecific claim about the dress being from the prince, Edric sprang toward her.

She barely dodged his blade—aimed directly at her arm with the self-imposed wound from their first match. He had almost drawn blood and ended the match before it began.

Rhielle pointed her blade at him from a safe distance. "Cheating? I thought monks were supposed to be honorable?"

"I'll do whatever it requires to win, Princess." He took two menacing steps forward, then lunged.

She hopped backward, nearly tripping on her long dress. "Stop calling me that!"

He circled her, backing her away from the railing. "You can't deny who you are, Princess."

"I'm not a princess," she hissed. "Stop demeaning me with a title I cast off long ago."

His forward movement slowed. "Demean you?"

She used his distraction to pounce, aiming for his broad chest, but he neatly sidestepped the attack, before resuming his steady press forward.

She kept her eyes on his blade. "You're like all the rest—my father, King Ruzgar, Prince Niklys. You see a princess as someone weak to be controlled. Well, I refused that title then, and I still refuse it now."

A new fury burned in his eyes. "You have no idea what you're talking about, Princess."

She slashed at him, but her dress tangled in her legs, and she had to dash back several steps to avoid his counter. Her eyes had finally adjusted to the overcast night, so she could see the direction Edric had been leading her.

Though it should have been obvious by the splashing of the fountain.

She was more out of breath than she should be for such a short match, her hand slick on her blade. She could remember none of the tricks she would normally use on opponents bigger and stronger than her. Panic hit her that she might lose, and even though the stakes of this match were insignificant, she still hated the thought of losing to him.

He lunged again, backing her so close to the fountain, a fine mist burned her bare arms. She gritted her teeth, unwilling to reveal how much it stung. She thrust one more time, and as he avoided her blade, he grinned, confident he had won. Rhielle stood wedged between him and the fountain. There was no escape.

A raindrop landed on his cheek.

Even though it hadn't landed on her, Rhielle still flinched. Edric's eyes widened, and he glanced up at the looming clouds.

Rhielle didn't hesitate before knocking the blade out of his hand. Edric grabbed her with both hands, lifted her off the ground and leaned her over the bubbling fountain until the ends of her hair floated in the water.

She held her blade carefully against his throat, though the splashing water soaked through her silk dress, burning like fire against her back.

"How unchivalrous of you, monk," she said through clenched teeth. "Using water to your advantage to injure me."

Edric looked conflicted, but he gripped her tightly. "It won't leave lasting damage, and it's the only weapon I have to get you to surrender."

"I'm the one with the blade to your throat. You're the one who needs to surrender."

His eyes narrowed. "You're only close enough to injure me because I haven't let go of you, Princess."

"Let go. Hold me under the water, if you want. I still won't surrender to you. I felt more pain when I dove off the cliff to save your life."

She'd meant the words to sound tough, like she could handle anything, but instead they sounded oddly vulnerable. A raindrop landed at the corner of her eye, and as she blinked, it raced down her cheek, stinging the whole way.

Edric's gaze traced the path of the raindrop tear, his face twisting in guilt and horror. He moved suddenly, spinning her away from him and the fountain, his body blocking the spray.

Rhielle's dagger lowered to her side as she watched him. She wanted to claim victory, but the words felt hollow.

A raindrop landed on her hand, and Edric flinched.

How dare he react to her weakness as if to his own? She bit down on a growl and stormed toward a stone gazebo to escape the rain. The faint moonlight couldn't reach inside the gazebo, which also let her escape his pitying eyes.

He followed her inside, and she moved further into the shadows to avoid his silent, looming presence. "You can leave now, monk. No need to worry about me escaping during a rainstorm. Go back to your room and stay dry."

She should take the same advice—get off the roof before the sky opened in a downpour, but she wasn't ready to return to the bright light inside the castle. She wanted to stay in the dark, barely protected within the small gazebo, with the sting of humidity buzzing against her skin. Only pain could relieve the strange anxiety clawing inside her chest.

Edric didn't answer, remaining silent as monks did.

She sagged against a flat stone pillar. "What do you want, monk?"

He chuckled darkly. "What I want is irrelevant, Princess."

"I told you to stop calling me that! I won't let you demean me with that title anymore."

He strode over to her in three quick steps. "Demean you? That's what you think I'm doing?" His voice was the low rumbling of the storm on the horizon. "Do you realize what the word 'princess' means to my people? A princess is a sign of the Goddesses' blessing, a divine birthright and true queen. Do you know how hard my country has prayed for a princess? How hard I prayed even as a child that my younger brothers would be born girls?" His lips twisted with guilt at the admission, yet he stepped closer, unwilling to give up. "A princess is a sign that life will continue, that Isandariyah will survive, that my mother wasn't cursed in giving birth to me ... A princess is so valuable I tried to make a deal with the devil herself to ensure Isandariyah gets her own." He swallowed, and his voice dropped to a deep whisper. "Whatever you hear when I say your title is not what I mean. Do you understand me, Princess?"

For the first time in her life, her title sent a thrill racing through her. She couldn't make his words fit into the world she had grown up in, a world where she had felt dominated and weak. But in his world, she was powerful and strong and cherished. That was the world she wanted to live in.

She spoke softly, her words floating somewhere between a command and an urgent request. "Say it again."

He was close enough to touch her, yet his arms remained carefully fixed at his side. She thought he might deny her request, so still was he, but he took a deep breath and whispered the word on an exhale. "Princess."

She heard it then. What the word meant to him. And she heard it echoed in every instance he had named her princess since the moment he discovered her identity. The weight of the honor he bestowed on her threatened to crush her, and she wanted to let it.

Time expanded around them as it had so many times before. She couldn't move, couldn't speak, couldn't draw breath—all she could do was hold perfectly still before him, waiting.

Rhielle was not the kind of girl who waited for anyone. But in this moment, he was the one with the decision to make.

Rain dappled the roses outside the gazebo and merged with the water in the splashing fountain. She breathed in the clean scent of rain and found the air to ask the question hovering on her lips. "What do you want, Edric?"

She saw what he wanted a heartbeat before he took it.

He crashed into her, pressing her against the stone pillar and drowning her in a kiss. Her body tensed, ready to resist ... to fight ... to defeat him ... when something strange happened.

Rhielle melted against him and surrendered—not to his desire, but to her own.

A small part of her screamed he would try to dominate her, to defeat her, to win, but the rest of her savored his lips on hers, trusting him to only take what she freely offered.

Despite him pressing her firmly against the pillar, she somehow didn't feel trapped. Just *held*.

She liquefied—flowing to match the shape needed, yet never losing the core of who she was.

She was Rhielle.

Captain.

Princess.

His lips never left hers as he drew her away from the pillar, weaving his arms around her waist. She pulled him closer, hands gripping his thin tunic, the heat rising off his body no match for her own. Her silk dress clung to her back, water dripping a steady trail between her shoulder blades.

But the water no longer scalded her skin.

She burned the water instead.

As she melted against Edric, the water sizzled down her spine, dissipating in a gentle mist. Steam usually irritated not only her skin, but also her lungs, making it hard to breathe. But somehow this fog soothed her skin, coating every inch of her in a dewy fog.

She wasn't sure about the status of her lungs, since she hadn't drawn a breath from the moment his lips met hers.

Thunder rumbled across the roof, vibrating the water pooled at her feet and shivering through the heavy fog inside the gazebo.

Edric lifted his head, and Rhielle finally drew a breath, though she would have been content to suffocate in his kiss. A flash of lightning brightened the gazebo, revealing the white fog within and the pouring rain without.

His mouth drifted open. "What? How …?"

Rhielle only had a vague sense of *what* and no clue about *how*. Alanna's words about her Spark came back to her. "I think the water decided it is fond of me …"

Edric's eyes lit up, and he stared at her in wonder. "I knew it. You have a Spark."

She lifted a hand, and the fog gathered in her palm, condensing into water. "I guess so, but I have no idea what I'm doing. What is this?"

He grabbed her by both arms. "It's a miracle, Rhielle. Sparks are blessings direct from the Goddesses."

Even inside the foggy, dark gazebo, she could see his face suffused with awe. She smiled at him, and his eyes moved to her lips.

And stayed there.

His smile slowly fell as he released her arms, his cheeks flushing with guilt. His hand floated to his mouth, and his fingers brushed his lips as if they were stained with sin.

"I have to go. Good night, Princess." He fled into the downpour.

She chased after him and grabbed his arm to turn him to face her. With every flash of lightning, she saw his guilt written plain. His regret stabbed through her chest, so she said something she rarely did.

"I'm sorry, Edric. I shouldn't have—"

"It isn't your fault, Rhielle. It was my choice. I ..." He trailed off as he stared at her. "The rain ... You're okay?"

She had barely noticed the rain, though once she focused on it, she felt it crawling across her skin. Not only did it pour in rivulets down her hair and back, but it crawled up from the soaked grass, streaming across her feet and curling around her ankles. It didn't burn, but it was vaguely unsettling.

She took his hand. "I'm fine. See?"

For a moment, the guilt on his face was replaced with fascination as he looked at her hand in his, watching the water stream away from him and attach itself to her.

He shook his head, allowing the guilt to triumph. "I'm sorry, Princess, I just need to be alone right now." He clenched her hand tighter. "But please, don't run away. Just give me the night to think." He swallowed deeply, as if the confession pained him. "And to pray."

She blinked the rain out of her eyes. Why shouldn't she let him go? Did she want him to stay on the roof with her, kissing her until the sun came up? Her answer embarrassed her enough to release his hand.

"Of course. You should go."

He chewed his lip, torn between running off and staying with her in the downpour. "I don't want to hold you captive anymore, but ... will you promise me you won't run away? Not until we talk again. After the ball tomorrow night?"

Rhielle didn't enjoy promising not to escape, but he looked so distressed. She sighed. "Fine. I promise I won't escape until after the ball."

He nodded slowly, accepting her promise as if he could trust a pirate's word.

Raindrops trickled off his lashes as he ducked his head with a final request. "And promise me you won't marry Niklys."

"You still think I'd—" She bit off her words. How could he think she had any interest in marrying Niklys?

Water droplets scattered as he flicked his eyes up to meet hers. "I won the match, remember? I forced you to surrender, so now you can't marry him."

"You didn't force me to surrender!" she hissed.

Which was technically true. Because when his lips had met hers, she'd willingly surrendered.

The point was too complicated to debate, but it didn't matter. The result was the same. "I promise I won't marry Niklys, okay?"

His eyes sparkled with pleasure, then immediately sank back into shame. "Thank you, Princess. We will speak tomorrow night." He bowed courteously, then marched back inside to make peace with his Goddesses.

Rhielle watched him go, the water drifting chaotically across her skin, until the liquid trails burned, just as painful as before.

30

Rhielle hid in her room all the next day. She hated herself for hiding, but she couldn't casually eat a meal with Edric now she knew what his lips tasted like. And especially now she knew how guilty he felt about it.

Pirates shouldn't feel guilty about anything, so they definitely shouldn't feel guilty about making someone else feel guilty. The belief that a single kiss was something to feel guilty about was preposterous.

But it wasn't just a kiss, was it? When Rhielle asked him what he wanted, the look in his eyes had been clear enough. He wanted more than a kiss.

He wanted *her*.

Despite his vows to the Goddesses. Despite her piracy. Despite every other reason a relationship was out of the question, he still wanted *her*.

The thought filled her with a sickening level of excitement and dread. He would never become a pirate. It was against his nature. But she could never give up the sea to live as a princess again. Even this short period on land was enough to make her skin crawl with the itch to escape.

Luckily, the discomfort was only from the lack of freedom and not lingering rainwater. Poppy had found her sopping wet and stumbling through the hallways after the incident on the roof, and had prepared a bath that was more bubbles than water, before tucking her into bed. The girl had brought her several meals throughout the day, trying to convince her to eat, but Rhielle's stomach churned so much, she couldn't even get out of bed.

Should Rhielle escape before the ball? Sure, she had promised Edric she would wait, but she was a pirate. He should expect betrayal by now. Besides, once she escaped, he could pretend he had never kissed her, and the awful regret would fade from his eyes.

Poppy had finally stopped nagging her about getting dressed for the ball and had wandered off to do whatever it was lady's maids did when they weren't with their lady. Rhielle sank deeper into her covers. What would be the easiest method of escaping the castle?

Her door flew open, and Alanna and Elliya burst in. Rhielle pulled the covers up to her chest and growled at the torture devices they carried.

A hair-curling tool, sharp hairpins, and a case full of makeup.

Alanna dumped a pile of silk on Rhielle's bed. "Time to get up, dear."

Elliya looked over her shoulder as she put the hair curler in the fire. "I know social events can be draining, Princess, but no more moping about."

"I'm not moping!"

Alanna raised her eyebrow. "So, you're lying in bed all day because of illness? That's curious, because a certain prince is suffering from the same affliction today as well."

She sat up in bed. "Edric is ill?"

Elliya gave Alanna a sly look. "He must be, since he's

refused to come out of his room all day."

Rhielle slouched back into the covers. "Oh ... Well, he's probably just praying."

Alanna's eyes lit with mischief. "Oh really? Does he have something specific he needs to atone for?"

Rhielle squeezed her lips together and refused to answer.

Alanna laughed brightly and tugged on the covers. "Come on, Princess. You're a lovely girl, so we don't have much work to do, but please put in a little effort."

Elliya tapped Alanna on the arm. "Maybe we should leave her be, Alanna. If she's too scared to face Edric after whatever happened last night ..." Her eyes clouded with pity as she started to tuck Rhielle back into bed.

Rhielle kicked off the covers and stood. "I'm not scared to face Edric." She straightened her pajamas, which had gotten twisted from rolling in bed all day. "And nothing happened last night."

"Whatever you say, dear." Alanna winked.

The door opened, and Poppy scampered in before Rhielle had time to argue. "I found shoes her size, and they'll match perfectly!" The girl handed the delicate shoes to Elliya, who cooed her approval.

Rhielle crossed her arms and adopted her fiercest captain stance. "Poppy! Are you responsible for this?"

The girl swallowed. "Um ... yes, Cap—" She glanced at the two other women. "Yes, Your Highness. I didn't know how else to help."

She wanted to yell at her, but how could she? Poppy had cared for her all day. She truly was a sweet girl who had given up everything to follow Rhielle as her captain.

Rhielle's shoulders sagged, and she sighed. "Fine. I'll go to the ball." She raised her arms. "Do your worst."

By the end, Rhielle had experienced torture even worse than when she was a child princess. Her hair had been curled and twisted and woven and pinned until her scalp felt pulled taut. With every blink, a fresh piece of glitter fell from her lid into her eye, and her lips were sticky, like they had been smeared with honey, except bitter tasting.

Poppy couldn't stop squealing with delight every time she looked at Rhielle, while Alanna and Elliya threw her knowing looks every time they mentioned Edric probably doing his own primping.

Rhielle almost gave up when they revealed her dress.

"Don't you love it?" squealed Poppy. "Jazhara found it in town. It's imported from Naermore, so you'll look like a true Naermore princess." She squeezed her hands at her chest like she couldn't contain her joy.

The shimmering blue silk dress was even more insubstantial than the draped piece of fabric she had worn the night before. She stepped into the dress herself but required help to fasten the row of buttons up her back. She could only take tiny steps thanks to the long, tight skirt, and the fitted sleeves and bodice limited her range of motion.

The fashion in Naermore restricted the women as much as their culture did.

"You are beautiful!" said Elliya. "It's hand painted like scales. You look like a mythical sea creature!"

Rhielle pulled at the high collar. "I'd rather be a shark."

Alanna tugged on the dress in a very personal way, until all Rhielle's bits had settled into place, then she stepped back and stared wistfully at her. "I wore a similar dress to my first ball."

Elliya shot her a warning glance, but Rhielle signaled for her to continue.

"It was when I was impersonating your sister." Alanna looked repentant. "I truly am sorry for any disrespect."

Pain stabbed Rhielle anytime she thought of her sister, but

it faded as she imagined Alanna in a similar dress. "Pardon me for speaking so bluntly, Alanna, but other than by wearing a traditional dress, how did anyone truly believe you were from Naermore?" With her golden brown skin and black hair, no one could possibly believe the woman was from the secluded country.

Alanna laughed. "Obviously, I wasn't chosen based on my appearance. Geeni gave me a rune that transformed me into someone she said resembles your sister."

Sick dread curled in her gut. "Someone who resembles my sister ... Do you still have the rune?"

"It's in my room!" said Elliya cheerfully. "Geeni left several runes behind when she fled the citadel, and I brought a few on this trip so I could continue to study them."

"Can I see it?" Rhielle whispered. "See her?"

"Of course, Princess."

Rhielle followed them down the hall to Elliya's room, with Poppy trailing on her heels. The closer she got to the room, the sicker she felt. Something wasn't right, though she couldn't lay her finger on it yet.

Elliya dug inside a trunk until she pulled out a small gold lamp with three runes shimmering on the surface. She handed it to Alanna. "You have the most experience with this."

Alanna grimaced. "The transformation is really unpleasant, but I'll do it this one time, just for you." She winked, then grew serious as she blinked a tear from her eye, then rubbed it on the lamp.

Alanna gasped, and as she leaned forward, strawberry blond hair covered her face. "I never get used to that," she said in a voice not her own, before she straightened, brushing the hair out of her face.

Rhielle clapped a hand to her mouth. The dread settled into an icy fear. "I know this woman," she whispered.

Elliya carefully took the lamp back from Alanna. "This is

actually the chosen form of a man from Tsanyin. Geeni stole his tears to make a rune that lets anyone take on this appearance. He was kind enough to gift us more of his tears so we could reimbue the runes for scholarly purposes."

Rhielle stepped closer to the woman who vaguely resembled her sister. "So anyone can take this appearance? No ... anyone who works for *Geeni* can take this appearance ..."

The strawberry blond woman shot a look at Elliya, then turned back to Rhielle. "You know someone wearing this woman's form? Who is she to you?"

There was a reason Geeni had known this form would be convincing as Princess Aliyabeth.

Because this was the woman her father had hired to cover up Aliyabeth's death.

31

Rhielle fled the room before Elliya and the replica of her sister's impostor could ask her any more questions. She had to get home—back to Naermore. Though she hadn't thought about it as her home for years, she couldn't leave one of Geeni's henchwomen as a spy in her father's house. She had to warn him.

She should have gone immediately to her ship, but instead she headed to the ballroom, taking dainty steps thanks to her ridiculously tight gown.

Rhielle couldn't leave without telling him goodbye.

It was foolish to find him. She didn't owe him an explanation. She was a pirate who could come and go as she pleased. It was only a single kiss.

Yet she went to find him to explain why she had to go. And she hated the part of herself that imagined he might want to come with her.

Even though she couldn't walk as fast as she wanted, Poppy still had to take running steps to keep up with her. "Your High — Captain ... what's going on?"

Music drifted from the ballroom. Dancing. Had she truly

considered actually attending this ball as a princess, just because Edric had asked her to?

She put her hands on Poppy's arms and spoke with quiet urgency. "I need you to go to the *Lady Tempest* right now, and warn them we will leave tonight. I don't know if you can simply sneak past the guards or if you have to tell them a story so you can leave, but you *must* do this. Do you understand?"

Poppy straightened her shoulders with resolve. "I won't let you down, Captain. I swear it."

Rhielle nodded sharply, and a proud smile spread across her lips. "I'll see you back on the ship, sailor."

Instead of her usual curtsy, the girl saluted, turned on her heel, and ran. Rhielle sighed, but she had to hope nothing bad befell the girl. She moved toward the music, then flung open the door, prepared to meet her doom.

It was exactly as she had imagined—too loud, too many people, too much perfume ... Everything and everyone was too much. She hugged the wall as she scanned the room for the red garb of a monk. All she had to do was find him, explain she had some urgent business in Naermore, then ... what? A handshake? An awkward hug? Would they promise to see each other again or admit what had been true all along?

A pirate and a monk had nothing in common, and it was time to say goodbye.

She choked down the grief that threatened to rise and resumed her search. Why couldn't she find him? He was always easy to spot in his bright red clothes.

Except he wasn't dressed as a monk tonight.

He wore the elaborate clothes of royalty, not the clothing of his order. Other than his monk clothes, she had only seen him dressed as a pirate, and this was even more shocking. He *had* said he was a monk no matter his clothing, but unease still shivered through her at the sight. Did his clothing choice mean something? After praying to his goddesses last night, had he made some sort of *decision*?

Terror rose inside her, though she couldn't pinpoint the source. She pressed closer to the wall and edged her way back toward the door. Saying goodbye was a bad idea. She should flee the country immediately.

Edric spotted her, his clear blue eyes halting her escape. She froze as she always did when he was near, though this time he was half a ballroom away. He stood among his brothers, and though they didn't resemble one another, they all stood with the same regal confidence. Edric didn't break eye contact as he shoved his glass into Hawthorne's hand without a word. Hawthorne nudged Jaemin in the ribs, waggling his brows in her direction.

What did they know? Had Edric told them what had happened on the roof? Or was it obvious from her expression?

She wanted to slap her hands over her reddened cheeks and run away, but she couldn't move from the wall as Edric made his slow approach.

He drew close enough to be heard over the music and cast an admiring glance over her dress of painted scales. "As a ship's captain, you are master of the sea, but tonight you truly look it."

Was the monk hitting on her? She tugged on her collar before it could strangle her. "Thanks. Um ... you look nice, too."

He glanced down, smoothing a hand across the front of his jacket. Was that a hint of doubt in his eyes? "Thanks."

He stepped closer, and with the wall at her back, she was reminded of when he pushed her against the pillar to kiss her. Despite the room full of people, his closeness felt breathtakingly intimate.

"Rhielle, I—"

"I have to go." She blurted the words before she could lose her nerve. "Tonight. I have to go tonight."

Hurt flashed behind his eyes, quickly replaced with concern. "What's wrong?"

"It's a long story, but the important part is my family is in danger. I have to return to Naermore."

Concern switched to alarm, then the faintest hint of suspicion crept in. "How do you know this? Did you receive word from them? Here?"

Her father had no idea where she was, but if someone told him she was in La Veridda, wearing a ball gown and talking to a prince, he definitely wouldn't believe them.

"No, they don't know about the danger. That's why I have to warn them. I'm so sorry, Edric. I—"

"It's fine." His eyes hardened, his emotions unreadable. "I already ordered our military off your ship. I won't hold you against your will any longer."

She wanted to tell him she hadn't come to the ball against her will, that she had chosen to come to find him, knowing it was stupid, knowing she didn't belong among all the glamorous people, but that she'd done it for the chance to see him one last time.

But there wasn't time. Wasn't time for her to tell the story of her sister's death and the hired impostor. Wasn't time to talk through everything until he understood, until the awful hurt faded from his eyes.

He was letting her go. She had won.

So why did she feel like she had lost everything?

"Edric, please believe me—"

"What are you two up to?" Prince Niklys stepped between them, holding two glasses of wine. "Isandariyah and Naermore aren't conspiring behind my back, right?" He laughed, but accusation tinged his words.

Edric's shoulders stiffened. "Of course not, Prince."

"Good. Because I have my own business to conduct with Naermore." He handed Rhielle a glass with a smooth grin. "In my country, we believe a lady should be handed a beverage the moment she steps into the room. It's only good manners." His eyes slid sideways, implying that Edric, and possibly his entire country, didn't know how to treat a lady.

Edric's jaw tensed, but he didn't offer a defense.

How had Rhielle forgotten about Niklys? He thought she was in La Veridda to seek a marriage proposal, and tonight would be the perfect night to find one.

She had to escape. Now.

She chugged her wine quicker than was proper for a princess, then handed the glass back to Niklys. "I'm still so thirsty. Will you bring me another?"

He stared at the empty glass, then laughed. "I think one glass is quite enough for now. Let's dance first, then I'll find you another." He shoved both glasses at Edric, then took her hand and drew her away from the wall.

Rhielle glared at Edric to rescue her, but he stared at Niklys with a mixture of jealousy and bitter regret. She tried to pull her hand away. "Thank you, Prince, but—"

"Just one dance, Princess, then we can have a conversation in private, like you requested." Niklys gave Edric a knowing glance.

Rhielle worried the wineglasses would shatter in Edric's hands. He'd get himself killed if he attacked Niklys in his own ballroom. Plus, an international incident would slow her escape.

She allowed herself to be drawn into the crowd, apologizing to Edric with her eyes as she surrendered herself to a dance with the wrong prince.

32

Dancing with Niklys brought back a flood of memories from her childhood. She knew the court dances, how to step lightly in delicate shoes, how to hold her partner properly while in a restricting dress. Her body moved on instinct, thankfully, since her thoughts were distracted by two princes.

Edric had handed off the wineglasses, or they would have shattered before the first note. He couldn't possibly believe she wanted to marry the prince. But then why did a terrible sadness fill his eyes? Was he truly so jealous of Niklys? Did he want to be the one dancing with her instead?

She tried to imagine dancing with the boulder of a man. He surely knew the court dances, too, but she couldn't imagine a monk dancing. Would his movements be stiff? Or would he shift between steps as freely as he had flowed through his morning prayers? When he kissed her, he had been as strong and steady as always, yet he had yielded to her as she had yielded to him.

She stepped on Niklys's toe, and it drew her attention back to the prince who currently held her in his arms. "I apologize,

Prince. Perhaps I shouldn't have drank the wine so quickly." Or perhaps she should have eaten at least one meal Poppy had offered her.

Just one of her many stupid decisions of the day.

Niklys chuckled. "Don't worry about it, Princess. My feet are not so weak as to be injured by a lady." He grinned as he twirled her in three rapid turns that made her head spin.

"You are in an excellent mood, Prince." She blinked to get her bearings. Edric was still glaring.

"It's a momentous night, Princess. I have a big announcement later." He winked and twirled her again.

She wanted to vomit, though whether from the wine sloshing in her empty stomach or the fact Niklys planned to announce their engagement tonight, she wasn't sure.

"Niklys, I don't—"

"I'm so grateful for everything that has happened these past two days. If you hadn't come ... If the Isandariyans hadn't told me the news about my illegitimacy ... everything would be so different now."

She stared at him, trying to comprehend his words. "You're grateful?"

"Oh yes!" He spun her again, his face the picture of delight. "I was never sure if King Ruzgar was truly my father. He treated me as if he doubted it himself, always favoring my younger brother, who looks just like him. But since I never knew for sure, I always acted as if I were his true son. Finding out he isn't my father means I owe him no loyalty. I'm free. And La Veridda is free as well."

"La Veridda is free?" His words made no sense. "You're abandoning the occupation?"

He laughed. "It's no longer an occupation. La Veridda is no longer under the control of Verkeshe, and neither am I. I am announcing myself as the new king of La Veridda, sovereign and no longer under King Ruzgar's control."

She tripped on his feet again. "You're doing what?"

"The best news is our country is suddenly much richer than it was. Now that I can stop paying bribe money to Geeni and a regular tithe to Verkeshe, I will have the money to bring this country back to the position of power it held before the war."

"Before the war *you* caused!" She shook her head to clear her thoughts. "Don't you have any loyalty to Verkeshe? Even if Ruzgar isn't your father, Verkeshe is your home."

"I've lived in La Veridda for the last fifteen years. I barely remember Verkeshe. This is my true home." He pulled her closer, gazing deep into her eyes. "Are you okay, Princess? I didn't mean to overwhelm you with this news all at once. We can go somewhere private to discuss further."

Her eyes shot to Edric still holding silent vigil. "No! Out here in front of everyone is fine."

Niklys frowned apologetically. "This is slightly awkward to say out loud, but I do hope you'll forgive me for not proposing."

"You *aren't* proposing?" Not that she had wanted him to, but she'd thought his intentions clear.

"Because of this turn of events, I will need to marry a woman from La Veridda. Probably someone related to the previous royal family. If only we knew where the missing La Veriddan princess is ... She would really help me win the people to my side. Do you understand?"

She blinked groggily, struggling to understand, but the wine, the spinning, the political schemes all swirled together in her mind. She glanced at Edric again. Why hadn't she hadn't danced with him yet? ... Because she needed to escape to Naermore ... How had she forgotten about that?

"I need to go." The words slurred embarrassingly, but she couldn't make her mouth function properly.

Niklys stopped dancing, yet still held her close. "Yes, unfortunately you do. I am truly sorry about that."

She stepped back, but her knees buckled, and she fell against him.

What was happening? She shouldn't be so drunk on only a single glass of wine ... Had he drugged her? She searched for Edric, and when she found him watching, she sagged in relief.

Until she realized his furious scowl wasn't at Niklys, but at her. He thought she was clinging to the prince in the same ruse she had pulled on him.

Niklys brushed a sweaty tendril from her face while he held her close. "You are a beautiful girl, and I would have been happy to marry you, but the Resistance has been hounding my soldiers for so long ... I have to do what's best for my country."

"The Resistance?" The words came out as a long slur. She attempted to raise a hand to signal to Edric that she wasn't faking, but she had to clutch the prince's jacket or fall.

"Yes, Princess. I'm trading you to them in exchange for a ceasefire." He slung her arm over his shoulder and called to the neighboring dancers. "Poor girl had a little too much wine."

They chuckled as he led her off the dance floor, away from Edric.

As Edric's furious expression faded from view, she was reminded of the little girl who cried wolf.

The wolf had finally come for her.

33

Rhielle hoped someone might stop Niklys as he dragged her out of the ballroom, but no one thought the situation peculiar. He carried her down a secluded hallway and propped her awkwardly against his hip as he opened a thick wooden door.

She glimpsed maps on the walls and a large table with a sea chart. Two La Veriddan soldiers dropped the files they were holding to salute the prince.

He carried Rhielle to a doorway at the back of the room as he called to them. "Go find the general's emissaries and bring them back to headquarters. The quicker the general gets her hands on the princess, the quicker the ceasefire begins."

As they hurried out of the room, he dumped her inside the closet filled with more files. She slumped in a pile, but he adjusted her limbs so a casual observer might think she was sleeping. He brushed her hair out of her eyes as he rested her head gently against the stone floor.

"Thanks for what you've done to ensure the future of La Veridda. I'll make the announcement about our new alliance."

He patted her cheek fondly. "The Resistance will come collect you soon, so just wait here." He eased the closet door shut and left her alone.

As if she had any choice but to wait. She couldn't move or utter a single word. She imagined all the people she would murder when she regained movement. Niklys was top of the list, of course, followed by the military lackeys who had run off looking for the general's emissaries. Then she'd murder everyone who'd watched her being dragged off the dance floor and stood idly by.

And Edric ... he would give her the excuse he couldn't trust her, but he should have still figured it out.

And last of all, the general of the Resistance, who had arranged for the ceasefire. Rhielle had worked alongside the Resistance for five years, but rarely heard anything about the general. And today was the first day she'd heard the general was a woman.

So even though Rhielle lived on a ship with all women pirates, and knew several female members of the Resistance, she had a sick certainty there was only one woman the general could be.

The closet door opened, and Geeni stood silhouetted, her pink hair tucked inside a bright scarf. She wore a traditional La Veriddan dress of draped fabric, as if she had been at the party. Perhaps she had been. Other than the unusual amount of gold jewelry, she looked like most of the partygoers.

Geeni clicked her tongue disapprovingly. "Oh, dear. How could Niklys leave you like this?" Geeni bent and examined Rhielle's pupils, before she plucked a rope from the draped fold of her dress and secured Rhielle's arms tightly near her waist. "Much better. You'd think someone with the ambition to be king would have more sense."

Rhielle tried to shape her lips into a curse but couldn't.

Geeni's lips curled into a grin as the door opened again. But instead of her Resistance lackeys, Edric called, "Rhielle?"

Geeni whispered a curse under her breath as she unwound a scarf from her wrist and shoved it into Rhielle's mouth. She stood in a graceful movement and pulled the door, leaving it open only a crack.

"Hello, Prince," said Geeni smoothly.

Through the crack Rhielle could see Edric edge past the large sea chart, his wary eyes on Geeni, who was hidden from Rhielle's sight on the other side of the door.

"What are you doing here?" His gaze darted around the room, taking in the military command post.

"Are you here looking for me?" Geeni asked conversationally.

"Um ... actually no, but—"

"Then relax! I have no issue with you. Continue on your way and forget you saw me."

He narrowed his eyes. "Where is Rhielle? What have you done with her?"

"What have *I* done with her?" Geeni laughed lightly. "Prince Niklys was the one doing things with her."

Edric's face darkened into fury. Thanks to the gag, Rhielle could only breathe a sigh out of her nose. Geeni was playing him, and Rhielle could do nothing to stop it.

"What do you need with her anyway? Don't princes have better marriage prospects than pirate princesses?"

His jaw strained, but he ground out his confession. "The Resistance is here. Mixed in with the crowd."

"Well, there's no need to warn her about that. After she finished playing with Niklys, she gathered several military secrets from this room, then escaped to her ship."

Rhielle wanted to believe he would call Geeni a liar, but her explanation was so plausible. Especially since Rhielle had jokingly told him she'd swoon inside Niklys's headquarters. Everything Geeni said was exactly what she would do.

Edric's lips pinched, but instead of calling her a liar, he mumbled, "I checked her room. Poppy was already gone."

"Well, there you have it," Geeni said matter-of-factly. "Your pirate princess tricked you. She pretended to be weak and in need of rescue, but she's been playing you for a fool this whole time. She's already fled with her crew. I bet you'll be the story she tells over drinks tonight."

Edric's face was so stricken, Rhielle wanted to scream. She strained to loosen her bonds, but her hands barely twitched. Why couldn't he be wearing the truth-seeker's ring? He would know Geeni was lying. But the woman's lies were too close to the truth, and Rhielle had no way of proving her wrong.

"So what will you do now, Prince?"

Edric swallowed his pain and aimed a hard look at Geeni. "I'm taking you with me back to Isandariyah."

Geeni threw her head back and laughed. "I can always count on a prince for a good laugh. No, dear. I will not come willingly with you. You're not wearing a sword, and no matter how many hidden daggers you have, you can't defeat my runes. The only way you could possibly stop me is if you sneak up and kill me before I spot you. And out of all your brothers, I know *you* will never do that."

Edric glared at her. "How do you know I won't?"

Rhielle could hear the shape of Geeni's smug grin. "Because I'm the last chance for an heir. You'll leave me alive, just in case I decide to do the right thing and get pregnant."

All emotion drained from Edric's face, and Rhielle knew this time, Geeni told the truth. Edric's shoulders slumped, and he turned, shutting the headquarters' door as he left the room without another word.

She still couldn't move as Geeni opened the closet door, dragged Rhielle out, and propped her against the wall.

Geeni took hold of Rhielle's face and looked at her with wonder. "How delightfully unexpected!" She rubbed her thumb beneath Rhielle's eye, wiping away a tear. "I honestly didn't expect this gift, considering all you've given me, but I'll take it." She lifted a gold seashell locket from her neck and dabbed the tear inside. When she snapped the locket shut, it started glowing.

Rhielle tried to speak, and this time her jaw actually moved despite the scarf. Geeni smiled benevolently and removed the scarf, perhaps accommodating her since Rhielle had just unintentionally gifted her a tear.

Rhielle slurred the word. "Gennnnerallll ..."

"You think I'm the general?" She laughed. "That job is much too tedious for me! I'd take you with me to Sehrine to meet her, but I'm going by ship, and no offense—I don't want to take you out on the open sea. But the Resistance has a lovely place set aside for you. Very *dry*." She winked. "Don't worry, though. I'll make sure they keep you hydrated during my visits." She patted the seashell locket fondly.

Geeni straightened, tucking a loose pink lock into her head wrap. "Thank you for taking such good care of my ship. I can't wait to see how fast she is. I hope your crew cooperates, because it will be very tiresome if I have to toss them all overboard."

Her ship? The *Lady Tempest* belonged to Rhielle. How dare Geeni think she could just steal it back from her?

"Shiiip ... runnnnne ... broken."

Geeni's eyebrows rose as the woman likely tried to translate the slurred words, then her lips turned down in a pitying frown. "No, dear. The rune is not broken. *You* are broken."

Rhielle blinked, which was all her body could do anyway.

Geeni grabbed her by the chin, looking her straight in the eye. "The rune never did anything for you other than light up —just a pretty display, nothing more. If the ship ever moved faster, it was your doing. Which means if it stopped working, that's also your doing. The rune is only keyed to me, but it was so nice of you to imbue it with so many tears. Thanks to you and your depressing thoughts, I have the fastest ship at sea."

She watched Rhielle for several long moments before walking out, leaving Rhielle alone, unmoving, but with completely dry eyes.

PART III

34

Rhielle stretched her fingers the moment Geeni closed the door. That she could move them at all was a good sign, and she chose to believe the same about the sharp needles prickling along her legs. She was grateful the drugs Niklys had given her had left her awake, because what Edric had said was her only hope of escape.

He had come to warn her of the Resistance in the crowd. She shoved down the thrill that he cared enough to warn her, even after he thought she had run off with Niklys, and she focused on his words.

Since the ceasefire hadn't been announced yet, he wouldn't have seen *uniformed* Resistance officers in the crowd, so the only way he would recognize them as the Resistance was if he had seen them before. And unless it was the two Resistance thugs they had beaten up together in Ravenna, it could only be one person.

"Oh, Little Captain ... why didn't you just come with me peacefully when I asked?" Commander Luca Saverio gazed down at her with arms crossed, while one of his officers stood watch at the door. "You're a mess!"

Rhielle was glad she looked a mess. It would help him underestimate her.

She opened and closed her mouth a few times, the slowness completely unfaked. "Drink?"

He stared at her flatly. "No drink. I'm under strict orders to keep you away from water."

"Just a sip," she begged. "Please, Commander?"

He frowned, then glanced at his officer at the door, before whispering, "One sip. No sudden movements, or I knock you out and drag you out of here, got it?"

She nodded weakly. He pulled his flask out of his jacket pocket and twisted it open carefully.

His lax attention to orders was severely disappointing. If she had commanded her crew to keep a prisoner away from water, they had better not be carrying around a flask in their pocket.

However, she didn't know how to make use of water in a flask. Geeni claimed Rhielle had a Spark, and after the night on the roof with Edric ... Well, something strange had definitely happened. But Rhielle still didn't know how. So perhaps the flask wasn't so unreasonable after all.

Because what she was hoping would happen was a long shot. A guess. Not only was Rhielle counting on Saverio being as straitlaced as she remembered, with water in that flask, but she hadn't had a sip of plain water in five years. She drank wine, rum, fruit juice, anything but fresh water.

She honestly had no idea what would happen.

He tipped the flask, and the water burned like fire. Even worse than the most disgusting moonshine she had tasted in the backstreets of Ravenna. After it seared her tongue and the roof of her mouth, it burned the entire length of her throat, and finally settled in her stomach, where it got into a nasty disagreement with the lingering poison.

The water won.

Just like she'd faked enjoying the moonshine, she

pretended the water was a simple refreshing sip. She breathed out of her nose, trying to dispel the fire, then spoke, her words slightly slurred. "Thank you."

Saverio carefully put the flask away and signaled to his officer, who rolled a large trunk into the room. He gave Rhielle a stern look. "I don't want to hurt you, Little Captain, but I will if you don't cooperate, do you understand?"

She dipped her head slightly, staring up at him with wide, innocent eyes.

Geeni had only tied her arms, and Saverio was foolish enough to not tie her ankles before he lifted her to her feet. "Time to get in, nice and obedient."

She let him drag her closer to the open trunk and the other officer. When he attempted to hoist her into the trunk, she fell against the other officer, swung both legs into the air—thanks to her ridiculously tight dress—and kicked Saverio right in the head. As he dropped, she grabbed the off-balance officer with her tied hands, and slammed his head against the trunk.

She felt mostly recovered from the drugs, but not so strong that she could easily dump the men inside the trunk, though she severely wanted to. Instead, she grabbed Saverio's blade, sliced through her restraints, and stole his water flask, just in case.

Then she headed straight for the docks.

∼

A local fisherman directed her to the empty berth where the *Lady Tempest* had been docked. How could she have let this happen? Geeni had stolen her ship and taken her crew. Were they okay? Would Geeni kill them? Dump them overboard? Enslave them?

She called out to a dockworker passing by. "The ship that was here ... When did it depart?"

He looked her up and down, perhaps thinking it odd to find a lone woman in a ball gown on the dock at night. He scratched his grizzled beard. "A young girl came by earlier, telling everyone to ready the ship to leave immediately. Less than an hour ago, more lady sailors arrived. There was so much yelling on that ship, a couple of us thought we should go sort it out!" He chuckled, as if sorting out a fight between lady sailors would be extremely rewarding. "But then the captain called down that they had settled their girl fight and would be on their way."

Rhielle's eyes narrowed. "And this captain ... I'm assuming she had pink hair."

He laughed. "Yeah, that's her. A mighty attractive lady who looks like she always gets her way."

"Yes," said Rhielle flatly. "We are acquainted."

She paced the dock, irritated at how pathetic her delicate heels sounded against the planks. She should have stopped by her room and changed into her pirate gear, except she had held the wild hope her crew would have defeated Geeni, and Rhielle would find the ship still docked.

But they were long gone, and she had no idea how to acquire a ship fast enough to catch them, especially since Geeni could use the rune, thanks to Rhielle's tears.

She couldn't steal a ship on her own, and definitely not quickly. Stealing the *Lady Tempest* had taken weeks to plan, and Rhielle suspected the theft had been guaranteed to succeed since Geeni had wanted Rhielle to use her tears on the rune.

She needed a fast ship with its own crew, but she had no money to charter one and no ready con to help her cheat one. And now, not only was the Resistance looking for her, Niklys's soldiers would be after her as well. All she had was herself—both identities: Captain and Princess. Where could she go where anyone would find her worthy enough for a ship?

She stopped her pacing directly in front of the docked Isandariyan ships.

Only one person in the whole city might give her a ship, though the thought of presenting herself to him after everything Geeni told him sent a thundering panic through her veins. But there was no other choice.

She had to beg Edric for a ship.

∼

Rhielle found Jaemin directing the crew as they loaded the flagship. When he spotted her, he tilted his head, then narrowed his eyes in suspicion.

Edric had told him.

"I'm surprised to see you here, Princess. Your ship is gone, and I assumed you would be on it."

Which role would serve her better with Jaemin: the pirate or the princess? She decided to start as an honest princess and go from there.

"Geeni stole my ship and took my crew. I need to get them back."

He crossed his arms with a hard look. Perhaps her tone had too much bossy captain in it for a firstborn prince.

"It sounds like something Geeni would do, but I'm hesitant to trust someone so unaccustomed to telling the truth."

She ground her teeth. "It's the truth." Why couldn't he wear the truth-seeker's ring when it was convenient for her?

"And what would you have me do about it?"

She looked him straight in the eyes, as if making a perfectly reasonable request. "I need a ship."

Jaemin's eyes widened, then he burst out laughing. "You think I'll just hand you a ship because you say yours is missing? I'd heard you've spent your days playing pirate, but I had no idea the scope of your operation. How many ships have you stolen with this act?"

Rhielle wanted to throw a punch, however, that might hinder her chances of getting a ship. If only she wore the clothes of a captain. Then she would feel strong, instead of like a weak girl in a silk dress. She took a deep breath and prepared to beg.

"Please, Jaemin. I have to save them. Maybe Edric—"

"You will not bother Edric with this." His sharp voice wasn't just full of suspicion—when it came to Edric, he was furious with her. He drew himself up, assuming his full role as prince. "Listen to me, *Princess*, I don't know what games you are playing with my brother, but they are over. And I'm not sure how you are involved with Niklys and his strange announcement tonight about a ceasefire with the Resistance, but honestly, I don't care. We are heading back to Isandariyah tonight—all of us. La Veridda can fight Verkeshe or among itself, but Isandariyah will not be involved."

As he spun on his heel and walked away, she felt the *Lady Tempest* and her crew slip out of her fingers.

She had no other scheme, no other plan. No one in La Veridda would ferry Princess Rhielle back to Naermore, much less would anyone help Captain Rhielle rescue her crew.

Rhielle was trapped on land with no escape.

She needed to run, to flee, anywhere ... away. She turned around.

And nearly stumbled over Edric.

35

Edric was dressed again as a monk, his soft shoes to blame for his quiet approach. How long had he stood there? Did he know her crew was missing?

Would he even believe her if she told him?

She needed a ship, she needed a crew, and she needed to hurry. The needs crowded together on her tongue, and if she opened her mouth, she wasn't sure if the words would come out as an order or a plea. But when she finally spoke, the words were neither.

"I'm sorry, Edric." She assumed he was most angry with her for what she'd supposedly done with Niklys, and even though she wasn't guilty of that, she had plenty more to apologize for. "I shouldn't have kidnapped you. Either time. I owe you so many apologies, Edric. More than I have time for. I—"

"You need a ship." His words were flat, emotionless. She couldn't detect anger or suspicion or acceptance ... If she knew what he felt, she could figure out the right words to get what she wanted.

But he gave her nothing, so she was left with telling the truth.

"Geeni is working with the Resistance. Niklys traded me to them in exchange for the ceasefire. She stole back my ship, with the rune now fully charged with my tears. She has my entire crew, and I'm terrified of what she will do to them." Such a quick explanation, yet the words had the bitter sting of confession.

The monk watched her in silence.

She sensed he was bracing himself for her answer to a question he was too afraid to ask. So she offered him the explanation to the question likely hurting him the most. "Niklys drugged me. That's why I swooned against him on the dance floor. I never wanted to marry him. I only pretended because I enjoyed how it upset you." That confession disgusted her, but it was the truth.

He still didn't speak. His blue eyes were shadowed on the moonlit dock, but they pierced her, as if he was trying to find his answer simply by looking at her.

Edric finally whispered, "Why were you leaving?"

And in his words, she heard his real question: Why were you leaving *me*?

After all they had been through—kidnapping one another, her saving his life, their kiss on the roof ... Why had she suddenly decided to run back to Naermore, with only a flimsy explanation, and leave him behind?

That question hurt him the most.

And she owed him the honest answer.

She wanted to say she had no time for the truth—the story was too complicated and would reveal a whole network of lies that would take so long to unravel, she'd never catch up to her crew.

But the real reason she didn't want to answer?

The truth was too painful to tell.

Edric's face was perfectly serene, yet she sensed the

churning storm beneath the surface. So she took a deep breath and told the truth.

"Five years ago, my sister, Aliyabeth, was killed."

His eyes widened. He couldn't have expected that start to her explanation.

"We were in Verkeshe while my father negotiated with King Ruzgar about who should have the honor of marrying the two princesses of Naermore. My sister would get married first, but I would soon follow. So I ran away. I found a Resistance ship operating undercover in Verkeshe, and the captain was willing to take on an unnamed recruit." She closed her eyes. "I didn't know my sister slipped out of the negotiations and followed me."

She shook her head, trying to shake off the regret. "She had come to drag me back home. Aliyabeth was always the reliable one, so wise … She should have been named queen of Naermore, but the law prevented it. Instead she was willing to surrender to our father and marry whoever he commanded." How could she still be angry at Aliyabeth? She shoved down the anger to finish the story.

"My sister snuck aboard to persuade me to return, but before I could convince her to let me escape, the Verkeshe military discovered it was a Resistance ship. The Resistance didn't care that they had two sisters fighting on board—they just fled out to sea. The Verkeshe caught up to us and destroyed the ship, killing everyone on board … Except me." She pinched her lips to keep them from trembling.

Edric opened his mouth as if he might speak, but she forestalled him, determined to finish her story while she still could. "My father didn't want to admit Aliyabeth was dead and give up half his negotiating power, so he hired an impostor and fostered the idea that my sister was reclusive. Before the ball, I saw Alanna's lamp and how it turned her into the exact woman playing my sister. So, my sister's impostor is one of Geeni's spies. I have to warn my father."

She exhaled, relieved the story was finally told. Her crew knew her identity as a princess, but even they didn't know her sister was dead. Unless her father had told his second wife, the only people who knew her sister was a fake were her father, the impostor, and herself.

And Geeni, of course.

Rhielle looked back into Edric's eyes. The churning storm had dissipated, leaving only a single question.

"What do you want, Rhielle?"

That was what she had asked him a heartbeat before he had kissed her on the roof. He had taken what he wanted, a kiss freely given, then had run away, guilt shadowing his eyes.

"I want ... my crew back."

He kept watching her.

"And I want to warn my father."

His eyes didn't falter as he waited for the answer.

She breathed, "I want ..."

Of course, she wanted him to kiss her. She wanted a gentle kiss to prove he had forgiven her for the kidnapping and the lies. And she wanted a fierce kiss to prove he desired her more than words could express.

She also wanted to kiss *him*. She wanted to grab hold of him, press him against a pillar as he pressed her, take a kiss he freely offered her.

She wanted him.

But he belonged to his Goddesses.

He had changed back into his monk clothes, though she didn't know if him wearing different clothes to the ball was significant. All she knew for sure was the last time they kissed, he had regretted it. And she couldn't bear to see that in his eyes again. Not after all she had done.

So his question remained unanswered, her incomplete

response hanging in the still night air. She wouldn't take what she wanted, even though she was a pirate.

He was the one treasure she refused to steal.

Edric breathed out a sigh, as if in resignation, then turned on his heel, striding toward the Isandariyan ships. "Come with me."

She took a skipping step to catch up. "You'll talk to Jaemin? Get him to change his mind?"

He snorted a laugh. "My brother does not change his mind."

They passed the ship Jaemin had boarded, instead walking to the Isandariyan ship at the end of the line. "Then what are we doing?"

He stopped and gave her a very serious look. "We're stealing a ship, Princess."

36

Edric headed directly to the ship's captain and asked her to tell him how much longer until they could depart. Overall, the Isandariyan navy was well managed and efficient, with an almost equal split of men and women crew. However, they would be even more impressive if they didn't keep ruining her plans.

Rhielle glanced around, trying to devise a way to steal the ship as Edric spoke to the captain. The woman was perhaps in her late fifties, her dark hair twisted into a tidy knot and her white uniform neatly pressed. She explained how they had followed Jaemin's instructions to the letter and would be ready to leave as soon as Hawthorne and both wives joined Jaemin on the flagship.

Edric shook his head. "Unfortunately, we need to depart before the flagship. It is a matter of some urgency."

The captain gave him a sharp look. "Is there something wrong, Your Highness?"

"We need to leave La Veridda as quickly as possible …" He clutched the collar of his tunic as if it were too tight. "My drink

... Niklys ..." His eyes unfocused, before he stumbled, falling against the captain.

"Edric!" Rhielle dove to help the captain as the woman struggled under Edric's full weight. How had Niklys managed to drug him, too? And why?

"Your Highness?" The captain lowered him to the deck with Rhielle's assistance. "What's happening?"

Edric's blue eyes fluttered open, and he clung to the captain's uniform, whispering, "Poison."

Rhielle's pounding heart slowed, and she raised an eyebrow. But before the captain could notice, she cleared her throat and played her role. "Niklys poisoned him! We have to escape immediately!"

The captain patted Edric's check, trying to get a response. "We have to get the doctor from the flagship."

Edric's eyes flew open, and he gasped, "Drazen!"

Rhielle didn't know what that word meant, so she wasn't sure what her next line should be.

Luckily, the captain understood. "Drazen? The wizard—um ... the queen's advisor?"

Ah, so that was the script! "Yes, a wizard! Edric needs magic. That's the only cure for this."

The captain looked torn, then bellowed, "All hands to stations! Prepare for immediate departure!"

Edric pulled the captain closer and whispered, "But do it quietly. We need to sneak away, or Niklys will follow." Rhielle thought he delivered the lines just a little too distinctly, but luckily the captain started dispensing hushed orders as she deposited the prince in Rhielle's lap.

Rhielle lifted his eyelids one at a time, peering into his blue eyes sparkling with mischief. "You're lucky it's dark, monk," she murmured. "Your performance wouldn't hold up in the light of day."

He grasped her dress and pulled her close, like a sick man seeking comfort. "You were worried," he rasped, the corner of his mouth twitching.

Slapping a sick man would spoil the illusion, so she just patted him on the cheek, a little rougher than necessary. "How far away do we need to get from your brothers before we admit to the captain where we're headed?"

"Once we are out on open water, I'll tell her," he whispered. "I've known her my whole life. I'm sure she'll understand why the ruse was necessary." He nestled his head in her lap, making himself cozy as the ship departed the port.

She found the experience surreal. Wearing a ball gown on the naval ship's deck, holding a prince sprawled on her lap, as they escaped from his brothers in port ... It was not where she'd expected her night to end.

If Edric wanted to fully commit to the part, he would keep his eyes closed, but instead, he stared up at her. He spoke quietly enough that none of the busy sailors could hear. "I didn't say it earlier, but ... I'm sorry. For what happened to your sister."

She swallowed, pretending her somber expression was only because of the poisoned prince.

He took her hand, like a sick man might. "We would never have been so flippant with the story of Alanna impersonating your sister, had we known the truth."

She stared at their clasped hands. "Yes ... I believe you."

He closed his eyes and blew out a heavy breath. "I should go speak to the captain before we get too far." He tilted his head to look at her again. "Where are we headed?"

A soft smile curved her lips—he had stolen a ship for her and didn't even know their destination. "Sehrine," she whispered. "Geeni is on her way to meet the general of the Resistance in Sehrine."

He nodded as if that explanation was enough for him, then

he hopped to his feet. Easy for him to do, thanks to his nonrestrictive clothing, but he kindly reached down to help her up, too.

"Curse Naermore and their Spirits-forsaken fashion," she grumbled, getting to her feet.

He chuckled softly, then walked to find the captain, head penitently bowed.

Rhielle walked to the stern of the ship as the city faded behind them. The other Isandariyan ships hadn't followed, but they could have if they had really wanted to. She imagined Jaemin on the flagship, arms crossed, glaring at her as she sailed away in his ship. "I promise to bring your crew and mine back home safely. But if I fail, I'll let the sea finally claim me, and you'll never have to see me again."

She saluted the imaginary Jaemin in the distance and went to help Edric apologize.

∽

The captain was not amused.

She listened to Edric's explanation with hands on her hips and lips pinched in disapproval. But since the prince outranked her, and she couldn't receive orders from her superiors on the flagship, she ordered the crew to turn the ship toward Sehrine.

Edric had also asked the captain to give Rhielle something more practical to wear. A very considerate request, but unfortunately, they only had uniforms on board, which the captain flat out refused to let Rhielle wear.

So Rhielle was stuck in a tightly fitted gown, trying to convince the captain to let her steer the ship.

Convincing the captain a princess could steer a naval ship was perhaps the most difficult request of all. And honestly, Rhielle didn't blame her. It didn't make sense.

When the captain reluctantly agreed, Rhielle pulled Edric

away from the woman's glare. "I don't know if this will even work. This ship is so much bigger, and without a rune—"

"It was never the rune, Rhielle. It was always your Spark. I noticed it from the beginning ... You weren't controlling the ship, you were controlling the sea. You just need to do that again."

"Oh, is that all?" she said flatly. "But I couldn't use my Spark the last time I was on my ship. Geeni says I'm broken."

He crossed his arms with a challenging look. "And you believe *Geeni*?"

"Well ..."

He pointed at the middle of her chest as if he were the captain giving orders. "Your Spark is not broken. You need to figure out how you used it before and do that again. You just used it last night on the roof, so ..."

He trailed off. He was reliving their night on the roof just like she was. She hadn't even realized she was using her Spark —it had been so effortless. Which differed completely from when she used her Spark on the *Lady Tempest*. On the ship, she battled the sea, forcing it to obey her will. On the roof, she had become liquid herself, melting against him as they kissed.

Perhaps they should ...

She cleared her throat, breaking eye contact. "I ... uh ... I'll figure it out." She stepped up to the helm, and apparently her posture was confident enough that the sailor stepped away, yielding control of the wheel.

She squeezed the handles of the unfamiliar wheel. Her ship was only a few years old, and the lacquered wood still relatively unmarred, but this ship was much older. Regular use had gouged the wood in places, but the wheel was smooth from the dozens, maybe hundreds, of hands that had steered the ship. However, Rhielle did something they probably never had.

She closed her eyes.

She tried to remember how she used to speed her ship

through the water. Even though it hadn't been her tear powering the rune, she needed to recreate the process.

Rhielle needed to think about her sister.

Telling Edric about her sister's death had softened the sharp edge of her emotions—the sadness was much closer to the surface, but the pain felt slightly diminished. Even with her eyes closed, she sensed him beside her, standing guard while she focused. She was safe in his presence ... safe when her Spark overwhelmed her and safe when she shared the secret grief she had held alone for five years.

Her sister floated into her mind ... only two years Rhielle's senior, yet so much more mature. She should have been queen. Should have ruled Naermore, with more wisdom and grace than their father had. Yet her destiny had been stolen, first by foolish tradition, and second by the sea.

Rhielle had been knocked out in the attack on the Resistance ship, only waking afterward, floating on a piece of the ship's hull and clutching her dead sister in her arms. Rhielle should have been dead, too, and had bitterly wished she were. She had cataloged her sister's bloodless wounds, yet none of them were serious enough to have killed her.

The sea itself had killed her.

Even though the Isandariyan ship didn't have a rune, Rhielle rubbed the tear from her eye and pressed it against the wheel. She whispered and knew the sea could hear her. "You stole her from me, and I can never forgive you for that. So you owe me. Take me to my crew. Right now."

The ship lurched as the sea fought her control. The wind had already been pushing the ship in the correct direction, but when she ordered the sea, the waves slammed against the hull, thrusting them forward, yet threatening to tear the ship apart.

"Stop it," she hissed. "You will take us to my ship, quicker than Geeni's rune will let her escape. Do it now."

She drilled her focus through the ship's hull, locking on to each wave, dragging the sea under her control. The ship shot through the water like an arrow released. She briefly wondered if Edric had tracked down some seasickness tea, but then even that thought drifted away as she focused entirely on her enemy.

She would defeat the sea if it was the last thing she did.

37

Rhielle woke from her battle with the sea as she had before—with a warm presence at her back. She blinked open her eyes and stretched her cramping fingers away from the wheel.

"Rhielle?" The warm presence shifted until he braced one arm behind her back while he turned to look her in the face. "Are you okay?"

She squinted up at the moon, which was too bright. "Did we make it?"

"We spotted the *Lady Tempest* about an hour ago and have been slowly gaining. They've stopped and appear to be waiting for us."

So Geeni was preparing for a showdown.

Good. Even though Rhielle was exhausted from her battle with the sea, she was ready to get her crew back.

Rhielle brushed her disheveled hair away from her face and tried to pull herself back into a semblance of control. Edric removed his hand from her back, but didn't budge from her side.

"Where's the captain?" she asked.

The captain approached slowly, her face lit with awe. "Do you need something, Princess?"

Rhielle opened her mouth to tell the woman not to call her princess, but she couldn't very well ask her to call Rhielle "Captain" on her own ship. "Raise the parley flag and ready a dinghy for me. I'm going to the other ship."

The captain saluted sharply. "Yes, Princess."

Rhielle relinquished the helm to a wide-eyed sailor, who proudly saluted her, then she turned to Edric and crossed her arms. "Well? I'm waiting to hear your objections to me going to the other ship."

He shrugged as if it was no big deal. "I assumed we'd have to face her again."

"No, not *we*, Edric. I—"

"I will not leave your side." His tone brooked no arguments.

She wanted to order him to stay, to protect him like she hadn't protected her crew, but a part of her desperately wanted him at her side. Which was probably pretty obvious, considering the number of times she had kidnapped him.

"Fine," she huffed, hiding her relief. She gave the captain a few last instructions before climbing down to the dinghy.

She cursed Naermore fashion again as she shimmied her way down the ladder, then while Edric rowed without her assistance, and then again as she shimmied up the other ladder. After her awkward wriggle over the railing, Edric took his place at her side as she finally faced Geeni.

Geeni's fashion usually had some hint of pirate—her tight vests, fancy boots, and a treasure load of jewelry on her neck and wrists. But now, she looked even more the pirate, thanks to Rhielle's hat, which she wore tipped at a jaunty angle.

Losing the hat to Geeni irritated her almost as much as losing the ship. But she bit her tongue and focused on the real reason she had come.

The ship was bright thanks to Geeni's gold lanterns shining with a flameless light, so Rhielle could clearly see her crew lined up on deck. It wasn't their bound wrists that kept them so still. It was Geeni's henchwomen, two with bows and three with swords, with one blade aimed at Poppy tied to the mast.

Poppy was back in her pirate clothes, but Rhielle still only saw the young girl within. Her lavender eyes held a trembling terror, but her jaw was set and her hands were fisted, though bound.

Geeni studied the Isandariyan naval ship in the distance. "I trust you've warned the navy I have no problem executing captives if their ship makes any aggressive moves. You're here under a flag of parley, which I will respect as long as they do."

Rhielle growled, "Release my crew."

Geeni put her hands on her hips, fully committing to her role as a pirate. "What are you prepared to offer me?"

"I offer you one of this ship's longboats. If you and your henchwomen row directly north, you should reach shore in a day or two. Consider the longboat my gift."

"You forget, dear, this ship is mine, including the longboats. What else do you have to offer?"

Rhielle ground her teeth. "Fine. Keep the ship. I'll take my crew in the longboats. You'll be free to go on your way."

"The service of your crew is compensation for the duration I let you use the ship." Geeni shook her head. "You are extremely ill-suited to negotiation, dear. So far you haven't offered me a single thing I don't already possess."

Rhielle knew the right offer, but the words froze on her tongue. Rhielle possessed only one thing Geeni wanted. She swallowed to get her mouth to form the words.

"Let my crew go, and I'll stay."

"No, Rhielle!" Edric grabbed her arm and whispered in her ear. "This is not the plan we agreed on."

Rhielle brushed off Edric's hand and glared at Geeni with arms crossed.

Geeni's lips curled into a smug grin. "You're finally catching on, dear. In exchange for you, I will release your crew. But not until we reach the next port."

"No," she ordered. "Untie Poppy and let them all go now."

Geeni raised an eyebrow. "I'll untie Poppy if you walk calmly to the mast and take her place."

At Rhielle's first step, Edric grabbed her again. "You can't—" He stopped talking when Geeni placed a dagger at Poppy's throat.

"Get your prince under control, Rhielle." Geeni turned up her nose at him. "Men are just too emotional for rational negotiations."

Rhielle pried her eyes away from the terrified girl to address Edric. "I'll be fine, Edric, but I need you to look after Poppy ... Please." She hated letting Geeni hear her beg, but Rhielle needed him to take her seriously.

The muscles in his jaw tensed. Would he refuse? But instead, he silently released his grip.

Rhielle straightened her uncomfortable gown and walked with all dignity to the mast, into Geeni's waiting arms.

A henchwoman lowered her sword long enough to cut Poppy's bonds. A tear trickled from the girl's eye as she watched Rhielle take her place. Rhielle jerked her head, and Poppy obediently scurried away from the henchwoman into Edric's arms. He held the girl protectively, though his eyes were locked on Rhielle.

Even though she was the prisoner, Rhielle spoke as if she commanded the ship. "You have me. Now let them go."

Geeni chuckled. "I told you I'd release them at the next port in exchange for you, and your good behavior got your girl untied. That's all I agreed to, and you have nothing left to bargain with."

Rhielle surveyed her crew gathered on deck. Jazhara and Chysu were close by, and despite their bound hands, they appeared ready to fight. They all watched her closely, waiting to see how she planned to defeat Geeni and take back control of the ship. She hoped they would forgive her when they realized she had no such plan.

"I do have something else to bargain with." Rhielle thought of her sister, and her eyes watered.

Hunger formed in Geeni's eyes, but she spoke coolly. "I already have your tears on this ship's rune. A few more isn't worth an entire crew."

"I don't want to trade my tears for the crew." Rhielle blinked slowly, careful not to let her tears spill down her cheek until the deal was made. "I'll trade them for my hat."

Geeni's hunger shifted into genuine confusion. "Your hat?"

"The one you're wearing." She nodded at Geeni's head. "I love that hat. So many pretty feathers."

Geeni's eyes narrowed as she tried to determine Rhielle's game.

Rhielle craned toward the hat. "Did you lose the red feather? I rescind my offer if you lost the red one."

Geeni ripped the hat off her head. "I don't know what kind of game you are playing, but you should stop now."

Geeni didn't know the game, but Rhielle's crew surely did. They shifted their feet, casting anxious glances her way.

"There's no game. Just give me the hat, and you can take this tear." She fluttered her lashes, and the tear dropped to her cheek. "I give you my word." Rhielle stared at her first mate and communicated her command. Jazhara gave an imperceptible nod.

Geeni crept closer, drawn by the tear, yet still hesitant. "You expect me to trust the word of a pirate?"

"You can trust this word." Rhielle cast one last glance at

Poppy in Edric's arms and remembered her sister again. "The word is ... *Now*."

Rhielle grabbed hold of the sea, and the ship surged, at the same time the crew followed her command and abandoned ship.

38

Geeni's henchwomen raised their bows to attack the crew, who awkwardly swam with bound arms, but the archers couldn't keep their feet well enough to aim.

Geeni chose a different solution to the problem. She brought her blade to Rhielle's throat and hissed, "Stop this ship. Right now."

Rhielle bared her teeth in a feral grin. She didn't think Geeni would kill her—not when Rhielle was a source of tears. But even if she died, the momentum of Rhielle's battle with the sea would push the *Lady Tempest* far enough away that the navy could fish her crew out of the water and escape.

A perfect solution with only one problem. When Rhielle gave the word, her entire crew had abandoned ship, with one notable exception.

Edric.

He had shoved Poppy into Chysu's arms and stubbornly remained on board. So when Geeni raised her blade to Rhielle's throat, Edric had stumbled toward them.

Geeni's eyes caught the movement, and she rubbed her

fingers across her bracelet, then moved faster than Rhielle could comprehend. One moment the blade was at Rhielle's throat, the next moment at Edric's.

This was not part of Rhielle's plan. If she hadn't been tied to the mast, she would have toppled the man into the sea herself. But instead, she was trapped with no way to rescue Edric and unable to stop the panic devouring her heart.

"Stop. The. Ship. Right. Now." Geeni's expression said she had no issue killing a useless prince.

The ship jerked to a stop. Not even the wind stirred the ship, so firmly did Rhielle root it in place.

Geeni gripped Edric from behind, and based on his labored breathing, she was using magically enhanced arms to crush his ribs. Her blade was rock solid against his throat as she summoned her henchwomen to her side with a word. The five of them moved in the blink of an eye, forming a menacing line of glowing runes beside her.

Geeni spoke calmly, with no hint of exertion at restraining the large prince. "Listen closely to me, *pirate*. The next stage of our trip will go one of two ways. Either you will behave all the way to shore, where you willingly step into your dry prison, or I kill the prince now and steal whatever tears you shed before I kill you and dump you overboard. Do you understand me?"

"I understand!" she gasped as if it were her lungs being crushed. "Please, Geeni! I surrender. Just let go of him."

Geeni threw Edric down at her feet, and said to her henchwomen, "Tie him up." Two women carried him to the other side of the mast as if he were as light as a small child.

"No, not beside her. Bring him over here by the helm. I want her to watch if I need to stab him because of her bad behavior."

Rhielle's chest constricted in terror as Edric struggled to regain his breath after Geeni's forceful restraint. His posture was so hunched ... Had Geeni broken his ribs? Rhielle wanted to squeeze the life out of Geeni, but she was too terrified to move in case the woman did much worse to him.

Once the henchwomen tied Edric to the helm, Geeni sighed in contentment as she sheathed her dagger and took the wheel. "Now then, I'll use this rune and get us away from here before your pesky Isandariyan navy catches up. I expect you to be a good little princess, quiet and obedient, okay, dear? If I notice the sea doing anything peculiar, then ..." She leaned toward Edric and drew a long pink fingernail across his neck.

Edric held still, but his stare at Rhielle said she should take the risk.

Obviously, she would not.

Geeni pressed her hand against the rune, and it glowed, even without a fresh tear. The sea slipped out of Rhielle's control as Geeni wrestled it away, and suddenly the ship jerked, then sped forward as Geeni commanded it with her eyes shut.

Rhielle tried to content herself that her crew had escaped. By now they would be safely aboard the Isandariyan ship, traveling at a perfectly normal speed in whatever direction their captain said. Maybe they would continue on to Sehrine in case Geeni really went there, or maybe they would go back to Isandariyah to gather more ships to search for the prince.

Either way, they would be much too late to help.

Maybe Edric could escape once they reached shore. Even if Rhielle couldn't get away, she would find a way for him to escape. Geeni had a cage planned for Rhielle, but not for Edric. Maybe Geeni would let him go.

Or maybe she'd just kill him.

Rhielle's thoughts churned as the sea buzzed angrily in her ears. She'd never been conscious enough to hear the sea as she battled it. The sea fought back, slamming vicious waves against the deck, grabbing anything not tied down. If Rhielle hadn't been tied to the mast, she would have had to cling to something like the henchwomen did, or risk being pulled overboard.

Geeni's brow furrowed in concentration, the raging battle clear on her face. Rhielle thought about all the times Edric had stood by her side, watching her battle the sea, protecting her from the rain, regarding her with awe. Now his body was still, but alert, like when they had sparred and he had waited for her to make the first move.

But she had no moves left. She had used every trick up her sleeve and had lost. And now Edric would suffer for it.

A raindrop landed on her cheek.

Anyone else on deck would think the drop was just splashing seawater, but it burned against her cheek like seawater never did. She glanced up as the dark cloud approached, and another drop landed on her forehead and burned its way toward her temple.

Edric's eyes widened as he sighted the storm cloud, then he frantically strained against his bonds. Rhielle shot him an angry glare. He would get himself killed!

The ship crashed to a halt as Geeni's eyes flew open, and she rubbed her hand against her pant leg. "What was that?"

Her henchwomen stumbled toward her, trying to gain their footing, but they couldn't tell what was wrong.

A second raindrop landed on Geeni's hand. She hissed as she looked up at the sky. "What's happening?" She stalked over to the mast and grabbed Rhielle's silk dress in her fist. "What are you doing?"

A raindrop landed on Rhielle's ear, and she flinched. "That's my supposed Spark. Water burns my skin."

Confusion creased Geeni's brow until a raindrop landed on her cheek, and she scrubbed it off angrily. "That's ridiculous. Sparks don't work this way."

A laugh burst from Rhielle, despite the raindrops trickling in burning lines down her scalp. "You thought you could just make the ship go fast. You didn't know about the downside to my Spark."

Geeni tightened her hold on Rhielle's dress. "I told you, girl —*you* are broken. Sparks don't have downsides. They start off small, sometimes imperceptible, then grow as your skill increases. If your Spark hurts you, it's because you are doing it wrong."

Rhielle wanted to taunt Geeni about stealing a broken Spark, but she had only ever known Alanna and Elliya to have Sparks, and Geeni had actual information on how they worked. "Tell me how to use my Spark correctly, then you can steal some tears that actually work right."

As Geeni narrowed her jade eyes, carefully considering the opportunity, Rhielle realized something about Geeni's runes— she only had as much magic as the person could use at the time they shed the tear. That Geeni was considering the offer meant if Rhielle's Spark grew stronger, Geeni would have a more powerful rune. Elliya had said Geeni either imprisoned people with Sparks or manipulated the unknowing owners for their whole lives to steal their Sparks. Geeni must walk a fine line in deciding when to steal their tears—either wait until they'd fully developed their Spark or capture them early enough they couldn't become a threat.

Understanding Geeni's depraved strategies thrilled her, though it was fairly useless information now that Rhielle was one of those she imprisoned.

Geeni bit her pink lip, then said begrudgingly, "When did the water start hurting you?" Apparently she thought it worth the risk to fix Rhielle's affliction if it meant she could use it herself pain free.

It had been hard enough to talk about her sister with Edric, and Geeni was the last person she wanted to tell. However, Geeni already knew the ending of the story.

"It was the day my sister died."

Geeni nodded as she considered the statement, revealing no hint she knew about Aliyabeth's death and had secretly provided the impostor. "Sparks are often triggered by traumatic events. When the Verkeshe attacked your ship, whatever latent magic you had must have coalesced into a Spark." She chuckled to herself. "How ironic that's when it happened."

A sick horror crawled over her skin that had nothing to do with the rain. "It was you? ... You sent the Verkeshe to attack."

Geeni brushed a hand down her arm to dislodge the crawling raindrops. "I didn't send the Verkeshe. I sent the Resistance to find you."

"But ... I discovered them myself ..."

Geeni snorted a laugh. "Really? A sheltered fifteen-year-old princess discovered an undercover squad of Resistance soldiers? No, they allowed you to discover them. Then they assisted your sister as she tracked you down. I merely wanted to kidnap you—I didn't know the Verkeshe would spot you. I control a lot of things, but I don't control everything." She sighed wistfully, then scrubbed her fingers through her wet pink hair. "It really was a shame your sister died. I wanted to collect the complete set of princesses."

Anger and grief swirled within Rhielle, the blame shifting from Geeni to the Verkeshe, to the sea, to herself, and back again. The rainfall steadily increased until rivulets poured down Rhielle's cheeks, and though it burned, she refused to let a tear fall. Geeni adjusted her stolen hat to protect her face, but her bare arms were now covered in rain. The water would claw its way across her skin, burning Geeni just as it burned Rhielle.

The ship rocked with a rogue wave. Geeni clung to Rhielle for support as a wave crashed over the side, soaking the deck in seawater.

"Stop it! Now!" screamed Geeni, stomping at the approaching seawater. "I swear I'll kill your prince if you don't stop."

"It's not just me!" Rhielle gasped as seawater soaked her dainty shoes. "The water reacts to our pain. We need to dry off."

Geeni glared at her, probably wondering if Rhielle was telling the truth. The rain picked up intensity, and as Geeni attempted unsuccessfully to scrape the water off her skin, another wave surged over the side.

She pointed at a henchwoman. "Bring me towels and something waterproof. I need to sail us out of this storm." Then she pointed at Rhielle while yelling at two other women. "Tie her up belowdecks, and for Goddesses' sake, keep her dry!"

The henchwomen scrambled across the strangely churning water on deck and loosed Rhielle's bonds. She considered fighting, except her skin hurt so badly, all she wanted was to escape the rain.

The women yanked her by the arms and dragged her past Edric. He was soaked, his hair and thin monk clothes plastered to his skin. He looked just like he had the night they had kissed on the roof. She hadn't noticed the rain then, even though it had covered every inch of her. But now she hurt inside and out, and nothing could stop it.

Another wave rocked the ship, and the henchwomen stumbled, letting Rhielle slip out of their fingers. She blinked, surprised by her sudden freedom, but before she could devise a plan, a wave smashed across the deck, knocking her feet out from under her, and swept her overboard, dragging her down to the heart of the sea.

39

Rhielle plummeted, the water pulling her down faster than a person should sink. She could still sense the waves surrounding the *Lady Tempest*, though they sped away, moving the ship ever forward. Deep below her lurked old currents, water more ancient than she could comprehend. The dark, primeval water drew her closer. So, this was it ... The end of her battle with the sea.

Today, the sea would finally defeat her.

As the water forced her deeper, she strangely felt no fear. This would be where it ended. The sea would kill her as it had killed her sister. So instead of kicking her way back to the surface, she just relaxed and let it take her.

She surrendered to the sea, as the prophecy had foretold.

The pain of the rainwater faded as the sea wiped it away, and the salt water didn't sting as it usually did. Her downward trajectory slowed, and she floated, hovering in place, neither sinking nor rising. She blinked her eyes open, and though it was dark, she sensed something she couldn't believe.

While water caressed her legs, her head and torso were inside a bubble of air.

She drew a tentative breath, then gasped as her lungs sucked in the air they had been longing for. She could breathe underwater? Was that part of her Spark? The experience was so surreal, she panicked, finally trying to swim to the surface. But as she kicked her feet, the water convulsed as if in pain. Water dripped inside her bubble of air and burned against her cheeks.

She halted her kicks, holding perfectly still, and the water rippled, reforming its bubble around her. A hysterical laugh rose in her throat. No, she couldn't breathe underwater. She could only surrender to the sea, then wait for magical things to happen. The lack of control clawed at her throat. Was the sea toying with her? Would she ever escape? Or was she now forever at its mercy?

Rhielle could do nothing but float within her pitch-black bubble of air. The only sound was her panicked breathing echoing off the rippling water. The sound brought back a memory, and she closed her eyes to remember.

She'd heard this sound on the day her sister died.

Rhielle could never remember how she had ended up on the broken hull, clutching her dead sister's body. If her sister had drowned, how had Rhielle found her without even remembering it?

Because the sea had helped her.

She remembered it now ... giving up ... her body slipping below the waves as the ship sank ... falling asleep underwater ... the waves washing her sister into her arms, then buoying them both atop the floating hull ...

"You saved my life," she whispered.

The sea didn't speak back, but the ancient water droned in the affirmative.

Despite her gratitude, she couldn't keep the bitter thought from spilling from her lips. "But my sister ... you killed her."

From the sea, she sensed images of children splashing in

the surf and sailors drowning beneath rough waves, seaweed fluttering as a school of fish passed by and a dolphin's blood mixing with the seawater as a shark circled. The life and death contained in the sea was beyond the ancient water's concern.

"But ... you saved *me*." Why would the sea save her? She had just been a fifteen-year-old girl—a princess, but what would the sea care about the politics on land? Why would the sea notice her at all?

She saw the answer in one of the sea's boundless memories: a small red-haired girl, barely five years old, standing on the shore.

It was the day Rhielle had first met the sea. Growing up as a young princess in a mountain castle, she had been told stories about the sea, but she hadn't understood until the waves crashed against her. The sparkling water had stretched far into the distance yet drew close enough to tickle her small feet in the sand. The beach was in La Veridda before the war, though young Rhielle had only had the barest concept of kingdoms and borders. But she'd understood two things, even as a small child.

The sea belonged to no one.

And she was deeply in love.

She had loved the sea from the day they met, and now, as the sea held her deep inside its watery heart, she knew the sea loved her in return.

She pressed her hands against her trembling lips. "I never realized you loved me. This whole time ..."

Rhielle had battled the sea every day since her sister's death. Each time she'd thought she had used the rune, she had been using her Spark to dominate the sea, to punish it. The water had convulsed when she tried to kick to the surface—how much pain had she caused the sea during her time as captain? No wonder the water stung her skin ... It was the only defense it had.

"I'm so sorry. I didn't know ... I just didn't know." A tear slipped down her cheek, and it plopped into the rippling water.

A deep hum reverberated through the water as her tears joined the sea. The sea shared a memory of the last time Rhielle had offered her tears.

Rhielle had tried to swim Aliyabeth's body to shore, but her sister had slipped out of her arms and sunk below the waves. Rhielle had dived after her, and when she opened her eyes underwater, her sister was alive. Aliyabeth's strawberry blond hair had formed a glowing halo around her face, and the sunlight filtering through the water had blurred the wounds on her skin. Her arms were no longer heavy and stiff, but graceful, like she was dancing. Underwater, Aliyabeth was alive, so Rhielle had left her there.

Rhielle's tears had watered the ocean as she floated all the way back to shore.

She gasped softly. The sea had provided the current to get her back. She'd had no energy, even to care for herself, but the sea hadn't let her go until she was safely back on land.

More tears fell, dropping like rain into the water. "I won't fight you any longer. I swear it."

The water rippled around her as if in an embrace.

She sat in the quiet bubble for several moments, waiting. Oh. The water might not release her unless she asked it to. Alanna had said the wind only did what she wanted because she asked very nicely and because it was fond of her.

If the sea loved her, perhaps it would do as she wished if she asked nicely. Considering she gave more orders than she made polite requests, she took her time to do it right.

She stroked the edge of the bubble, petting the water as if it were a cat. "Um ... Sea? Can I ask you a favor? I left someone very important to me on that ship, and—"

Rhielle shot through the water faster than her ship had ever sailed. She tried to take a gasping breath, and her lungs found nothing there—she had left the air bubble behind. She sensed the water restraining itself from entering her mouth, but there was no air to breathe as she zipped through the water toward the ship.

As she passed through the currents, she sensed their individual thoughts along with the greater thoughts of the whole. The sea only had a rough understanding of human physiology, so it didn't understand why her lungs burned after such a short time with no air. Capturing a bubble of air was complicated. It required the sea to avoid crushing the air and sending it fleeing back to the surface. The sea couldn't do that while speeding her through the water.

In her panic, she almost kicked her legs to propel herself, but she stopped, remembering her promise. "Please!" she begged with no air.

The current shifted, and shot her toward the surface, where the water lightened.

Rhielle burst out of the waves in a spray of water, her lungs dragging in air as her body floated, more buoyant than she should be. The sky had brightened with the first hint of dawn, and on the horizon sat the *Lady Tempest*, trapped unmoving in the waves.

She closed her eyes against the brightness of the early dawn sky and imagined herself back in the depths of the sea, then she pressed her hands on top of the water, resting them on the surface as if on glass. "Thank you," she rasped.

The sea answered in a scream.

Geeni was using the rune, fighting the waves, battering the sea, who only held the ship in place because of its love for Rhielle. She could tell the sea to release the ship, but that wouldn't solve the problem. The rune held tears that only knew how to command the sea, not surrender to it. As long as the rune existed, the sea was in danger.

Rhielle stretched out her fingers along the surging water,

spreading her awareness to the sea beyond and below. "Sea, my love, I vow to protect you now and for the rest of my life. Please, I beg you to listen as I make this request *very nicely*. Will you please drag my ship down to the bottom of the sea?"

The sea rippled in a delighted shiver and complied.

40

The ship sank faster than Rhielle had expected. Ships with hulls broken by battering rams took time to sink completely, but the *Lady Tempest* sank in a disturbing manner. The water crawled over the sides of the ship, and slithering rivers poured up the masts, flowing up the sails in a steady stream. Water infiltrated the entire ship, flooding each cabin and hold, until the *Lady Tempest* sank below the waves as if she had never been.

Rhielle had no time to grieve the beautiful ship, because her mind was firmly focused on asking—*begging*—the sea to please honor one more request. If the sea was like her crew, she could have shouted many orders at once, including a request for the sea to chase Geeni and her henchwomen as they escaped in a longboat.

But she refused to hurt the sea by bending it to her will, so instead she surrendered to the sea, trusting it loved her enough to listen to her one-word prayer.

"Edric."

She repeated his name over and over, even when the sea stole her breath, carrying her deep below the waves. His name reverberated in her mind, and she sent it pulsing through each wave and current. Her lungs constricted, unable to draw air or water, and her head spun. Was her body slowing its sharp descent? Or was it her thoughts that slowed?

Her body stopped, and as she hovered in the water, a light glowed in the waves. Before her eyes could focus, Rhielle slipped through the water and fell inside a bubble of air surrounding the helm.

Rhielle thudded to the deck in a puddle of warm silk, the bright glow of Geeni's flameless lantern burning her eyes. She gasped in a breath as she scrambled to her feet. Edric was just as she had left him, sopping wet but breathing.

Her hands shook violently as she tried to untie the knots binding him to the helm. "Oh, Edric ... I'm so sorry for dragging you down here. I didn't know what else to do. I can't imagine how terrifying that must have been—"

"I knew you would come for me." His voice was calm ... completely unafraid.

The second his bonds loosened, he cupped her chin in his hands, staring deep into her eyes. "I love you, Rhielle, and I cannot bear to be separated from you again. I will follow you to the ends of the earth or the bottom of the sea, but I will not leave your side." He stared at her with the devotion he usually reserved for his Twin Goddesses.

He was close enough to take a kiss if he wanted it, but he waited patiently for her.

"Edric ... I can't ask you to forsake your Goddesses for me."

His thumb brushed a seawater tear on her cheek. "I'm not betraying the Goddesses by loving you. I was searching for an Isandariyan heir, but you are the princess they sent me to find. You are proof of their blessing. Proof everything will be okay."

Her breath caught in her lungs, and she whispered, "But you belong to your Goddesses."

He leaned closer, the warm vapor of his breath tingling her

lips. "I belong to them even if I don't serve in their shrines. But I can also belong to you."

Her icy resolve melted, and she flung herself against him. One of his hands wove into her hair, the other wound around her waist, as he kissed her with the ferocity of a drowning man. Her fingers dug into his strong back, pulling him closer, breathing him in.

She wanted to live forever with him on this shipwreck under the sea. The outside world didn't exist—it was only the two of them, kissing, forever and ever, with dripping seawater sizzling beneath her fingertips ...

Edric stopped kissing her, his lips twitching into a grin against hers.

She opened her eyes. His eyes were already open, a silly grin spreading across his lips as steam billowed around their feet.

Rhielle relaxed her tensing fingers, sliding them off his back to rest on his chest. Even with her magic going wild, she didn't want to let him go. "Perhaps we should save the kissing for later."

His blue eyes sparkled as he tucked a rogue red tendril behind her ear. "I'm looking forward to it." He glanced up, where the water rippled around their bubble of air. "So, how will you get us out of here?"

He spoke with complete confidence in her. He had never doubted she would swim to the bottom of the sea to find him, and now he believed she would lead him back out again. She hoped to be worthy of his trust, now and always.

"The sea will carry us out, but we won't have enough air for the whole trip. I imagine we'll pass out, but we should revive once we can breathe again ... hopefully."

He didn't appear concerned about her uncertainty—he just held her loosely around the waist, and said, "I'm ready when you are."

She cleared her throat and spoke in a calm, clear voice. "Sea … my love?"

Edric's eyes widened. He had only heard her threaten the sea, so he must find her tone surprising.

She took a deep breath and waited for him to do the same, before she asked, "Would you mind carrying us to dry land?"

The pocket of air dissipated in fizzing bubbles as they shot upward, firmly wrapped in each other's arms.

41

Rhielle sat by the window of her apartment a few blocks from the Isandariyan docks and stared at the sea. She hadn't been down to the dock in a week—all the ships, both big and small, saddened her too much. The *Lady Tempest* had been a beautiful ship, and she missed it deeply, but she missed her crew even more.

After she had washed up on a deserted shore with Edric in her arms, they had kissed in the waves for quite some time, until the Isandariyan naval ship sailed directly in front of them. After the ship's captain had fished Rhielle's crew out of the sea, they'd followed a strangely direct current that led them right to the shore where Rhielle and Edric had washed up.

Edric had remarked he wished the current had been a little slower, and though Rhielle had agreed, she had still greeted her crew with open arms.

After Rhielle had sent a courier with a secret message to her father about the impostor, she and the rest of the crew had sailed with the navy back to Isandariyah, where Edric had found jobs for everyone in the crew. They were so busy, she'd barely seen them all week. How could they adjust to life on land so quickly when she still spent most of her days moping around?

Obviously, Edric kept her from spending her *entire* day moping, but he couldn't be with her all the time. He was a prince with responsibilities, so he couldn't always distract her from how badly she missed the sea. He'd been even busier than usual the last few days, though she didn't know why. Though he remained devoted to the Goddesses, he had given up his responsibilities as a monk, which should give him more free time, but the sun had almost set and she hadn't seen him all day.

She was still preparing her rant when he burst through the door and planted a kiss on her cheek. "I've missed you so much!"

Rhielle crossed her arms. "You could have come by before now."

His eyes twinkled mischievously. "I've got a surprise for you." He pulled her out of the apartment, down to the busy street below.

She could barely keep up with him. Even though she was again wearing pants and boots instead of silk and heels, her clothes just didn't feel right. She tugged on the sleeves gathered at her wrists, the blouse fancier than her pirate clothes, and more in line with Isandariyah's fashion than what she was used to.

The nights she dined at the palace with the other princes and their wives, she would wear a dress out of respect, but she still hated it. Although she begrudgingly had to admit her fondness for the Isandariyan dresses Alanna and Elliya had kindly introduced her to—the dresses had very roomy pockets. She appreciated the ease with which she could hide treasures or weapons, even at a fancy meal.

As she hurried to catch up to Edric, she breathed deeply, savoring the taste of the sea on her tongue. She should have come to the docks much sooner, if only to greet the sea. As she drew closer, the sea trembled with excitement.

The sea wanted to see her.

And it also knew the surprise.

She took several skipping steps to catch up, then nearly ran into Edric's back as he pulled to a stop in front of a truly stunning ship.

The ship wasn't new—Rhielle could tell from the smoothly worn wood hull—but her trim was freshly painted, and the new sails gleamed white. She was a regal ship—powerful, yet elegant. An absolutely breathtaking flagship of the queen's navy.

The naval crew stood before the ship in proud formation on the dock, with their white uniforms neatly pressed and gold buttons shining. They saluted the prince as he approached, dragging an open-mouthed Rhielle along behind him.

"Good evening, Captain," said Jazhara.

Rhielle whipped her head around, finally studying the faces of the crew. Her entire crew was here, including some sailors she had met on the Isandariyan ship she had stolen with Edric.

"What are you ... Did you join the navy?"

Chysu's lips quirked in a crooked grin. "This is the job your prince found for us. Do you not approve?"

"I ... um ..." Rhielle shook her head, trying to picture a group of pirates in the queen's navy. "It's very unexpected."

Jazhara glanced at Edric, who couldn't stop grinning. "We've heard this ship will have an excellent captain, which might have convinced us to enlist."

Edric turned to Rhielle, the first glimmer of doubt shining in his eyes. "Obviously, it's your choice, Rhielle. I just know you will never be happy on land. And Isandariyah needs someone who will protect us and protect the sea. If you accept the job, this ship is yours." He pointed at the name engraved on the ship: *Heart of the Sea.*

His eyes shot back to the crew in formation, and a small soldier marched forward, a white jacket held reverently in her hands. Poppy lifted the jacket, offering it to Rhielle. "Captain?"

Rhielle answered her question by taking the jacket. Poppy saluted her sharply before falling back into formation.

Rhielle pulled on the fitted jacket but could barely fasten the buttons with her shaking hands. As the uniform settled over her shoulders, she sighed. This was the clothing she had been searching for. Life as a pirate had granted her freedom and taught her to protect those she loved, but she was done running away. It was time to stand her ground and fight for what she cherished.

Edric helped her with the top button, his hands steady and warm against her neck. "I'll have my own uniform, of course, but I need to warn you ... I won't be calling you Captain."

A laugh threatened to burst forth, but she covered it by raising an imperious eyebrow. "Do you think I will give you special treatment, letting you address me as you wish, sailor?"

A smooth grin curved his lips. "No, it's because you've been promoted. I'll have to call you Admiral."

Her mouth dropped open, but before she could speak, he gathered her into his arms and whispered in her ear, "But when we're alone, I'll still call you Princess." He captured her lips in a kiss before she could command him otherwise.

EPILOGUE

Geeni washed up on shore, fuming mad and ready to scrape off her skin—if only it would stop burning. She trudged awkwardly through the waves as they clawed at her ankles, fighting her till the very end.

The moment she made it past the water's edge, she ripped the seashell locket off her neck and tossed it back into the sea. If she hadn't stolen that last tear from Rhielle the night of the ball, she would have died when the *Lady Tempest* was sucked beneath the waves. But even though the Spark had been useful for escaping on the longboat, Geeni refused to use it ever again.

It was just not worth the pain.

The sea had fought back by tossing her and her henchwomen out of the longboat before they made it to shore. The women looked like a pack of bedraggled cats as they squeezed the seawater out of their hair and clothes, and Geeni patted down her pink hair sticking up like horns. She probably looked worse than her henchwomen, considering the water didn't burn them as it had burned her, but they wisely kept their mouths shut.

She stomped away from the shore and looked along the

beach to get her bearings. She still needed to get to Sehrine to see the general. The girl had been useful in her job with the Resistance army for the last several years, but considering the alliance with Prince Niklys, Geeni needed to set her on a new path.

Geeni had to admit the general was a hard worker. The girl had been adopted by farmers at a young age and was always up before the sun, then working late into the night to finish her chores.

Geeni swore the girl never slept.

She needed to hold tightly to the general, now more than ever. When Geeni had failed to capture Rhielle and her sister five years ago, she'd unfortunately lost her chance to collect the full set of princesses. She still hoped to eventually capture Rhielle, but even if she never did, she absolutely couldn't lose track of the two princesses she'd kidnapped to start the war.

To be continued in
A Spark of Harvest: A Sleeping Beauty Retelling

AFTERWORD

A big thank you to Nia Quinn for her thorough editing. If any issues remain, it's because I snuck it past her after the final edit.

Thanks to my family and friends for the consistent encouragement. Your support means the world to me.

And to Kent ... Thank you for always having my back. You are the prince of my dreams.

Final note: I researched nautical terms for this book, but I sincerely apologize to any sailing aficionados if I got anything wrong. If I did, it's because honestly, I got most of my naval lingo from Star Trek.

Sci-fi nerds can also love fairy tales.

ABOUT THE AUTHOR

Susannah Welch lives in sunny South Florida with her brilliant husband and a magically hypoallergenic cat. She enjoys singing and dancing and showing off. She likes her stories with a little bit of drama, and a whole lot of sparkle.

facebook.com/susannah.welch.author
instagram.com/susannahwelchauthor

Milton Keynes UK
Ingram Content Group UK Ltd.
UKHW021928220724
445827UK00012B/73/J

9 781958 568163